Reunion

Marty Almquist

This is a work of fiction. While, as in all fiction, the literary perceptions and insights are based on experience, all names, characters, places, and events either are products of the author's imagination or are used fictitiously.

ISBN-13: 978-0-9852624-3-3

ACKNOWLEDGMENTS

For me, life is about connecting, and staying connected, to those I love. It's pretty simple, really. That means making the effort to find ways to see family and friends whenever possible, even though we are all now spread across the country. Sometimes it's a call, sometimes it's Facebook, sometimes it's a Words with Friends game. The writing of this story has been a different kind of connection—achieved through reliving those college and grad school experiences that we had and using those to build a fictional story.

As always, I have to say thank you, first and foremost, to Nellie Sabin, the most amazing woman and editor. She gives me structure and helps strip away all the "noise" of too many words and paragraphs leading nowhere. And a big thanks to my other staunch supporters, through their creative genius, and that's Rosalia Diaz and Cassa Leonard. Thank you, Sharon Rogolsky, for taking the final look and catching the typos and inconsistencies that were STILL there even after multiple readings.

And finally, thank you to Peter, who is my rock and my better half. You keep me balanced, and centered, and always laughing, mostly at myself.

France was my spiritual homeland: it had become a part of me, and I a part of it, and so it has remained ever since.

--*My Life in France*, Julia Child with Alex Prud'homme

Chapter 1.

It looked like any other piece of junk mail from the Foundry College Alumni Association, but as Melanie dropped it into the trash, the colorful picture inside the fold caught her eye. Retrieving it, she read: "How about Paris and a Wine Tour with your favorite college classmates for a week?" Then came a description of the hotel, in the heart of the Latin Quarter; visits to a variety of restaurants, monuments and museums; and a wine tour in Burgundy. She and Gary had only been to Paris once before, when he was still in graduate school. That trip had been about seeing as much as possible on as little money as possible, staying in cheap hotels and picnics in the park. This trip looked both fun and educational, not to mention delicious!

These days the only trips they took were to Bethany Beach each summer, and to visit alternating sets of parents at Thanksgiving and Christmas. She looked down at the dates: September 16th through the 23rd. That could work. They would be back from dropping Craig at UCLA by then. Maybe this was a chance to recapture some of the excitement that came with going somewhere new. And, she realized with a shock, this year marked twenty-five years since she'd graduated in 1989! How could that be?

She dialed Gary's number and, putting on her cheeriest voice, said, "Hey, how's your day going? Oh, I got home early—I had a meeting downtown so I just came home afterward. One of the advantages of being a consultant. What's your schedule look like? Okay, I'll assume I'll see you in a couple of hours then. What? No, nothing special, just figured I'd check in. Oh, and we got a brochure in the mail from the Alumni Association about a trip to Paris and Burgundy that looks like fun. No, that's okay if you're in the middle of something. I'll see you in a bit."

Hanging up the phone, she felt both drained and angry. When had chatting with her own husband become so awkward? Recently he made her feel like such an intruder into his day. She wasn't asking him to talk for hours. *Why couldn't he just be friendly, for heaven's sake?* She picked up the brochure again, trying to summon the feeling of excitement she'd had.

Pulling out her work calendar, she saw that she was scheduled to send final reports to two of her clients at the end of August, and a preliminary report to two others by Labor Day, so the timing of this trip definitely worked for her. Now it would just depend on Gary's schedule. She turned on some music, then opened her laptop to work until he got home.

****

Gary couldn't go. He worked for the State Department and had to attend a meeting in San Francisco that week. Melanie finished putting the dishes in the dishwasher and turned to toss the brochure in the trash, but couldn't stop looking at the picture on the front. It showed four people at a café table, laughing, with cocktails in front of them and Notre Dame behind. The picture had been taken right at sunset and everything was wreathed in a golden glow. She suddenly, desperately, wanted to be one of those people. Life these days was full of tension, with work and at home. Wouldn't it be great to leave all of that behind?

Why did Gary's meeting have to fall that week? She knew, from the little bit of talking they still did, that it was a critical one for his job advancement, but frustration over the whole situation left a bitter taste in her mouth. The brochure taunted her with its promise. She moved toward the trash but again stopped before throwing it away, struck by a new idea.

Just because Gary couldn't go, did that mean that she couldn't go? On the one hand, she knew he'd be angry and frustrated if she took a trip like this without him, but he was already angry and frustrated. These last few months had been exhausting. Maybe some time away would help her figure things out.

Sifting in her mind through possible traveling companions, she quickly discarded friends through work as not the right fit. The best option would be someone who had been at school with her. But who? She had never made it back to the campus for any of the alumni reunions. California was simply too far away from Virginia and besides, the priority for vacation time and money had always been to see family.

Suddenly it hit her. Angie, Gigi, Emily and Julie—four acquaintances at college who had become real friends in the five years *after* graduation, when they'd all moved to the Boston area, some for graduate school, some for jobs. They had done everything together and everything on the cheap—free summer concerts in the park, student-discounted movies and plays, and eating family style, with everyone contributing a course. She had so many great memories from that time.

Early on, they had come up with the idea of indulging once a year in a big trip together, to get away from the tensions and stresses of daily life. Each January they would meet for the Trip Planning meal. All five women would gather, accompanied by a revolving assortment of boyfriends for Emily, Gigi, and Julie. She and Gary had been together since Foundry, and had come to Boston together so he could go to MIT for graduate school. Angie and Joe had also been together at Foundry and had gotten married in his hometown, Portland, Oregon, right after graduation. They had then moved to Boston so Joe could go to Tufts.

The evening always began with a lively discussion of the merits and challenges of past trips, then moved on to ideas for the upcoming adventure. They always traveled in early September, before the next year's coursework started for those in school. September was the start of their New Year, and the trip marked its beginning. They'd had some wonderful trips: to Spain, the Caribbean, Mexico, and, of course, that one trip to Paris.

The tradition had lasted five years, but by that last trip, only Melanie, Gary, Angie, and Joe were left. Looking back on it now, Melanie remembered that Gigi and Julie had both moved away by then. Emily had still been in Boston, but was no longer on speaking terms with the rest of the group.

After leaving Boston, Melanie and Angie used the trip as a way to make sure they saw each other once a year, since they now lived on opposite coasts—Melanie and Gary in Virginia, and Joe and Angie in Portland, and were both starting families. Angie was in fact already pregnant with Mary, the first of their two girls, when they left Boston, and Melanie was soon pregnant with Craig. Eventually, conflicting schedules and geographic distance got to be too much and the trips stopped. Melanie now realized with a start that it had been eight years since their last trip together.

To stay in touch, she was now friends with Angie on Facebook, and they talked on the phone every month or so, but she missed having in-depth, face-to-face conversations. She had never felt comfortable sharing too many details of her life on Facebook. It felt too public, and she was always reading about embarrassing situations that were the result of privacy settings gone wrong and personal information released into the public domain. She did like to post on Facebook when she felt strongly about an issue, and she also liked to use it to see what other people were doing. Though Gigi and Julie were on Facebook, they rarely posted anything, so she didn't have much of an idea what was going on in their lives. She knew they now both lived in Europe and that Gigi had a daughter, but not much else.

Coming back to the present, Melanie decided that her first step had to be to try to contact everyone, making it very clear that she was asking for them to go on a "girls only" trip. It was a long shot, she knew—but what if it worked?

Filled now with purpose, she grabbed her laptop and sent a Facebook message to Angie. She sent a regular email to Gigi and Julie, not trusting they would check Facebook quickly enough. Her final task was to track Emily down. This trip felt like a great way to reconnect with her. Melanie spent a couple of minutes trying to find her on Facebook. There were several "Emily's" with no picture, but she wasn't sure enough she'd found the right one to risk it. Switching tactics, she went instead to the Foundry website with the link to the alumni directory and there she found an email address she felt confident was for the right Emily.

In her message to everyone, Melanie referred to the brochure and gave a brief outline of the basics of the trip, closing with a reminder of how much fun they'd all had traveling together.

She didn't know if including Emily would be awkward, but it felt right to try. She told herself she would definitely go if at least two of them said yes—and she would tell Gary *after* she booked the ticket.

Chapter 2.

Gigi

Gigi opened the email from Melanie and, after reading it through several times, leaned back in her chair. She let the view of the olive trees in her backyard blur slightly as she let her mind drift back to those days in the Boston area. She, Emily and Julie had shared a tiny apartment in an ancient row house near Harvard Square in Cambridge. She had known Emily at Foundry, and when both had chosen to move to the Boston area after graduation, they agreed to find a place together. Within the information packet from Harvard that Emily had received, there was a description of housing options, and it quickly became apparent that to afford *anything* in Cambridge, even a rent-controlled apartment, they were going to need a third person. Emily had reached out to Julie, a friend from Powell, one of the sister schools to Foundry. Julie confirmed that she, too, was headed to Boston for graduate school, and would be happy to join them.

Slightly terrified, but filled with anticipation, the three began their new life in Cambridge. Both Emily and Julie started their graduate programs that September, and Gigi started at a small piano-tuning school in Boston, using money her father had left her. The apartment they found was old and tired, but a quick coat of paint and some colorful rag rugs on the hardwood floors had brightened the gloomy interior. A few trips to local thrift shops for furniture completed the transformation.

Not long after they moved in, Julie had run into Melanie at the farmer's market in Central Square, and Melanie said that she and Gary lived just a few blocks away. They, in turn, had been hanging out with Angie and Joe, who lived across the river in Brookline. Soon all seven of them were having regular dinners together.

Gigi smiled as she thought about their annual vacations. The trip they had made to Spain had been her first real exposure to Europe, and she had fallen in love with the slower pace of life. After two years of school, then two more years working as a piano tuner for a variety of private clients around Boston, Gigi had heard of an opening in a repair and restoration shop in Turin, Italy and—very boldly for her—she had gone to work there, thinking that it was a great moment in her life to spend some time in Europe. Now, twenty years later, she found herself still in Italy, married to an Italian, with a twelve-year-old daughter. Where had the years gone?

Gigi rummaged around in the pile of papers on her desk until she found the brochure. Opening it, she re-read the descriptions of the week's activities and allowed herself a moment to imagine herself there. It would be fun to reconnect with her old friends. She loved her life and her home in the rolling hills that surrounded Turin, but sometimes it felt very far from everyone and everything.

Setting the brochure to one side, she tried to research the other women—frustrated, as always, with how slow their Internet service was. Paolo had told her that it would change in the next few years when the telephone company upgraded their equipment, but for the time being, they were too far out of the city to be covered by the faster service offered in town. When the connection finally showed as a strong signal, she tried to see what she could find out about everyone. On Facebook she was connected to Melanie, and through her, she found both Julie and Angie, but there were too many choices for women named Emily with no photo to guide her.

The slow Internet service gave Gigi an excuse for not being more active on Facebook, but the real reason was that she was shy and preferred to socialize in person with her small group of friends. Being physically so far from the others had also made keeping in touch that much more challenging. Clicking through Facebook now, she noticed that Angie seemed to post only pictures of her husband and her kids. Moving to Julie's site, it looked like Julie was living in London. That was great—she would love an American friend relatively close by! Maybe Julie would sympathize with some of the cultural issues and traps Gigi faced sometimes. Now she was regretting she hadn't tried to find her before.

After a few more minutes of looking at Facebook and at the website for the trip, Gigi was overwhelmed with longing. She just *had* to go! It was a perfect way to reconnect—it wasn't far from home, and therefore wouldn't cost too much to get there. And it would be good for Mariella and Paolo to spend time together without her. With Paolo away so much for his wine export business, Gigi was responsible for overseeing Mariella's daily activities, like piano and soccer practice. He didn't realize how time consuming that could be and sometimes gave Gigi a hard time about not doing anything. This could be a chance for him to experience that side of their life for himself.

That thought led her to another reason she wanted to go. Gigi would love an outside perspective on her current dilemma—one that was causing a major disagreement in her marriage—Mariella's education.

Mariella had just started middle school, and Gigi had assumed, after hearing about her niece and nephew's experiences in middle school in Chicago, that Mariella would soon be talking about all the projects she was doing on the computers at school. She and Paolo had taught Mariella to use their home computer and she was quite proficient. But when Gigi went for her first visit to Mariella's classroom, she noticed there were only a few computers along one side of the room. Technology was obviously not part of the curriculum, at least not at the level that Gigi expected. In her conversation with the teacher, she learned that they simply did not have enough computers for everyone, and it had also become obvious that having a computer at home was a luxury many of the families couldn't afford.

And there lay the problem. Gigi wanted Mariella to go to college in the U.S., and she was sure that any good American college would require proficiency with computers. An American college education, in Gigi's mind, was a critical component of a happy and successful adult life for Mariella, socially and intellectually. She would never achieve that if she stayed in the rural Italian school system.

But what other options were there? Private school? But private schools cost money. And though Paolo's business was growing, it was not robust enough to cover that expense—at least, not yet. One immediate solution that seemed financially viable would be to send Mariella to middle school in Chicago, where she could live with her aunt and cousins. It was obvious that the Chicago school system considered computers a critical component of learning. Mariella would then have a strong base of computer skills, and it would give Gigi and Paolo time to find the best high school option. That might very well be a private high school back in Italy, and if so, they would have had the interim years to put money away. Gigi was not firm about many things, but she felt strongly that Mariella needed to get accepted into an American college.

But Paolo did not see the immediate urgency of the computer issue, and he did not want Mariella to spend time away from them. Most importantly, *he did not see the value of an American college education*. So far Gigi had not been able to explain clearly to him why it was so important to her, but it was something she had decided in the very first days of holding Mariella in her arms, and she remained firm in her resolve. She hoped that by talking about it with people who were her friends and who were also American, she would find the words to convey the logic of her arguments and better support her position.

For Gigi, it was simple. An American education for Mariella would also be a connection back to Gigi's own American roots. Gigi saw Mariella's exposure to, and understanding of, American life as a way to retain that part of herself that had been physically left behind when she made Italy her permanent home.

Gigi knew her sudden longing to go was also because she missed American life and American friends. When Gigi had left Boston that first time to work in Italy, she had thought that it would be for a short-term adventure, a learning experience to build her resume. But then she had met Paolo, and suddenly she was faced with very different choices. Most of the time, she was sure she had made the right decision. But living in a foreign country, no matter how wonderful, could be stressful. This alumni trip could be a break from that.

She thought back to the first time she had become aware of that stress. It had been on her first trip home to

Chicago to see her family after a year in Italy. That first evening at home, she had been struck by how relaxed she felt. She found herself telling stories about her year away, and marveled at the ease of it. Her shoulders loosened and her stomach lost its perpetual knot of anxiety. She knew how to make people laugh and she knew how to cajole her parents. Social interactions felt easy. Part of it was the language—in English she didn't have to think before she spoke. But there was more to it than that. She suddenly realized that it was also a cultural thing. In Italy there were lots of small nuances to simple everyday conversations.

She was always a little on edge, paying attention to what she said to be sure she was not offending someone by accident. In Chicago, there was none of that tension because she knew the social rules instinctively. Things like children's books or TV shows that everyone had grown up with were shared points of cultural reference that she didn't even think about. A reference to a Flintstones episode made her laugh out loud, and she was reminded of a similar reference to an Italian cartoon at one of the first parties she and Paolo attended together. It had caused a similar burst of laughter within the group, but Paolo had had to explain the joke to her.

As Gigi shut down the computer and got up to start dinner, she let herself think about how relaxing it would be to hang out with Americans and reminisce about college and about the good times they'd all had in Boston. And how much she would love sharing stories about Mariella and Paolo, and about her life in Italy. She wondered if Julie had children. She hadn't seen any sign of children on her Facebook page, but you never knew. Now that she thought about it, she didn't even know if Julie was married. And how had she ended up in London? Ah well, all of those questions and more would be answered if she went on the trip!

But how would she present the idea to Paolo? She had never asked to do anything like this before. What would she do if he objected?

****

Angie

Facebook alerted Angie to an incoming message. Now that she was almost an "empty nester" she felt she had time to spend online, chatting, catching up and—she had to admit to herself—playing silly games.

It was a message from Melanie Russell. Melanie's use of Facebook was like her personality—when there was an issue she cared about, she was passionate about it and posted often, but most of the time her focus was on other things and you didn't hear from her. The last posts had all centered on her son's graduation from high school, which had been in the spring. Angie read Melanie's email, and then read it again. What on earth was Melanie thinking? Angie couldn't just take off and go to France! And it specifically said that it was a "girls only" trip, which would mean going without Joe. Her stomach tightened at the thought.

Angie looked through the pile of unread mail in the kitchen and found the brochure. The picture was certainly inviting. The people were clearly enjoying themselves, and Notre Dame looked both regal and enticing. Could she really be considering such a crazy idea?

This fall, both girls would be away at college, and she knew that she was going to miss them terribly. This would be a way to start the fall on a positive note, with a fun adventure. But would she be able to do it on her own? She didn't speak

French and had not been back to Europe since those early trips from Boston so many years ago.

Would she be able to figure out how to get around? Or would she even have to? You'd think most decisions for the trip would be pre-arranged by the alumni staff. Opening the brochure, she saw there was a shuttle from the airport if you arrived within certain windows of time, so that wasn't an issue. She *would* have to figure out where to get some French money before she went. What did they use now? Euros? Maybe her bank could help her figure that part out.

Angie sat and thought for a long time. What if Joe didn't want her to go? Would she go anyway? There was no *logical* reason he should object. He would be fine on his own for a few days. She felt a tingle of excitement. Wouldn't it be *great* to see her old friends again? And what fun to sit at a café near Notre Dame again! She couldn't even imagine what that would be like after all this time!

Turning back to the computer, she decided to answer Melanie before she could lose her courage. "I definitely want to come. Joe is having some back surgery, but his sister will be here that week (*where had that lie come from*?). I look forward to seeing you and the others! I will send a follow-up message when I have my actual itinerary." She clicked "Send," and with a deep sigh, got up to go tell Joe.

****

Julie

Drops of rain joined into rivulets to run down the windowpane, chasing each other to the bottom. Behind them the sky was light grey, forming a solid, bleak backdrop to the day. Julie sighed. It was days like this that made her long for those blue skies of California. London weather could be like that—no change for days—just a slow lightening each damp morning before a slow darkening again as the afternoon wore down. It was one of the few things she didn't love about her new home.

Turning away from the window, she took a moment to look around the living room and felt a warm glow, happy to be surrounded by things that reflected her taste and style. Simply furnished, the apartment suited her. She liked clean lines and open spaces, and she had combined Danish furniture in soft beiges and browns with bright dabs of color in the throw pillows and in the modern paintings on the walls. She lived in a wonderful building built in the 1890s, and she loved the juxtaposition of its old exterior with the modern interior she had created. She had now been living in London for five years, and the apartment reflected the passage of that time in various small ways, from pictures she had found in upscale galleries, to unique treasures she had found at the neighborhood flea markets. And she was slowly developing a set of close friends, people who liked to do the things she liked to do. People who didn't care about the latest gadget on the market and who didn't talk for hours about technologies that were incomprehensible to her. She'd been very happy to leave those people behind in San Francisco.

She liked her life in London very much. But there were days like today when she found herself touched by melancholy and a sense that something was missing. If she was honest with herself, she knew it was not "something" but "someone." A "special someone" to share life's daily adventures with.

To distract herself, Julie moved over to her desk and opened her email. To her surprise, she saw an email from Melanie. She and Melanie had only been in touch sporadically over the years. When she had moved to California to be near her parents, her life had filled with new friends and then, after she married Ryan, the two of them spent most of their waking hours building his business. Over time, she had had less and less contact with friends from her graduate school days.

After her divorce and subsequent move to London, she had deliberately removed herself from contact with everyone from her past, wanting to completely start over. After a couple of years, however, she had found herself thinking more and more about people she had been close to, and had gotten onto Facebook to reconnect with a few people, including Melanie.

Opening up Melanie's email, she noticed immediately that it was addressed to their old circle of friends from Boston. Intrigued, she read Melanie's invitation to join her for a "girls only" trip to France hosted by Foundry's Alumni Association. Forgetting the grey skies, Julie thought back to those days in Boston, reliving some of the good times. What innocents they had been! All just starting on the great Adventure of Life in a world that felt shiny and new. She had spent two years getting her master's degree in accounting, and two more years at one of the most prestigious accounting firms in Boston, before accepting an attractive offer from a firm in San Francisco. She had been well on her way to becoming a partner when she met Ryan Wood, a shy, but adorable computer science engineer who had just started working for a newly-formed company called Google. Google's grandiose visions about the future of computers fed Ryan's own ambitions for opening his own company, and he vowed that one day he would find a way to share his own brilliant ideas with the world.

Julie and Ryan had met at a local bar. She took herself back to that night, remembering how deafening the noise level at the bar had been, with everyone demanding drinks in loud voices while trying to hear each other over the sound of the basketball game playing on the three television sets above them. It had been during March Madness and Stanford was playing, which meant that the crowd was ebullient. Julie had agreed to come out to have one drink with people from her office and had immediately regretted it. Bars were really not her idea of a good time. She had decided to finish her drink and make the excuse of finding the ladies' room so she could sneak home to her soft couch and quiet apartment. There she could help herself to a bowl of chili from the crockpot that was even now bubbling away, and watch the Masterpiece Mystery she had recorded. Taking a last sip of her drink, she noticed someone else standing slightly apart from the crowd, also nursing a drink, and also looking like he would rather be anywhere but there. He was cute, with brown hair that curled slightly where it met his collar, more the result of a missed haircut than a fashion statement. He had small, round glasses that gave him a professorial air, and he glanced up just as she looked in his direction, meeting her gaze with a shy smile before ducking his head back down. His shyness made him instantly appealing—the opposite of the conceited blowhards she'd been fighting off all evening. She decided to stop by on her way out and see if he was as interesting in person as he was from a distance.

A year later they were married, and four years after that Ryan had started his own company in their garage. They had both worked hard during those years, and her promotion to partner by then had provided the start-up capital he needed. She had occasionally thought about having children, but Ryan was dismissive whenever she brought it up. He would point out all the work still to be done for his business to be successful, promising to address the idea of children at some future date.

Ryan's company proved to have the right product at the right time. It was 2002 and people were picking themselves back up after the "tech wreck" of 2000 and 2001. He had his choice of qualified software engineers who had lost everything. It took him just two years to find the additional venture capital funding he needed, and another two years for his company to go public. The rest, as they say, was history. Ryan became a multi-millionaire. For three years after the company went public, she had worked hard to move their marriage to a new, more intimate level, but without success. She finally asked for a divorce, and the look of confusion on Ryan's face had been a confirmation of his total lack of awareness of their non-existent relationship. The end had all been very cordial and without fuss. As far as Julie knew, Ryan was still sitting in his converted garage playing on his computers.

But Julie found that she could not stay in San Francisco. Everywhere she turned, she ran into people who were friends of Ryan's, or people who thought she was insane for divorcing one of the "shining stars" in the field. By then, both of her parents had passed away—her mother from ovarian cancer, and her father of a heart attack within a year of her mother's passing. She knew it wasn't logical, but she felt he'd really died from a broken heart. Her parents' marriage had been a source of inspiration for her, which added to her subsequent despair when she could not find that same happiness with Ryan.

So with her ties to San Francisco gone, and a generous settlement from Ryan in the bank, Julie's future was wide open. With no idea where to turn, she signed up for an expensive spa and yoga retreat in Arizona, and set off to decide what the next chapter of her life should be.

Her thoughts during that next couple of weeks kept returning to the six months she had spent at the London School of Economics during her junior year at Powell. It was where she had developed both her love for accounting and her love for travel. When she returned home, she knew what she wanted to do. She sold most of her belongings, packed the few family heirlooms that she wanted to keep into a storage facility, and bought a first class ticket to London. Within six months, she was furnishing her beautiful apartment. Her life was now filled with art exhibits, music concerts, and theater outings. Generally, life was good.

Even so, every now and then when one grey day followed another, she found herself longing for those early days right out of college, when the future had looked so bright. Watching every penny had been hard, but somehow it had also made each indulgence that much sweeter. For Julie, their Annual Trip had been the best of those indulgences. Each year it had taken all of her creativity and thrift to find enough money to travel, but it was always worth it.

Coming back to the present, she smiled ruefully. The Julie of today didn't need to worry about what things cost. But she also didn't have the daily interactions and challenges of a career, which could be so energizing. She had enjoyed her freedom immensely these past five years, but she had begun to ask herself what she should do with the rest of her life.

Julie went to the website for the trip and checked to see who had registered. Because she had been at Powell, she didn't know a lot of Foundry people, and was nervous about being totally dependent on the group that Melanie was proposing. What would the others be like today? It was an interesting mix of personalities: Melanie, with her loud laugh and wild stories; Emily, who was probably still prickly and defensive; Angie, who had always pretty much gone along with whatever the group wanted; and finally Gigi, who had been so focused on her music that she had never had time for much else. Would they be able to rekindle their old camaraderie? Julie loved the thought of reconnecting and remembering those fun, early years. *Why am I overthinking this?* She thought to herself. *I can certainly afford to go, and if I hate it, I can just catch a train back home.*

She typed her response to Melanie, confirming her decision to go, and clicked "Send." A reunion in Paris would be fun, and now that she felt more comfortable and settled in London, maybe it was time to think about opening herself, and her life, back up. She had no desire to return to California, ever. But maybe it was time to see if there were parts of her former life that she wanted to include in her new world.

****

Emily

The house in Cambridge smelled musty. Not surprising, considering how long they'd been away in Vermont, but Emily had had all of the fans blowing non-stop since their return and thought the stale smell would have dissipated by now. She turned back to the computer screen and squinted. Only 1,200 more emails to go! She never took her computer when they went to their home in Vermont because she considered her time there as purely recreational. It was a welcome break from the constant demands of email. If someone really needed her, there was always the telephone. Instead, she would load up her Kindle with all the books she hadn't read during the year, and throw in a jigsaw puzzle or two for good measure.

It was also a time to get back into a healthy lifestyle. She and Ben took time for long hikes or bike rides together during the day, and every evening they cooked whatever they'd found at the local farmer's market.

This summer had been especially nice because Emily was now officially retired from her teaching job at the community college. With no need to worry about the fall class schedule, the summer had truly been an escape and a chance to relax.

As she skimmed the first few emails, Emily realized she was still getting notices about various activities surrounding the start of fall classes. She had posted an automatic response on her college email address about her retirement, but it would obviously take some time for her name to be removed from the many mailing lists.

She continued her way through, quickly moving all emails related to teaching to a separate folder to be reviewed later. A moment later she stopped in shock, amazed to see an email from Melanie Russell. *Melanie Russell?* Could it be the same Melanie from all those years ago?

Surely not. But how many Melanie Russell's were there? She quickly skimmed the message, and as she read, her amazement grew. Yes, it was the same Melanie, and she was inviting Emily to join her on an alumni trip to Paris! With Angie, Gigi and Julie! Her finger immediately moved to the delete button, but she paused, her finger hovering. Seeing those names had triggered a flashback of anger and frustration, but she needed to think this through.

During Emily's fourth summer in Boston, she had started dating one of her professors, Ben Williams. This alone would have been shocking enough because of their age difference, but he was also already married. It had caused a scandal at school and explosive, heated debates within their small group. Because everyone in their group knew and liked both Ben *and* his wife, they reacted very personally. The arguments had eventually led to Emily's departure from the apartment and from the group's social life. Forced to choose between the group and Ben, she had chosen Ben.

There had been enough said in those heated conversations that, for Emily, reconciliation was impossible. She recalled how disgusted they had all been at the time, and how she had not asked a single one of them to her wedding.

The episode still stung. But it *had* been a *long* time since then—over twenty years, she now realized. In truth, reconnecting with those four was something she had thought about at various times over the years when she got copies of the alumni newsletter, or when she saw an email from the alumni office. But each time her residual anger had stopped her. Now here was Melanie, holding out the olive branch. Who was she to immediately dismiss that?

Emily remembered how much fun they had all had together in the beginning. She recalled the bright pottery dishes they had found at a yard sale, and the games they would play to choose who got the best mug for morning coffee. There had been an old set of pots and pans that Julie had brought from home, and one pot in particular whose handle they'd re-attached with electrical tape, because somehow it made the best sauces.

Now Emily racked her brain, trying to recall what she might have read about any of them. She didn't use Facebook, which seemed to be most people's preferred method for staying in touch. Pulling up the Foundry website, she did a quick search and saw that Melanie and Gary were still in Virginia, and Angie and Joe were in Portland. Gigi was in

Italy—now that was interesting. And Julie was in London. There were certainly stories behind both of those moves.

Emily sat back in her chair, considering. Maybe this was the right moment to reconnect. The emptiness of her own fall schedule had been looming as both a threat and a promise. Certainly a trip to Paris would be a fun way to start her first year of transition, as she decided what she would do next. Ben had already decided to take a year off to write his next textbook, and Emily had used that as her official reason to stop teaching, claiming that they would be doing some traveling. The real reason was that she was simply tired of the routine and of academic politics, and she was ready to start something new.

Ben was already happily buried in research, and had recently expressed concern about how she was going to spend her time. She knew he would love this idea—he had been gently suggesting that she consider reconciliation for a while now.

She sorted through the pile of mail and located the alumni brochure. The tour started in just three weeks! She needed to first confirm there was space available, and next would be a search for flights. *If* there was still space, and *if* there was a reasonable flight, she would email Melanie.

Emily's heart quickened with a mixture of excitement and dread. Who would come? What would they be like after all this time? And how would she feel when she saw them again?

Chapter 3.

Charles De Gaulle Airport was noisy and crowded. After more than twelve hours of travel from Portland and very little sleep, Angie was exhausted. It was also disconcerting to have it be early morning when her body was convinced that it should be late evening and close to bedtime. It was all very disorienting. To calm herself down, she began to scan the crowd at the baggage carousel, playing her favorite game of trying to figure out what people's stories were. It was a game that she had started when the girls were young, to distract them whenever they needed to wait somewhere, and she had enjoyed it so much that she did it even when she was waiting somewhere by herself. Her natural curiosity about people, and her sincere interest in them, had also led to a career of volunteering for a variety of non-profit organizations.

Now looking across the baggage carousel, she noticed that a young couple across from her was having an argument, and their baby, who must have been exhausted after such a long flight, was wailing, adding to the stress of the situation. She felt a momentary impulse to go over and offer to calm the baby while they got their luggage, but dismissed the thought. After all, she was a complete stranger, and for all she knew, they might not even speak English! But she still found herself willing the mother to look her way and see her sympathetic smile.

The notice above the baggage carousel said there were incoming bags for her flight as well as a flight from Boston. Was it possible that Emily might be here? Melanie had confirmed she was coming. After twenty years, would they even recognize each other? Angie had tried to find Emily on Facebook, but there were a lot of Emilys and since she wasn't sure whether she should look for Emily Wright or Emily Williams, she soon gave up. The alumni website had a picture, but it was obviously an old one.

Angie eyed the bags pushing their way onto the carousel and then, looking beyond the luggage, she saw her. It had to be Emily. The same short, straight, brown hair, the same round face. She was wearing a tight pair of black jeans with boots, and her coat was brown with swirling designs in dark blue. Very artsy, very Emily.

At the same moment, Emily glanced up and their eyes met. For the first few seconds, Angie saw shock, then uncertainty cross Emily's face. Angie decided to make the first move and began to weave her way through the various obstacles of people and bags of all sizes.

"Angie?" Emily's tone was cool, and her smile was slightly condescending.

"Emily!" Angie decided to ignore the lack of welcome and, after an awkward moment, gave Emily a hug, not sure if it was the right thing to do. Making her own voice cheerful, she said admiringly, "How could you not have changed after all this time?"

Emily's look was slightly smug. "Ben and I take good care of ourselves. It's always been important to both of us." She paused before asking, "How have you been?" Her pitying glance made it obvious that she had already formed an opinion, and it was not positive.

Angie tried not to sound defensive as she replied, "I'm doing fine, thanks. A little heavier than college, obviously, and my blonde hair is now courtesy of my wonderful hairdresser—and don't look too closely or you'll see all the wrinkles. I'm starting to look like my mom!"

"Aren't we all?" Emily replied, though it was obvious she didn't mean it. They stood together for a moment, sharing an awkward silence and an obvious regret for having decided to come.

Angie cleared her throat, determined to break the tension. "This is going to sound crazy after so much time, but I'd like to apologize." She paused. "We said some ugly things to you way back in Boston, and I've wanted to say I'm sorry."

Emily was silent. She looked away and her face did not soften. She looked back at Angie. "It was not fun, and it hurt for a long time." She paused before continuing. "But I told myself that was over twenty years ago, and I should come on this trip to see if we could all start again." She paused a second time, then said, "I'll be honest—I'm wondering if I'm too old to change my ways…."

Angie was silent. It was obvious they had gotten off on the wrong foot. Her tone became brisk. "Well we're here now. Let's make the best of it, shall we? First thing is to find our bags and then find the shuttle."

They were both silent as they made their way through customs and out to the curb, where they found a large van with a hand-written "FOUNDRY COLLEGE" sign taped inside the window. Climbing into the middle seat, Angie turned to Emily and tried again. "Can we start over? Tell me a little about what is going on in your life."

Emily's tone was slightly defensive as she said, "You know I did end up marrying Ben?" At Angie's nod, she continued, "We never had kids. I've been teaching history at the local community college. Ben turned 65 this year, so he's taking a one-year sabbatical to write a textbook. I decided to take a break, too."

Angie felt a moment of shock. Sixty-five?? How could that be? Her thoughts were interrupted by Emily holding out her phone, saying, "Here's a picture of me with Ben at our lake house in Vermont." Angie studied it. Ben had white hair, but still had the wonderful smile and twinkling eyes that Angie knew had attracted Emily to him in the first place. He was lean and looked tanned and relaxed.

The driver started the van, and as they pulled into traffic, Angie felt a jolt of excitement. They were in Paris! She turned to share her feelings with Emily, but Emily had turned to look out the window. Angie had always prided herself on her patience with difficult people and her ability to smooth over uncomfortable situations, but now she felt a momentary irritation. *Isn't she going to ask about my life?* she wondered. She decided to pretend that Emily had. "I'm sure we'll be repeating some of this when everyone's together, but Joe and I have two daughters, Mary and Anne. I don't know if you knew I was pregnant when we left Boston?" There was an awkward silence and Emily shook her head, still looking out the window. Angie continued. "Anyway, they're both in college now. Mary is a junior at Ohio State and Anne is just starting as a freshman at Willamette. We live in Portland. Joe's mother passed away last year, and he wants to stay close to his father, who has Parkinson's."

"How's your husband's back doing?" Emily asked rather indifferently. Melanie had sent out another group email that had given everyone some background on members of their group.

"Oh—he's good. Thanks for asking."

There was silence again, and Angie was puzzled. *If Emily came on this trip to make amends and start over, she's certainly not trying very hard. What is wrong with her?* Determined to draw Emily out, Angie pulled out her own phone. "Here's a picture of the four of us last summer." Knowing that everyone would be showing pictures of their respective families, Angie had chosen one that had been taken on a trip to the mountains the previous spring. Mary, Anne and Joe had all gone for a hike while she found a spot in the sun to wait for them with her book and iced tea. She had never enjoyed hiking the way Joe did, and was relieved when the girls came along to keep him company, providing her the opportunity to stay behind.

Emily reluctantly turned to look at the screen, taking the phone and holding it closer to the light from the window. After a moment she said, "Joe doesn't seem to have changed much, though I don't remember him having so many freckles. And your girls are gorgeous." Her grudging tone belied the compliments, and again Angie felt irritation swelling up. It made her even more determined to stay positive.

"Thanks," she said with a false brightness in her voice.

As the silence lengthened, Angie's felt confused and very alone. Her initial excitement at seeing Emily had turned into frustration and now, sinking back into the cushion of the seat, she felt exhausted and worried. Was the entire week going to be like this? Maybe she was overreacting because of the jet lag and her embarrassment at her own appearance. *How* had Emily managed to stay so skinny? Angie could feel the button of her jeans pressing into her stomach, and she shifted slightly to try to relieve the pressure. *A little heavier. Who was she kidding? She knew from each new diet that she was forty pounds heavier than in college.*

Suddenly Angie wished fervently that she had never come. The others would probably all look fantastic too, and she would be the fat lump next to them. With a sigh, she looked out at the traffic and began to formulate her strategy for leaving. Joe would be angry with her for spending all that money only to turn around again, but all of a sudden, she couldn't imagine facing the pitying glances of the others. *What had she been thinking?*

****

Melanie

Melanie quickly glanced around the hotel room before setting her bag on the bed to unpack. Pulling out her phone, she saw it was 9:00 in the morning. Her eyes felt gritty, but overall she felt fairly rested. She had managed to sleep quite a bit on the plane. She went over to inspect the bathroom, and in doing so caught sight of herself in the mirror. Her dark brown hair was now the product of a hairdresser visit every six weeks, and she'd had it done just before coming on the trip so it would be at its best. She also now wore glasses full-time, and she had chosen a rimless style because it hid the small pouches that had formed under her eyes. Overall, she felt she looked pretty good, weighing just about fifteen pounds more than when she was at Foundry. She had carried an extra ten pounds for several years after having Craig, but had finally lost that when she started jogging.

Turning back to look at the room, she had a quick moment of doubt about her decision to share a room with Angie. It had seemed like a good idea on paper, but the reality was proving much smaller and tighter than she had imagined. The furniture did look expensive, sleek and modern, but the overall amount of space was not what Melanie was expecting for the price. There was just enough room for the two single beds and a small dresser between. The armoire on the opposite wall had two shelves and one hanging rod. Hopefully Angie had packed lightly so they could fit everything in.

The program pricing had been targeted toward couples, assuming double occupancy, so she and Angie had agreed they were comfortable enough with each other to stay together. Certainly the savings would help with other expenses and save Melanie from further arguments with Gary.

After putting a last sweater on her shelf, Melanie sat on the bed with the packet of reunion information she'd picked up at the front desk. It had the updated itinerary, and she liked what she saw. The only event on the agenda today was dinner at a nearby restaurant at 8:00 this evening. Wow—she hoped she'd still be awake! It might make sense to catch a quick nap at some point. Pulling her notebook out of her carry-on bag, she checked her notes on the arrival times of the others. Angie's plane should have landed by now, and Emily's too. But Gigi's and Julie's trains wouldn't get in till around 4:00, so it would be a while before they saw them.

Grabbing her purse, she headed downstairs to sit in the café across from the hotel entrance and keep an eye out for new arrivals.

****

Melanie had just finished her *café crème* and *croissant* when she saw the shuttle pull up and watched Angie slowly get out. She looked a lot heavier than Melanie remembered, and Melanie guessed that was why she didn't post pictures of herself on Facebook.

Glancing beyond Angie, she watched the next person get out and suddenly realized it was Emily. Melanie called out enthusiastically—to the horror of the Parisians sitting near her—and the women turned and waved. They made motions of going in to register and she waved back, indicating that she would wait at the café for them.

Pulling out her new journal, Melanie opened to the first page to start a chronicle of the trip. She felt a small *frisson* of pleasure as she held the new pen in her hand, writing the first words on the crisp, blank page. Organizing her thoughts like this had always calmed her. When her thoughts were organized, she felt in control of her life. Gary sometimes kidded her about her obsession with writing everything down and about the row of notebooks that lined one shelf in their bedroom, but she was looking forward to recording her experiences and impressions during this trip.

Arrival at the hotel: 8:30 AM. I'll be sharing a room with Angie. The room is nicely furnished, but small. I hope I left enough space for Angie in the armoire. I am now having my first café crème and croissant sitting across from the hotel. Emily and Angie have just arrived and it's 10:00 AM. Angie looks heavier, but Emily seems the same. Julie and Gigi are both coming by train and will get here this afternoon.

She wondered for a moment what Gary would be thinking when he got up in the morning. Would he miss her? She decided she would put all thoughts of Gary on the back burner until her brain was less fuzzy, but she was looking forward to talking to Angie about it. Maybe, if they all got comfortable with each other, there could even be a broader discussion with everyone. Only time would tell.

****

Emily

Emily's first impression of her room was that it resembled a cruise ship cabin: small, but efficient. Everything looked crisp and new. A simple, white comforter covered the single bed and there was a narrow passage between it and an armoire.

Opening a door past the armoire, she found a tiny bathroom. The toilet and sink were both on one wall, and on the opposite wall was a small, enclosed glass shower. It was spare, but complete. She liked it.

Emily unpacked quickly, neatly stacking the pants, blouses and sweaters she'd brought, as well as her one black skirt. She was very deliberate in her choices when traveling, always wanting to bring things that could be combined in a variety of ways. Her biggest concern and biggest challenge were to find ways to feel chic and creative while not packing a large suitcase. She knew that her physical appearance had an enormous influence on her mood.

She got to the bottom of her bag and pulled out her other pair of boots and her black pumps. Her shoes were where she spent the most money—soft, supple leather, and handmade. She had always cared more about her shoes than any other article of clothing. *Well, almost,* she thought, glancing over at her coat. It had been a special purchase at a local, high-end store in Vermont. It had not been cheap, but as soon as she saw the soft wool, dyed into muted swirls of color, she knew she had to have it.

Sitting on the bed, she allowed herself a moment to think back to seeing Angie at the airport. She had been shocked at how big Angie had gotten and she knew she had not been able to hide how she felt. All of her good intentions about being pleasant and starting over with everyone had just flown out the window. Health and fitness were so important to her—she couldn't help her negative reaction! Grudgingly she tried to cut Angie some slack. *You don't know anything about Angie. You don't know about her life, or what she's going through. Stop judging and just give her a chance.* But what could have happened? Was it from having kids, maybe? Or just bad eating habits? She smoothed her shirt over her own tight stomach. She knew she looked good for her age. Both she and Ben were still active, working out at the gym at home, and then taking their long hikes and bike rides in Vermont. She knew it was probably easier for them because they had no kids, but still, in Angie's case she felt like there was something more going on. Angie looked twenty years out of date, as if she had stopped caring what she looked like.

And that apology. *Was she for real?* As if she could somehow erase the hurt of all these years with a simple sentence. Emily felt mildly disgusted. Angie was like a big puppy dog, her brown eyes begging for forgiveness after chewing up your favorite pair of socks. Her round face added to that impression, plus her curly hair falling down in two big bunches over her ears. Emily vehemently hoped the shuttle ride wasn't an indication of the days to come or she'd never make it through the week. Hopefully everyone else would be more—she didn't know—more cosmopolitan, more worldly. Her quick glimpse of Melanie, sitting over at the café, had been reassuring.

She needed to get past this feeling that things weren't going to work and go say hello to Melanie. She had never been a quitter and she wasn't going to start now. She grabbed her coat, checking to make sure her purse held her credit card and some euros. Running down the three flights of stairs instead of taking the elevator, she briskly headed for the street.

****

Emily, Angie and Melanie

Angie was already sitting with Melanie at the café and the two seemed engrossed in a serious conversation. Emily hesitated, experiencing, with a sickening sense of *déjà vu*, that feeling of being excluded that had marked those last months in Boston. She knew Melanie and Angie had maintained their friendship after Boston, and that now they were rooming together.

As Emily approached the table, Melanie rose to give her a quick hug, and Emily's doubts receded. Melanie looked chic, almost European, in a dark grey sweater coat. Her behavior, however, was distinctly American. Her earrings bobbed wildly with her gesticulations as she started a new story, and Emily was instantly transported back to Boston. Melanie had not changed a bit.

The waiter appeared and Melanie laughed when she saw Angie pull out the exact same Berlitz language book that she had brought. The waiter looked pained.

"My *café crème* and *croissant* were delicious," Melanie said as the other two looked at the menu.

"So, I guess it's a dumb question, but it looks like some variety of bread and some variety of hot drink are basically the breakfast choices?" Angie asked.

"Yes, from what I can see. I guess they aren't the eggs and bacon sort."

Angie said ruefully. "That's too bad. I'm starved."

Emily thought about the granola bar in her bag, but didn't offer it, silently thinking Angie didn't need it.

Angie turned to the waiter and gathered her courage. *"Un café crème et un croissant, s'il vous plaît."* From his grimace, she could tell that she had mangled the pronunciation.

Emily smiled and said flawlessly, *"La même chose, s'il vous plaît."* The waiter smiled at her before turning away.

"What does that mean?" asked Angie.

"It means 'the same thing,'" said Emily. Almost apologetically she added, "Ben had a French exchange student living with us a year ago and I picked up a few words." She didn't add that she and Ben had made several trips to Paris over the years. She was afraid that Angie would either take it as bragging, or it would lead to more of Angie's fake exclamations of enthusiasm.

"You obviously did something right. He looked positively cheerful compared to when I gave him my order," Angie said.

Emily shrugged before saying, "French waiters. I think it kind of goes with the territory."

There was an awkward silence. Melanie rushed to fill it, saying, "According to my notes, Gigi and Julie both arrive around 4:00, though they come into different train stations. Julie is coming into *Gare du Nord* through the Chunnel, and Gigi comes into the *Gare St. Lazare*." She paused and then said with a laugh said, "Of course, I have *no* idea where either of those is, so I don't know how long it will take for them to get here." After the waiter set down Emily and Angie's orders, she continued, "What I *do* know is that I will need a nap this afternoon if I'm going to be coherent tonight at dinner." She continued, "This morning though, I'd love to take a walk to try to get oriented. Are either of you up for something like that?"

Emily spoke first. "I slept pretty well on the plane, so I would."

Angie's heart sank. She was so exhausted! But she could sense Emily's disapproval again. She looked at Melanie. "I'm pretty tired, but I think I could handle a *short* walk. I will definitely want a nap after that!"

Melanie said kindly, "Well, you traveled the farthest of anyone."

Angie looked at her gratefully, but said nothing. There was another awkward silence as Emily and Angie ate their *croissants.* Melanie reached for the check, feeling concerned. *Well, it's been a long time since we've seen each other,* she chided herself. *It makes sense that we're uncomfortable with each other.* Out loud, she said, "Let's pay and get going. Looks like we each owe 6 euros. Is tip included?"

Angie looked blank, so Emily spoke up. "Yes, it's always included."

Melanie was glad that Emily seemed to know her way around. That would be a big help when they were doing things on their own outside of the program schedule.

Angie was frowning as she looked at Emily, and Melanie wondered if something had happened between the two of them on the van ride from the airport. She would have to ask Angie later when they were in their room.

All three stood, gathering purses and putting on coats. Melanie reached over to touch Emily's sleeve.

"Your coat's gorgeous."

For the first time, Emily's smile was warm. "I picked it up at a small specialty store in Vermont last year. I just couldn't resist it."

"It definitely looks like you. I would have picked it out for you in a heartbeat," Melanie continued.

Angie watched their interaction with growing bitterness. Emily had been so cold and distant on their ride in. Was it jet lag or had that attitude been specifically directed at her? *I apologized—what more am I supposed to do?* She thought. She shrugged into her own coat, feeling the tightness across the middle as she buttoned it. She was feeling embarrassed and wondered again if she should just call Joe tonight and go home.

Melanie spoke up. "I had a chance to look at the map before you two arrived. There's a famous park not too far away—the Luxembourg Gardens. It's right up this street, *Boulevard St. Michel*. Have you heard of it? I thought we could walk up that direction. We can certainly stop anywhere in-between, but having a destination will keep me more alert. Okay?"

Melanie and Emily headed for the sidewalk and Angie meekly followed. She might as well see a little bit of Paris, even if she decided to go home early. She just hoped they wouldn't want to go too far or too fast....

****

Gigi

When Gigi arrived at 4:30, she headed directly upstairs to unpack. Her trip from the train station had been uneventful. Her French was rusty, since she hadn't done much traveling recently, but it was close enough to Italian that she was able to figure out how to buy a subway ticket and which metro stop would get her to the hotel. It had been fun figuring it all out, and it made her realize that she hadn't done much on her own in a very long time. Paolo was always there and handling everything. Most of the time that was fine with her, but today's success had given her a renewed sense of independence.

She wondered if she should call home and check in. She knew Paolo would want to know that she had arrived safely at her hotel. She pulled out her phone to dial the number, but then hesitated. The problem was that if she called, it would give Paolo a chance to complain if something wasn't going exactly as planned, and she would have to listen and be sympathetic and pretend that she wished she were there with him. And it *would* be pretending, because she *didn't* want to be there—not at all. Her feeling of excitement had grown as she had gotten closer and closer to Paris, and she had to admit that she was feeling happy, and maybe a little bit selfish for enjoying herself so much. She knew that she would miss Mariella and Paolo at some point, but at the moment everything was fresh and new. She quickly texted Paolo a message, saying that she had arrived safely, but that her phone service seemed spotty so she would try calling him later. It was an easy white lie that made her feel less guilty.

Her window faced the Seine with a sliver of a view of a café across the street. Enjoying her solitude, she unpacked slowly and then went to the window. She could see a few of the tables in front of the café and for several moments she watched the activity there, hoping to catch a glimpse of a familiar face. There was a woman sitting at one of the tables who looked like Julie, and Gigi thought about going down to the café—but suddenly a man sat down at the table. She watched for another few minutes, becoming more certain it was Julie, but not wanting to intrude.

She decided instead to continue taking advantage of her newfound freedom, so she took the elevator down to the lobby and headed outside, leaving through a door that exited onto a back street. Feeling an exhilarating sense of being invisible, she took random turns onto small streets, letting her body choose where it wanted to go. She had a map in her purse, but was enjoying the freedom of not checking it. Gigi wandered for an hour, stopping to gaze into shop windows whenever something caught her eye. She passed what looked like a small club and she thought about how much fun it would be to go listen to some live music. She and Paolo rarely did that anymore. Maybe there would be time to do that one evening?

At 6:00, she found a café that faced the Seine and sat at an outdoor table to have a coffee. Her sense of invisibility continued as she watched the couples and small groups all talking around her. No one took any notice of her. No one looked at her strangely for being on her own. The waiter came over and she managed to say *"Bonsoir"* and order a *café crème* without dying of embarrassment.

It all felt good. She felt independent and self-sufficient and just a little unpredictable. The past hour had been completely out of her normal scope of existence. She felt a bit rebellious, as if she were trying on a new personality.

Gigi pulled out the itinerary and list of attendees to check for any last-minute changes. She wondered again if anyone had a daughter Mariella's age. It would be a fun extra benefit of the trip for sure. Gigi found that talking about Mariella usually helped her relax in the first awkward moments of meeting new people. Looking at her watch, she decided that at 7:00 she would stroll back to the hotel so that she could be ready to meet everyone in the lobby at 7:30. She cringed momentarily, imagining the larger tour group.

Would the friendship within their smaller group buoy this new sense of independence? Or would she revert back to her usual strategy and make herself invisible.

Chapter 4.

Getting off the train in Paris, Julie paused a moment to take in the sights and smells that were so different from London. She'd started the journey at the St. Pancras train station, which was bright and airy, the ceiling stretching far above the hallway that was filled with scattered groups of people headed in different directions. Shops of all sorts lined each side of the walkway, showing their wares behind bright glass windows. It was neat and orderly, but also a little sterile.

Now, in sharp contrast to the other end of the Chunnel, was the *Gare du Nord* train station. It was darker, with lower ceilings. It felt older, and a little shabby. But the smell was the real difference. Here she could smell coffee, fresh baked bread, and a whiff of perfume as a well-dressed woman walked swiftly by on her way to some important rendezvous. Paris held a hint of the unknown, of the mysterious. All was proper at St. Pancras, all was in its place. *Gare du Nord* was a chaotic swirl of people, all intent upon their respective destinations. Heading for the metro, she could hear someone singing and the sound of an accordion, and both were slightly off-key. Checking the large wall map, she reviewed her route and set off.

Twenty minutes later, Julie emerged into *Place St. Michel,* which was at the base of *Boulevard St. Michel,* the center of life on the Left Bank. This was the area known as the Latin Quarter, full of students and tourists. Blinking at the sunlight that was now breaking through the scattered clouds, she made her way across the square to the hotel entrance, hearing three or four languages swirl around her even in her short walk. In no time she was checked in and made her way upstairs to her room.

Plopping down on the bed, she realized she was nervous about seeing everyone again. It surprised her, but upon reflection it shouldn't have. It had been such a big change to move to London, and she dreaded the thought of explaining the history behind it over and over. There weren't *that* many people that she wanted to fully inform, so she'd have to figure out a quick response to use most of the time.

After unpacking, Julie headed downstairs and walked across the street to sit at a table with a clear view of the hotel's front entrance. Looking at her phone, she saw that it was 5:00 and ordered a beer.

Glancing up from reading the description of the wine tour, she saw a taxi pulling away from the hotel. The figure pausing at the entrance seemed familiar. Shading her eyes to get a better look, she watched him look slowly around the square, his gaze stopping when it got to her table. There was a moment's hesitation as each examined the other. Julie's heart skipped a beat as she realized it was Sam Evans. She had seen his name on the list and wondered how she'd feel when she saw him again. Now she knew.

Sam Evans. Brilliant student at Foundry, even more brilliant student at Harvard Business School, and currently President and CEO of one of the better-known tech companies in Silicon Valley. He had drifted in and out of their Boston social activities, sometimes participating in the larger group events. She and Sam had shared a slow dance one cold February night that had led to a kiss and the promise of much more… but when the time had come to leave, she couldn't find him and had walked home alone. The next morning, she had convinced herself that it had just been a flirtatious kiss and told herself to get over it.

During her years in San Francisco with Ryan, Julie had wondered whether she would run into Sam. She heard about him at various industry events, and she knew that Ryan and Sam saw each other occasionally. She wondered now, for the thousandth time, if Sam had ever asked about her, or if he had even known that she and Ryan were married. She had never told Ryan that she knew Sam—it didn't seem necessary. She really didn't feel like she "knew" him in any true sense of the word, so what would that accomplish? Julie and Sam had never crossed paths again. But deep down, she did sometimes wonder about that night….

She saw that he was smiling, and suddenly he was walking over to where she sat, pulling his luggage behind him. She rose, her heart fluttering.

"Julie? I didn't know you were coming on this trip."

"Hey, Sam." She stopped, breathless, mentally kicking herself for feeling so flustered. "It sounded like fun, so I figured I'd check it out."

How dumb did that sound? She quickly added, "Uh, I mean, I live in London, so I figured it's an easy train ride over, and I thought it would be fun to reconnect with folks from school."

He looked surprised as he settled into a chair next to her. "You live in London? I thought you were in the Bay area."

She couldn't tell from his comment if he had known, or cared, that she was married to Ryan. Keeping her tone neutral, she said, "Yes, I was living there after I left Boston—got married to Ryan Wood in fact."

He nodded in confirmation. "He's done very well for himself."

She continued. "Yes, he has. Well, he's still there—and I'm now in London." She reached blindly to take a large sip of her beer.

There was an awkward silence, as he seemed to search for something to say. He spoke again. "I didn't realize you'd split up.... I'm sorry."

"You know how these things go." She tried to sound nonchalant, but the words came out a little stiffly. "Anyway, what about you? You're still Head Fred at Avanti Technology, right?"

He laughed. "Head Fred? I like that better than CEO! Yeah, I'm still there." He added, "I had to come to Paris to oversee the opening of our office here, so I arranged to stay an extra week for this."

"Have you stayed in touch with a lot of people from school?" Julie asked. Her heart was slowing back to its normal pace.

"Not really, but the brochure convinced me. You know the picture on the front of those people sitting in a café? That made me want to leave California for good!"

She laughed. "I think that photo had the same effect on everyone."

He went on. "It promised such an escape from reality. You know the Silicon Valley routine. I don't need to tell you how artificial it feels. Lots of people who want to be your best friend, but only because they need you or they want money." He suddenly looked tired. "I really get sick of it. It starts to feel like you can't trust anyone to be your friend, to just like you for *who* you are instead of *what* you are." He looked over at her, obviously discouraged.

She nodded. "I totally agree. And it sucks you in. I hadn't realized how superficial everything was—including my relationships—until I left. Once you realize it, you can never feel the same again. Ryan's pretty oblivious to that sort of thing."

There was a moment of silence and she wondered if she'd revealed too much. She asked quickly, "So, how about you? Any family?" She already knew the answer, of course, because as soon as she saw that he was on the list of attendees, she had gone online to find out whatever she could.

He nodded. "Wife and two kids. Jack is 19 and Lucy is 20, so we don't see them much except when they're home in the summers." He pulled out his phone and pulled up a picture of the family. It looked like it had been taken at a beach and everyone was windblown and smiling. His wife was beautiful, she noted with irritation. Both of the children looked a little like him.

"Very nice. Where are they in school?"

"Jack is at USC and Lucy went east to Brown."

"Wow—not stupid kids, that's for sure." She smiled at him.

He smiled back with pride. "Nope—guess they get that from their mom."

"Yeah, right," she drawled. "You're so dumb that you became CEO at 42." All of a sudden she wondered if she'd made her homework too obvious.

He smiled, and she felt her heart flutter again. Wow, he had not lost *any* of that boyish charm. His reddish hair now had streaks of gray, and he carried himself with such confidence. His hair had always been wavy, and she thought maybe it was a little thinner, but to her, he looked the same as he had all those years ago.

"So is your wife going to join you here?"

He looked uncomfortable for a moment before replying, "No, I told her she wouldn't really enjoy it. Too much re-living the 'old days' from school that she wouldn't know anything about. You know how people get—they start telling stories that start with "Remember when you…." And it's *never* something you want to remember, to be honest. Let alone share with a spouse!"

Julie laughed. "Well, that's probably true! Though the fact that it's a week in Paris and also includes wine-tasting in Burgundy would make me want to come!"

He looked sheepish. "Yeah, you're right. I had to kinda talk that part down." He grinned and added, "I guess I really just wanted to come on my own." Julie had to fight the little flutter of delight she felt at that news.

What was she *thinking*? Just because his wife wasn't here, he *was* still married, for God's sake! Intellectually, she could tell herself that all day, but emotionally, she was letting herself enjoy the simple pleasure of sitting across from him in a Paris café.

She got a little lost in his blue eyes and suddenly realized he was saying something. She brought herself back from her thoughts. "Sorry?"

"I was just saying, who else do you know who's coming?"

"Do you remember the group I hung out with in Boston? My roommates—Gigi and Emily? Or Melanie, or Angie?"

He was silent for a moment before nodding. "Vaguely, now that I think about it. I *do* remember the great parties you all threw in that tiny apartment."

She grinned. "How *did* we manage to fit so many people into such a small space?"

"Didn't need a lot of room—just a table for the drinks and food, and some room for dancing! So are they all coming?"

"They are! Melanie—remember her? Loud and always telling crazy stories? Anyway, she got the idea that she wanted to come and her husband couldn't, so she emailed me, Gigi, Emily and Angie and suggested we all come for a 'girls' trip. No spouses invited." She stumbled for a moment. "I mean, for those who have spouses…."

"Got it," he grinned. "That's a great idea—at least as long as the spouses don't mind."

Julie smiled. "It turns out Emily's husband is writing a book, Angie's husband just had back surgery, and Gigi's husband is staying home with their daughter. And as I already told you, I don't have one, so it all worked out." She paused before adding, "Actually, now that I think about it, I don't know why Melanie's husband didn't come."

"It'll be fun to see them again," he said. He saw she had the packet sitting on the table and, with a questioning look asking for permission, he reached over and took the list of attendees. "Hmmm…. Let's see who else is coming." He smiled at her. "I've been so focused on opening the office that I haven't even looked at the packet."

They both looked at the list in silence for a moment and she was acutely aware of his arm brushing hers as he leaned over to read the names.

"Oh good," he said. "Greg is coming. We had some good times when we lived on the same hall junior year. Oh, and look—Todd, too. He was always pretty quiet. I wonder what he's doing now? Where did the years go? I don't think I've seen anyone in twenty years!"

Julie nodded. "Hard to believe, right?"

"So you didn't go back to any of the reunions on campus?" he asked.

"Nope. Those first years in Boston, I had no money. When we moved to Palo Alto, I got all wrapped up in making partner at my accounting firm and helping Ryan get his company off the ground. There just wasn't time for anything else. "

"Oh, I know how that goes." After a short pause, he added, "And then kids take up any time that's left, right?"

She was silent and when he looked at her face, he looked embarrassed. "Oh, I mean, if you have kids...." He let his voice drift off.

Julie deliberately kept her tone light as she answered, "We never got around to it. To be honest, I was living with a kid so who needed another one?" She tried, but failed, to keep the bitter tone out of her voice. He reached over to touch her hand.

"Sorry. I didn't mean to pry."

"No problem." Julie changed the subject. "What kind of person am I to have not even offered you anything to drink?"

He smiled and she felt that flutter again, deep in her stomach. It might be a first sign of trouble to come, but at the moment she just knew she didn't want it to end. He moved his hand away from hers and looked crestfallen. "I should get back over there and unpack this bag." He stood. "See you at dinner tonight?"

She nodded and smiled, then let herself check him out as he walked back to the hotel. This could be a *very* interesting week.

Chapter 5.

Angie collapsed onto the bed and closed her eyes. She had just finished squeezing her clothes into the tiny armoire, but "moving in" had only added to her feeling of despondency. *What was she doing here?* she asked herself for the millionth time.

Following Melanie and Emily as they made their way to the Luxembourg Gardens, Angie had watched them chat away about the sites they wanted to visit and people they hoped to see, but it was as if she were experiencing everything from behind plastic wrap, the sounds and smells muted. She knew one reason for this was her exhaustion. She knew another reason was the horrible shuttle ride with Emily. That initial encounter had almost brought her to tears. Angie was a very positive person, and being treated so coldly had really hurt. Then there had been that snide waiter, looking down his nose at her when she asked for her coffee. Was it her fault she didn't speak the stupid language?

Tagging along behind Melanie and Emily, Angie had felt a lump growing in her throat. She had purposely filled her thoughts with pictures of her beautiful daughters until the pressure had faded.

At the Luxembourg Gardens, they had watched a group of small boys floating their sailboats on the pond. The park was enormous. Winding paths of light-colored gravel enclosed green grassy areas. Benches and metal chairs along the paths were filled with people of all sorts, enjoying the sunshine—some reading, some chatting, and some simply watching the children who ran back and forth, chasing each other. It was a garden that was both orderly and yet full of life, with so many people using it. Melanie commented that if you lived in a tiny apartment—and she had heard that apartments were generally very small in Paris—it made total sense that you would take advantage of the nice weather and come out to enjoy all this beautiful space. For Angie, it was a completely new way of looking at things. Having a roomy house and a big back yard—very typical for their neighborhood—she hadn't really thought about the space they occupied, inside and out.

When Melanie and Emily stood up to continue their walk, Angie had told them she wanted to unpack and they should go on without her. They had made a half-hearted offer to accompany her back, but after a moment they set off, with Emily reaching over to grab Melanie's arm to show her something. Angie's loneliness came back full force and she had to fight back tears. She was tired and alone in a foreign country, and home felt a million miles away.

Now, lying down, she felt utterly exhausted, but she was afraid if she went to sleep she would never adjust to Paris time. Looking at the clock on the nightstand, she saw that it said 11:30. Her brain felt fuzzy and full of cotton, so it took her a moment to count backwards the nine hours of time difference to figure out it was 2:30 in the morning in Portland. No wonder she was exhausted! Joe would be sound asleep in their king-sized bed. Feeling her eyes closing, she decided it wouldn't hurt to take a short nap, and even as she finished the thought, she was asleep.

Buzzing, what was that buzzing? Slowly opening her eyes, Angie focused on the unfamiliar surroundings and, for a moment, had no idea where she was. Awakening further, she remembered that she was in Paris. She looked over at the other bed, hoping that Melanie might have returned, but the room was empty. The buzzing was a large fly, trying desperately to find its way out into the bright sunlight.

Getting up slowly, Angie fumbled a moment with the window clasp, and as the fly made its way to freedom, a cool and refreshing breeze came in from outdoors. It had turned into a beautiful day—a clear blue sky with a few white, wispy clouds scattered across it. The clock on the nightstand now showed it was almost 6:00. She had slept for more than six hours! She knew she should feel refreshed, but instead she felt lethargic. It reminded her of those early years with the children, when she would be up with them at two or three in the morning, then have this foggy feeling the entire next day. She had a sudden pang of longing for those days. It had been hard, with both children so small, but it was also the time when she had felt the most needed.

Well, she knew what *she* needed now, and that was coffee. Locating her purse and room key, she made her way to the tiny elevator and down to the lobby.

Pausing at the door, she looked across the street and saw a woman sitting alone at one of the café tables. Was that Julie? She was supposed to arrive around 4:00, if Angie remembered right. Yes, it looked like her—same straight brown hair, shoulder length. Her head was bent toward something open on the table.

Smiling at the thought of not having to sit alone, Angie started across the street. Drawing closer, Angie could see that Julie had earphones on, and that her tapered fingers were lightly tapping on the table as she read. Angie hesitated, not wanting to interrupt, but enjoying the chance to examine Julie more closely without being observed.

Julie had on a perky pair of orange-framed reading glasses and Angie could see that her shoulder length brown hair was liberally streaked with grey. She also now wore bangs that framed her face nicely. She was also still slim—*how did all these women keep their figures?* Angie found herself slightly irritated by that fact as she moved toward the table.

Glancing up, Julie looked startled before recognition seemed to dawn and she stood up to give Angie a hug, pulling out her earphones and pushing her hair behind her ears.

"Angie! It's great to see you! Want a beer?" She indicated her now empty glass.

"No, thanks, but I'd love some coffee."

"Sure. Do you take milk in it?"

"Yes, please." Julie spoke a couple of sentences to the waiter, and Angie was relieved not to have to order for herself again.

"Wow—thanks for that! I didn't know you spoke French."

Julie blushed. "I don't really, but now that I live in London, I come over here fairly often to visit, so I've picked up some basic phrases."

Angie asked the dreaded question. "What brought you to London, anyway? Last I remember you were in California."

Julie hesitated before answering, "Well, life threw me a few curves and I ended up there." She didn't seem to want to say more, so Angie moved on to other topics.

"Have you seen anyone else yet?"

"Only Sam Evans. Do you remember him from Boston?"

Angie thought for a minute before nodding. "Oh, yeah, that tall guy who was at the business school? He came to some of our parties, if I remember right."

"That's the guy. Anyway, he arrived about an hour ago and saw me sitting here so he came over for a minute. How about you? Have you seen anyone?"

"I was with Melanie and Emily earlier. Emily and I arrived at the airport at the same time, by coincidence. We rode in the shuttle together."

Julie looked surprised. "I wondered if Emily would come. Considering how we left everything...."

"I know—I wondered the same thing. Well, she's here, though it'll be interesting to see how much fun she'll have."

"What do you mean?"

Angie's voice turned bitter. "She's got a chip on her shoulder a mile wide. You wouldn't *believe* her attitude when I tried to apologize. First, she nearly bit my head off, and then she basically ignored me."

Julie looked concerned. "That doesn't sound very pleasant. I'm sorry to hear that."

Angie took a shaky breath. "It's okay. I just told myself that I'm not going to let her attitude affect mine." Julie could see that Angie was hoping her own words would convince herself.

"Well, just keep in mind we're in Paris—what could be greater than that?" Julie's tone was deliberately bright.

Angie's sorrowful look, framed by the hair that fell on either side of her face, suddenly reminded Julie of Eeyore. It would have been funny if it hadn't been so obvious how unhappy Angie was.

Angie said abruptly, "I don't think being here is great. In fact, I've been feeling like I don't belong here at all."

"Oh no, don't say that!" Julie patted Angie's hand soothingly. "Paris is a great city and this week is going to be an adventure. The five of us back together again, just like the old days."

"But it's not like the old days. Back then, I had Joe with me, Melanie had Gary, and Emily didn't act like I wasn't good enough for her."

Julie looked nonplussed for a moment before saying, "Just think of it as a little vacation from all your family responsibilities, then. A great city, delicious wines, and new people to meet." Julie was horrified to see tears begin to flow down Angie's face. "Angie, I'm sorry. What did I say?"

Angie gulped, picking up the small paper napkin from under her *café crème* to wipe her eyes. "I'm sorry." She looked down in silence, trying to pull herself together. After blowing her nose, she turned back to Julie, her eyes red-rimmed and pleading.

"It's just.... It's just that.... Well, I don't speak French. And I'm fat. And Emily hates me. And I miss Joe and my girls already." Her voice suddenly got louder. *"Why in the world did I agree to come?"*

Julie looked around, distressed by Angie's tears and embarrassed by the scene she was making. Then she felt ashamed of herself. "Angie, it'll be fine. You're exhausted—you came a *long* way and that makes everything seem harder."

"That's what I keep telling myself, but I just took a six-hour nap and I don't feel *any* better." Angie put one hand up to her mouth to stifle sobs. She was losing her battle to keep her composure.

Signaling the waiter, Julie spoke a few quick words and he soon returned with a small glass, which he set on the table, eyeing Angie warily.

"Here, try this," Julie said, pushing the glass gently toward Angie.

"What is it?" Angie sniffled and eyed the glass warily.

"It's sherry. We'll call it your pre-dinner aperitif. It might help to calm you a little."

Angie took a small sip, grimacing slightly. After a moment, she took a larger gulp. "It's pretty good."

"I'm glad you like it. Here, have some of these nuts that came with my beer."

Both sat silently as Angie polished off the sherry and all of the nuts.

"Thanks. I did need something stronger than coffee."

Julie looked relieved. "I'm glad it helped. And it won't be long until we head to dinner. Once you have some good French food in you, you'll feel *much* better about everything."

Angie looked at the empty bowl. "Are there any more nuts? I'm starving. I slept through lunch."

Julie signaled to the waiter once more, who quickly brought another small bowl of nuts. As Angie poured them all into her hand, Julie watched her in alarm. "So tell me—how are you and your family? You have two girls, right?"

Angie was cheering up as she discussed her family, but after listening to twenty minutes of Angie's life history, Julie realized that it was going to be difficult to escape in time to freshen up before dinner.

"That all sounds really great! Hey, I'm sorry to interrupt, but I would love to head back over to the hotel to tidy up a bit—if that's okay?"

Angie stopped her monologue. "Of course, that makes total sense. Sorry—I've been going on and on. Let's pay up."

"Why don't I treat this time?" Julie smiled. "I'm sure there will be other chances for you to buy me a drink. Consider this your welcome to Paris."

Angie smiled. "That's very nice of you. Thanks. I do feel better!"

The two women walked back across the street, and as they entered the lobby, they saw Melanie and Emily coming in from the opposite side.

"There you are!" Melanie greeted them, smiling broadly. "And you found Julie!" Melanie gave Julie a quick hug of welcome, but immediately grabbed Angie's arm, saying, "Julie, I know we have a *ton* of catching up to do, but Angie and I need to get back to our room to get ready for dinner. See you back down here at 7:30?" Emily and Julie both nodded, and smiled at Melanie's retreating back. They could hear her gushing, "I'm *so* glad you made it back safe and sound, Angie. I was worried about you. But you won't believe the *great* market that Emily found!"

Julie turned to Emily. "She hasn't changed, has she?"

Emily shook her head with a smile. "Nope. I've been the object of all that energy for the last few hours so I'll let Angie have her turn."

Emily fell silent and Julie suddenly felt awkward, remembering Angie's comments about Emily's attitude. Julie decided that the easiest course was to just give Emily a hug. Emily looked startled at first, but then hugged her back.

"How was your trip?" said Julie, feeling relieved to have broken the ice.

"Good. I slept quite a bit on the flight. And how was your train ride?"

"Easy. Much easier than for you guys, for sure."

"Do you come over often?"

Julie nodded. "Quite a bit, actually. The Chunnel has made it so easy to go between London and Paris. You hop on in London and poof! In two hours, you step off in Paris."

Emily nodded. "I envy you that."

Julie said, "I love it." She looked at her phone and added, "Emily, I'm sorry to pull a 'Melanie' on you, but if you don't mind, I would love to freshen up as well. See you back down here shortly." She gave Emily another quick hug before heading for the elevator.

Emily was glad Julie seemed so normal and approachable. After the rough start with Angie at the airport, she had begun to doubt her own ability to "'start over." During her walk with Melanie, she had started to relax, and now it looked like getting to know Julie again would be pretty easy as well. She and Julie had been very close once—maybe they could find that friendship again.

Emily went back outside, pulling out her cell phone and mentally calculating the time difference. Could she catch Ben? It was just after noon in Cambridge, so he might be home getting a bite to eat. She wanted to talk to him about her day. She'd already gone through a roller coaster of emotions—first anger and frustration with Angie, combined with disappointment with herself for being so intolerant. But then things had gotten much better in her walk with Melanie, and now her quick conversation with Julie had made her feel hopeful. She wanted to share all of that with Ben. He was the one who had been so confident that she should come—to take this chance to mend the old hurts and start over. And she did want to. She just wasn't sure she could.

"Ben? I thought I might catch you. Do you have a second to chat?" Taking a deep breath, she continued. "No, no, things are okay now, but they started out rough. I rode in with Angie from the airport and Ben, she looks *terrible*. Really overweight and kind of pathetic, to be honest. I tried to be patient, and to do what *you* would have done. I really did. But I couldn't get there." Emily was silent for a moment, feeling ashamed again of her behavior. "You know how I get, especially when I'm tired. No tolerance." She paused, listening, and smiled gently. "I know—I wish you had been here, too. You are so good in those situations." She took a deep breath. "Anyway, I then spent the afternoon walking around with Melanie—and *that* was an experience. She hasn't changed at all." She paused, listening to Ben's response, and feeling reassured by his calm voice. "And then I got back here and Julie had arrived and you know what she did? She just reached over and hugged me. It really made me feel good." She paused again, and then said, "I know—I do want to make this work. Okay, I'll call you in a couple of days. I love you." Hanging up, she felt calmer. She would keep reminding herself of his advice—to keep an open mind and an open heart.

Chapter 6.

Gigi took one last look at herself before heading downstairs to meet everyone. One advantage of being just over five feet tall was that she could see most of herself in the mirror that hung on the inside of the bathroom door. Overall she was happy with what she saw. Her shoulder length hair was still primarily blond, and she liked to think of the gray streaks as her own natural "highlights." Her hair was still wavy and reasonably thick. Her eyes were now edged by small wrinkles, but she told herself they were laugh lines. She'd always worn contact lenses, so there was no outward change there. She'd also really tried to stay active and keep her weight in check. She walked whenever possible, finding that it was easy to do since she made daily trips to the local grocery, butcher, and bakery. That was one very good thing about the European lifestyle.

Looking at herself with a critical eye, Gigi suddenly worried that she looked too "European." She was wearing a flowing, printed top that she'd bought in a small shop in Turin. Its green and gold stripes set off her green eyes, and she had always liked it, but now she wondered if it would look strange to this group. After a moment, she shrugged. They knew she lived in Italy, if they'd read anything on the Alumni website, so she wasn't going to let herself worry about it.

She paused at the bottom of the stairs, feeling nervous as she glanced around the large group gathered in the lobby. Searching for a familiar face, she recognized Julie from the earlier glimpse at the café, and thought that one of the men next to the reception desk was the man she'd seen at Julie's table.

Julie was standing with three other women, and Gigi realized with a start that the large woman was Angie. She was wearing a pair of jeans that looked a size too small, and her blouse's buttons were straining to stay closed. She had obviously made some effort with her hair, but it was also obvious that she needed more practice.

Next to Angie was Melanie, in a beautiful dark red long jacket and several rows of beads. Her dark hair had been swept up into a low bun at the nape of her neck, and her dark eyes sparkled. Her earrings swung as she talked and, as usual, she was in the middle of a story. Emily was standing next to her, and she looked over, meeting Gigi's eyes. There was a split second before her face brightened with recognition, and to Gigi's surprise, she came over to give Gigi a hug.

"Hey you! We wondered if you'd gotten lost en route from Turin."

Gigi blushed. "No, I ended up doing a little exploring on my own after I unpacked."

Emily nodded. Under her breath, she said, "Didn't want to tackle this group too early, huh?"

Gigi smiled. "You guessed it," she confessed. "I've never been very good at this 'meet and greet' thing."

"It's easy once you say hi to one or two people," said Emily, and then added, "Especially for you, with no 'baggage.'

Imagine how I felt, knowing how we had all left things in Boston?"

Gigi's look became contrite. "I am very sorry about all that. We were a very judgmental group, weren't we?"

Emily nodded, her look slightly strained, but then added, "I can't say I handled it very well myself. Looking back now, I can see how crazy it must have seemed to all of you at the time."

Gigi looked sympathetic. "This is going to sound corny, but one thing I've figured out is that no one can ever predict where love will lead them. Look at it this way—you two are still together, aren't you?" At Emily's nod, Gigi continued. "So it was the right thing after all."

Emily smiled gratefully. "You make it sound so simple when you say it like that, but you're right. It *was* the right thing, and it still *is* the right thing—for me and for Ben." She looked thoughtful. "Thank you for understanding that."

Gigi smiled, and both women felt the importance of the simple words. It was the first step toward renewing their friendship.

"You ready to jump in?"

Gigi took a deep breath and followed Emily toward the front doors. She found herself swept into a crowd of laughing, talking people and, after a short walk, they were filling up a small restaurant, choosing seats at several long tables. Gigi found herself next to Julie and across from Emily, Melanie and Angie.

There were carafes of wine already in the middle of each table, as well as baskets of fresh bread. Melanie's eyes were sparkling. "The old gang together again!" she exclaimed, raising her filled glass high.

All five women clinked glasses. It really was quite an accomplishment to be all together again.

"So what happened to you this afternoon, Gigi?" Melanie asked. "Find some cute Italian on the train?"

Gigi vainly tried to think of something clever to say, not wanting to admit how much fun she'd had just spending time on her own. She didn't want to start the trip looking like she was being anti-social. So she replied simply, "I'm here now, isn't that the most important thing?"

"Ha! Yes—you're right!!" Melanie's face was slightly flushed and Gigi wondered if she'd already been drinking.

"When did you all arrive?" Gigi asked.

Melanie answered for everyone. "Well, I arrived first. Then Angie and Emily caught the shuttle from the airport and arrived together. I took them to see the Luxembourg Gardens after we had our *café crèmes*." Gigi noticed that Emily grimaced slightly at Melanie's pronunciation.

Melanie took another sip of her wine before continuing. "Angie came back to the hotel for a nap, but Emily and I ended up walking all over the Latin Quarter." There was a slight pause before she added, "We did find time to have a beer on *Boulevard St. Germain*. I couldn't tell you exactly where. Emily found our way back—she has a great sense of direction!" She looked at Emily affectionately.

Emily raised an eyebrow and said wryly, "We might have had two beers."

Melanie's laugh boomed across the restaurant. "Oh, I guess you're right. And I'm thinking that my jet lag may be making them go just a teensy bit to my head." She giggled.

Emily handed her the basket of bread. "Might be a good idea to have some bread, then."

"Good idea." Melanie grabbed two of the baguette slices and immediately stuck a large piece in her mouth. A waitress who had been hovering nearby chose this moment to dart in and hand everyone menus, and the next few moments were spent in relative silence as they all tried to make their choices. Gigi glanced down and, with a small smile, suddenly realized they were in an Italian restaurant. She enjoyed the irony and thought it would be fun to see how it compared to her favorite restaurant at home. She was relieved that no one asked her for help with their orders, even though she was—as far as she knew—the only one fluent in Italian.

Soon everyone had ordered, and Julie turned toward Gigi.

"How *are* you?" She glanced over to be sure that Melanie was busy talking to a man on her other side, then turned back to Gigi with a conspiratorial smile. "Looks like we have a few minutes."

"Things are good."

Julie remembered that Gigi had never been a big talker. "Tell me what's going on in your life. I found you on Facebook, but all I know is that you're married and you have a daughter."

Gigi nodded. "You may remember I went to Italy to work as a piano tuner after I finished my apprenticeship in Boston?" At Julie's nod, she continued. "Well, I met Paolo through one of our clients. His family owns a vineyard and he's in the wine export business. The vineyard is small, but it's part of a larger cooperative of vineyards nearby, so they actually do quite a bit of exporting throughout Europe."

"That sounds great! And your daughter?"

"Mariella." Gigi reached into her pocket to pull out her phone. Scrolling for a moment, she then handed it to Julie.

"She's gorgeous! How old is she? Ten? Twelve?"

"Twelve. She just entered middle school."

"She must speak both English and Italian? That will be a tremendous asset as she gets older."

Gigi nodded, but inwardly her thoughts immediately went back to her ongoing concerns on that front. She hoped she would have the chance to pull Julie aside in a quieter moment and get her opinion. "What about you? Any kids?"

Julie shook her head and lowered her voice. "No kids. I was married, but we never got around to having children."

Julie looked like she didn't want to discuss it any further so Gigi changed topics. "How do you like London?"

Julie beamed. "I love it! I moved there about five years ago after my divorce." She looked like she was going to say more, then stopped.

Gigi waited to make sure she wasn't going to continue before asking, "I've only been to London once and what I remember is grey skies and people standing politely in line for the bus. How do they say it—'in the queue?'"

Julie laughed. "Yes, we definitely have both of those things, but we have lots of other fun things, too!"

"I'd like to go back, and bring Mariella. She could use practice with her English."

Julie laughed again. "*I* could use practice with British English! I'm always finding myself saying things that are *not* appropriate, though I don't mean to!"

Gigi nodded vigorously. "I know how you feel. I was thinking about that on the train ride here—how stressful it can be when you're always watching what you say."

"That's what happens to me, too," said Julie enthusiastically. "Just the other day, I was at dinner with some neighbors—an older couple who have been wonderful to me—and when I'd finished my meal and she asked if I'd like another helping, I said, 'No, thank you, I'm stuffed.' I meant it in a positive way—that I'd enjoyed her cooking so much that I'd eaten more than I should have. But she got this shocked look on her face, and then started laughing."

Gigi looked puzzled. "Why? Does that mean something different there?"

Julie nodded. "Apparently 'stuffed' means pregnant!"

Gigi laughed out loud, then looked around embarrassed. She turned back to Julie. "Believe me, I could tell you lots of those sorts of stories, too."

Feeling at ease already, she decided to add, "It's actually something I'm worried about for Mariella—that she won't fit in with Americans."

"That isn't all bad—Italians and Italy are great, too!"

"I know, but I want her to go to college in the States, and I think that'll be hard if she's only experienced life in Italy."

Julie looked thoughtful. "Maybe." She paused before continuing, "I guess I can see both sides." She had no opportunity to comment any further, because suddenly there was a loud burst of laughter and Melanie was standing up at her place, weaving slightly.

"I want to propose a toast." Her voice was slightly slurred and Angie had a panicked look on her face. "I asked four of my *best* friends to come on this trip and they are all here!" There were cheers and whistles from several people.

"Okay, Melanie, simmer down!" shouted a large, red-faced man at the end of the table.

"Shut up, Greg!" Melanie retorted. "I won't give a big speech—I just wanted to raise my glass in a toast to reconnecting with friends."

"Hear, hear!" There were several clinks of glasses and as Melanie sat back down, pizzas began to arrive, followed by the low murmur of conversation as everyone began eating. Glasses were refilled and then, as dessert arrived, several other people stood to recount stories from college and there was lots of laughter.

Gigi glanced over at Melanie and Angie, and she could see that they both were looking glassy-eyed. Looking at her phone, she was shocked to see that it was 10:30. Where had the time gone? And the people who had come from the States had been awake for many more hours than she had. Glancing over at Emily, she could see that Emily was thinking much the same thing. As if on cue, both stood up. Julie looked over and seemed to also sense the mission, and the three gently persuaded Melanie and Angie to join them and quietly slip out of the restaurant. Emily had one hand under Melanie's arm, and Melanie appeared to be having trouble walking in a straight line. Angie seemed in better shape, though obviously exhausted, so Julie and Gigi put Angie between them and walked two steps behind Emily and Melanie, talking quietly as they made their way back to the hotel.

Gigi was thankful that someone had been paying attention to their whereabouts. It looked like Emily was taking responsibility for getting them home safely.

Fifteen minutes later, they were in the hotel lobby. After seeing Angie and Melanie safely to their room, Emily, Julie and Gigi tried to control their giggles as they made their way up one more flight of stairs to their rooms, which, it turned out, were lined up along the third floor corridor.

Emily said. "Well, I wonder how much of that dinner Melanie will remember?"

Julie shook her head. "I just hope she doesn't have a giant headache tomorrow."

Gigi giggled—something she only did with her closest friends. "When she stood up, I was really afraid she was going to break into song or something!"

Julie nodded. "I know—wild and crazy Melanie!"

Emily was silent, then looked at both of them. "This was fun." She paused. "I'm glad I came." They could see that it took some effort for her to say it.

Gigi nodded and squeezed her hand. "Me too."

Emily asked, "You mean you're glad *you* came or you're glad *I* came?"

"Both, of course!" Said Gigi, giggling again.

Bidding each other good night, the three women slipped into their tiny rooms.

Emily lay back on the bed, feeling mentally exhausted She let herself think back over everything that had happened, reminding herself again about Ben's advice to keep an open mind.

Had she been too harsh with Angie on the ride in? Angie had certainly been easier to deal with at dinner. Well, she'd see how things went. They didn't have to become *best friends* or anything. She rolled over, and was soon asleep.

Julie couldn't stop thinking about Sam, despite her efforts otherwise. She kept going over their conversation at the café that afternoon, and trying to decide if there had been any hidden messages there. As she drifted off to sleep, she admitted to herself she was hoping there were.

All the socializing had exhausted Gigi, but she was also exuberant that she had held her own throughout the evening. She had enjoyed the conversation with Julie, and talking about Mariella and her life in Italy had made her see it in a whole new light. It had been the right decision to stay all those years ago. But what would be the right decision for Mariella?

Chapter 7.

Melanie grimaced at the sunshine in her eyes. Turning over, she felt her stomach gurgle dangerously. Gently putting her legs over the edge of the bed, she allowed herself to sit up slowly, waiting for the room to stop spinning. Glancing over, she could see the lump that must be Angie in the other bed.

What had happened last night? She remembered walking around with Emily, and the couple of beers they'd had in a sidewalk café, and she remembered meeting everyone in the lobby and walking over to a restaurant. Pizza, that's right. They'd had pizza. She remembered it was good, and that the wine also tasted good—too good, apparently.

Gingerly, she moved to the bathroom, drank two glasses of water, and took two Excedrin. After brushing her teeth and taking a hot shower, she started to feel more like herself. Opening the door into the bedroom, accompanied by a cloud of steam, she saw that Angie was now awake.

"How'd you sleep?"

Angie looked glum. "I think taking that long nap in the afternoon was a mistake. I went to sleep right away when we got back, but woke up in the middle of the night and felt like I was awake for hours."

"What time is it anyway?"

Angie reached over to squint at the clock. "About 9:00."

Melanie picked up the itinerary. "This says that the hotel serves breakfast until 9:30, so maybe we can just make it. Do you mind if I dry my hair while you shower?"

Angie looked away before answering with a tentative "Sure."

It was obvious she didn't mean it. Angie was apparently self-conscious.

Melanie quickly changed tactics. "You know—now that I think about it, there isn't a plug in there for blow dryers anyway. I'll use this one next to my bed."

"Okay, if that's easier." Angie's look of intense relief belied her words.

"Let me grab my makeup bag and I'll just use the mirror in the armoire."

Twenty-five minutes later they both headed to the elevator, Angie's hair still damp. Entering the dining room, they immediately saw Emily and Julie and made their way to their table.

"Room for two more?" Melanie asked, trying to keep her tone bright.

Julie nodded, giving her a close look. "You doing okay this morning?"

"Absolutely! Slept like a rock," she added brightly.

Julie and Emily exchanged glances, but said nothing.

"Where's Gigi?"

"Oh she's eaten and is now off on a walk," said Emily. "She said she was going to look for a present for her daughter."

Gigi was, at that moment, retracing her steps from the day before, in search of a particular scarf shop she'd passed. Turning a corner, she saw it in front of her. The window display was amazing. The owners had created a giant pinwheel of scarves of all different colors that revolved slowly. She saw that the door was open and went inside.

"Bonjour, Madame."

The saleswoman looked up from the counter. "Bonjour, Madame."

Scarves were very much a part of women's apparel both here and in Turin, so she felt sure Mariella would love one to add to her collection. The scarves were organized by color so Gigi made her way to the corner that held variations of red and purple. Purple was Mariella's favorite color.

She quickly found one that that had a deep purple background interspersed with soft bands of white. Pulling out her purse, she exchanged a few basic sentences about the weather with the saleswoman, and felt very proud of her accomplishment—both in the purchase and the conversation.

Hurrying back to the hotel, she ran upstairs to drop her package in her room before joining the rest of the group in the dining room.

Meanwhile, Melanie and Angie were just finishing their breakfast. "Ah," Melanie said as she set her coffee cup back down. "Now that's what I needed." Her stomach appreciated the warm milk and her brain needed the hot coffee. She had a new appreciation for *café crème* and its medicinal qualities. She looked sheepish for a moment as she looked around at the others. "I might have had just a tiny bit too much wine last night."

Emily laughed and then, with a drawl, said, "Yeah, we figured that out."

"I assume I have you two to thank for getting me home safely? I swear I wouldn't have had a clue which way to go from the restaurant."

Julie nodded. "Luckily, Emily paid attention when we walked over. Speaking for myself, I was so busy getting re-introduced to people and scoping everyone out that I didn't have any idea where we were." She had been searching for Sam, but left that out. "Emily and I have been trying to remember people's names and faces."

Julie took a surreptitious look around and said quietly, "Here's what we have so far. Sitting over in the corner behind you is Sam Evans. Do you remember him? He used to come to some of our parties in Boston." At Melanie's nod, she continued. "Sitting with him are Greg, Todd, and John. Don't know much about Greg or Todd yet, except that they seem to be here on their own."

Trying not to be too obvious, Melanie turned her chair so she could glance back at the table. "I know Greg. He was a History major like me. We had a couple of classes together. Now I remember seeing him in the lobby last night. Wait. Didn't I yell at him at the restaurant?"

Emily laughed and nodded, and Melanie groaned.

"I definitely recognize Sam Evans, too. He's still gorgeous, isn't he? I don't recognize the other two. Have any of you connected to the Wi-Fi here at the hotel?" asked Melanie. "We could check online to see what the alumni directory says."

Julie nodded. "That's not a bad idea. I did some research before I came, but I only looked up people I remembered and I don't think I knew Todd." She deliberately kept her face neutral before adding, "And John wasn't on the list of attendees. I would have remembered."

Melanie looked at her more closely. "Okay, that's an interesting tone of voice. Which one is John?"

Julie looked mischievous. "He's the balding one that's a little overweight." She paused while Melanie snuck a quick look.

Continuing, Julie said, "I don't think he was at the dinner last night either. At least, I don't remember seeing him. Maybe he was a last minute addition."

Melanie looked confused, but intrigued. "Why do we care?"

Julie looked at Emily and they both burst into laughter, trying hard to hold it in. In a stage whisper, Julie said, "That's *John Cameron.* Does that name mean anything to you?"

Melanie sat silent for a moment before shaking her head. She looked over at Angie, who said, "No, I don't think I knew him."

"Well, let's just say that he was a popular guy freshman year. With the women, at least. And a big party man." Julie paused dramatically before adding, "And Emily and I have just figured out that we both slept with him!"

Melanie choked, her coffee splashing out onto the checkered tablecloth. After a moment, when she could breathe again, she dared to look up. Her expression sent them into more gales of laughter and this time, Angie joined in.

"*Seriously*? That is unbelievable!" Melanie's eyes were streaming. Mopping her eyes with her paper napkins, she added, "Now look what you've done to my mascara!"

Julie said, "Sorry. Think about how *we* felt. We couldn't believe it at first, but when you look closely, it's him."

Emily added, "And as you may recall, Julie was at Powell, not at Foundry, so it's no wonder we never had this conversation before!"

Melanie shook her head, grinning. "Now *that's* the kind of juicy tidbit that these college trips are supposed to produce! I *like* it!"

Angie felt left out. *She* had not slept around in college, and was not really comfortable with this turn of conversation. She tried to separate herself by pretending to read the label of her yogurt container. Maybe she could go get second helpings and remove herself entirely. Glancing down at her cell phone, she saw that it was 9:00. At home it would be 1:00 in the morning, she thought sadly, and for a moment wished she were lying in bed next to Joe.

Melanie said, "Thank God for *café crème*—I almost feel normal again." She turned back to the others. "So quick, who else should I remember from last night?"

Emily spoke up. "Over at the table in the other corner are Judy and Wayne. I met them last night, and I know you were introduced, too. Judy was in our class, but I don't remember her. She said she was a Biology major. I didn't take any science classes so it's not too surprising that we never crossed paths."

Angie brought herself back to the present, wanting to join back into the conversation. Wiping crumbs off of her blouse, she said, "Next to them are the two professors on the trip, Professor Savalini and Professor Dupont. Actually, I guess we're supposed to now call them Joelle and Michel. I took French from Joelle when I was at Foundry, but never had Michel. He's a French History professor. Joelle introduced me to him last night."

Emily said, "I'm sure we'll hear from them today. We're supposed to get on a bus at 10:30 to get a quick overview tour of the city."

"I'm glad we're doing that," said Melanie. "As someone who was only here once, and a *long* time ago, I could use it." She turned to Julie. "Do you come over often?"

Julie nodded. "It's so easy with the Chunnel."

Angie spoke up. "I'm sticking *right* by your side, Julie. I do *not* want to try to find my way back here again. I almost had a panic attack yesterday coming home from the Gardens. And I wouldn't have the first clue how the subway works." She looked like a scared rabbit and Julie remonstrated her gently.

"C'mon, Angie. You need to stop looking at this trip as a scary thing and start looking at it as an adventure."

"That's easy for you to say. You're used to traveling to different countries and dealing with different kinds of people on your own. But I'm not. What I'm used to is having Joe around to take care of everything." She paused for a moment. "When the email came from Melanie, I thought at first that I'd have to say no, since I knew Joe wasn't invited, and *of course* I couldn't imagine doing something like this without him." Angie was silent for a moment and then, when she spoke again, her tone had changed. "But then I kept looking at the brochure and I started thinking, 'Wait a minute. Why *can't* I do this on my own? It would be fun to go somewhere new, somewhere exotic.'" Her gaze was intense. "I had sudden visions of this crazy, carefree life I would get a chance to experience." There was another pause and then her shoulders slumped. "But the reality has already proved a lot scarier than the dream."

Julie spoke first. "Angie, you can depend on us to help you through any problems that come up."

Angie looked grateful, and said, "I appreciate that. But I also don't want to be a burden on anyone."

Melanie held up her fingers in a Girl Scout pledge. "As your roommate, I take my responsibilities seriously. I promise to make sure you don't get left behind anywhere."

"Okay."

Emily's look was skeptical. "Oh, yeah, right—like last night?"

Melanie looked sheepish. "I know—I blew it last night. But that was the jet lag. It won't happen again."

Melanie took a last sip of her coffee before standing and stretching. "Okay, let's get out of here and onto that bus."

Julie laughed. "Sounds good. Let's go!"

****

Julie deliberately got on the bus behind everyone else and used the delay while people were finding places to quickly scan those already seated. She spotted Sam in the back, sitting with Greg and Todd. She noticed with relief that John was not with them. Sam looked up just as she got on and waved her back to where they were sitting.

"Guys, this is Julie. Have you all met yet?" He motioned for her to sit next to him and she did so, feeling his arm brush hers. "Julie, as I told you yesterday, Greg and I lived on the same hall junior year, and Todd was always hanging out with us. Greg's room was always the starting place for a party."

"Nice to meet you," Julie said with a smile. "I was at Powell, instead of Foundry, so I guess I'm not officially supposed to be on this trip, but Melanie invited me."

"No wonder you don't look familiar," said Greg. He was a big man, with a ruddy complexion. His grey hair was cut short and was sticking up in a crew cut style. "I saw you sitting with Melanie at breakfast. Did she tell you I was also a History major?"

"She did," said Julie. She looked around the bus again. "Where's John?"

"Oh, you knew John?" Sam's look was questioning.

Julie smiled. "A couple of us knew him freshman year." Her eyes sparkled, but she didn't explain.

Sam searched her face for an explanation, but when she just smiled, he continued. "Poor John. He apparently caught something on the flight over and has been in bed since. He came down to breakfast this morning, thinking he would join us, but decided his stomach wasn't quite steady enough yet for a bus ride."

"That's a shame." Turning to Greg, Julie asked politely, "So where do you live now?"

"Rochester, New York. I run a small furniture manufacturing business that my father started. Cheap labor and good materials in Rochester. We just introduced a recliner that's selling like hotcakes."

Greg looked ready to talk her ear off and Julie was *not* ready to get sucked into a conversation about upstate New York. She turned to Todd and said, "And what about you?"

"I'm in St Louis. I work for a large accounting firm."

Julie said, "Oh, that's what I used to do. I was in San Francisco."

Todd brightened. "Really? Who did you work for?"

"Rush & Rush."

"That's a great firm. They have a small office in St Louis."

Julie smiled. "I had forgotten that. How about you?"

"Sullivan & Moore."

Julie nodded. "I've heard of them. Have you been there long?"

"About five years. I'm married and my wife, Jane, is from the area."

"Oh, is she here, too?" Julie took a quick look around the bus.

Todd looked unhappy. "Unfortunately she couldn't come. She's a teacher and they just started back to school."

"What a bummer to miss a trip like this."

Todd nodded. "I know. We talked about it, but with the economy the way it is and teachers getting laid off right and left, she was nervous about being away. She didn't want to risk being part of the next round."

Julie wondered to herself why he had still decided to come, but before she could ask, he continued. "I admit I was going to just throw the brochure away, but she told me that she thought it would give me a chance for some 'guy time' with Greg and Sam. I've told her a lot of stories about both of them. She and I agreed that I would scope out the best things to do so we can enjoy them together when we come back."

Julie nodded. "That was nice of her! I'm sure this trip will give you lots of great ideas for when you bring her back."

Sam nudged Julie's arm and she turned back to him. Joelle had a microphone and was pointing out the sites, but it was hard to hear her from the back of the bus. Sam said, "Hey, stop talking and pay attention to what we're passing. You've already missed the first part of the tour."

She smiled. "Okay, boss." Being near Sam made her feel young and a little rowdy—she wasn't sure why. It also made her feel like doing things outside of her comfort zone. She found herself pointing out of the bus, saying in her best, 'tour guide voice,' "And on your right is the D'Orsay Museum, and as we cross the bridge, you will see the *Grand Palais* on your left, and the *Petit Palais* on your right."

Sam's eyes widened, and then he gave a loud guffaw. "Who needs a tour guide when we have Julie?"

Greg and Todd both clapped their hands and Julie blushed.

Sam said, "Keep going." He let his arm rest along the back of the seat behind Julie's head, and she let herself lean back onto it for a moment before reluctantly sitting forward and continuing. "To your right are the Tuileries Gardens and if you go down through there, you'll end up at the *Louvre*. This very wide street that we're driving up is the *Champs Elysées* and it will take us to the *Arc de Triomphe*. You can actually go to the top of that. Did you know that?" When they shook their heads, she added, "There's a little observation balcony on top. It has a great view of the city."

"I'd like to do that sometime." Sam's gaze turned from the monument and he looked into her eyes. She felt that flutter again in her stomach. Turning quickly away, she continued, "Um, and now we're crossing over on the *Pont D'Iena* bridge to circle back to the Eiffel Tower. Hard to believe it got built back in 1889! And now, we're heading into the Latin Quarter and toward the Luxembourg Gardens, then down toward *Place St. Michel* and the hotel."

They all looked out at the cafés, stores, and swarms of people. Arriving at the *Place St. Michel,* the bus didn't slow down. Julie turned to Sam again. "Looks like we're not done yet." She pointed to the left. "Here, on the *Ile de la Cité,* is where *Sainte Chapelle* is. It has the most amazing stained glass. I think it's on our itinerary to visit it." There was silence for a few moments as they drove across another bridge and up several streets lined with shops. Julie spoke up again. "And that's the original *Opéra* building. Behind it are a couple of the largest department stores—*Au Printemps* and *Galleries Lafayette.*"

Todd spoke up from his seat. "Wow, there are also mobs of people. Not really my thing, I have to admit."

"Mine either," Julie agreed. "Though the buildings are really spectacular."

"Everything's beautiful in Paris!" Greg chimed in loudly. Looking down the bus, he shouted, "Hey, Melanie, here's the shopping district. Don't you girls all want to hop off and buy some fancy lingerie?" Julie knew he was trying to be funny, but the joke fell flat.

Melanie turned back to them, obviously annoyed at being interrupted in her storytelling. "Greg, maybe you should buy some for your lady love?"

Greg shouted back. "Don't have a lady love. Maybe I should buy some for you?"

Melanie wagged her finger playfully at him. "You're lucky my husband isn't here to hear you talking like that." She quickly turned back to Emily and Angie.

As they made their way back to the hotel, Sam started telling a story about a previous business trip to Paris when he had taken a boat tour that ended up being conducted entirely in Chinese. Julie was grateful to be taken out of the spotlight and turned to look out the window at the changing panorama of people and bright shops. When the bus stopped, Joelle stood up again at the front to announce, "We are planning to go to the Cluny Museum at 3:00. It's 12:30 now and there are lots of small cafés and restaurants around to choose from for lunch. We thought you might like to have the chance to wander a bit, so we did not reserve anything for the group. Please meet back here at 2:45 and we will walk next door to the museum."

There was a general hubbub and shuffling as people gathered their things and moved off the bus. Sam turned to Julie.

"Want to grab a bite somewhere? Or are you eating with Melanie?"

Julie hesitated, and Sam said under his breath, "Greg is eating with Wayne and Judy to get to know them—he has apparently made it his goal to get to know all twenty-five people on the trip before the week is through." He paused before adding, "So Todd and I were just going to find a quiet spot."

Julie tried to decide if there was any hidden meaning behind the invitation, but found herself instead just enjoying how blue his eyes were. "I'd like that. I'll just let Melanie know when we get off. She's our unofficial Commander in Chief."

Descending from the bus, she saw Melanie, Gigi, Angie, and Emily waiting for her, and she hurried over. "Do you all mind if I eat with Sam and Todd? They've asked me to join them."

Melanie looked irritated for a minute, clearly hoping for some more "girl" time, but her tone was cordial. "Of course. You certainly don't have to ask permission from us."

"I know we all want to spend time together. I'll meet you guys back at 2:30 and we can all go through the museum together."

"That works." Melanie's gaze was assessing. "We'd like to get to know Sam and Todd better, too. Maybe we can sit with them at dinner."

"Good idea." Julie hurried back to where Sam and Todd were waiting and with a wave backward, the three set off for a café that Todd had noticed a couple of blocks back.

Melanie turned to Emily, Angie and Gigi. "Well, *that's* interesting. Renewing an old friendship with Sam?"

"Now Melanie," warned Emily. "Don't get that crazy mind of yours working overtime. She was sitting with them and they probably want to finish whatever conversation they'd started."

"Yeah, maybe." Melanie turned and looked around them. "That little street looks like fun. Let's go find somewhere to eat down there."

As they set off, Gigi remembered that she had seen Sam sitting with Julie at the café table yesterday. She knew Julie was divorced. What was Sam's situation? She wouldn't say anything to the others, but she decided to keep her eyes open—just in case.

Emily fell into step next to Gigi. "Well, it looks like Melanie has decided she will find us a place to eat." She grinned, and Gigi smiled back.

"This street has quite a few restaurants, so I'm sure she'll choose a good one."

Emily said, "From my experience with Paris, it's generally hard to choose a bad one."

"Have you been here often?"

"A few times. Ben is a Classics professor, and whenever we come to Europe we try to spend a couple of days in Paris." Emily paused, before adding, "But how about you? I would think it's pretty easy to come to Paris from Italy, right?"

Gigi shook her head. "We're geographically close—certainly much closer than you are. But financially and culturally, Turin is a long way from Paris."

Emily looked interested. "Julie told me your husband owns a wine export business. Does he travel much?"

Gigi nodded. "He does, actually. But I don't often go with him. Our daughter, Mariella, is twelve, and with her school and sports activities, we're usually pretty busy. And I still have some piano tuning clients."

Emily nodded, but thought to herself, *Piano tuning seems like a pretty flexible job. I wonder why she doesn't go with him?*

Gigi pulled out her phone to pull up Mariella's picture, and Emily studied the picture for a minute before saying, "She's beautiful. She looks older than twelve to me, though I'm no expert."

Gigi nodded. "I think so too, and so does Paolo. He's very protective of her." Gigi paused. "Paolo is a very traditional Italian in lots of ways."

Emily looked surprised. "I would have said the fact that he's staying home with her this week reflects a very 'modern' attitude."

Gigi answered quickly, and her tone was defensive. "He *wasn't* happy about doing it. I really pushed him to let me come."

Emily could see the steely determination behind Gigi's words, and it was a side of Gigi that she hadn't seen. She was curious to know why this trip was so important to Gigi, but before Gigi could say more, Melanie interrupted.

"This place looks affordable and interesting!" She was standing next to a sandwich board with a hand-written menu on it. "And I've never tried couscous before. C'mon!"

Soon they all had steaming plates in front of them.

"Are you sure this is safe?" asked Angie, who was poking her fork into the chicken leg that was sitting on top of a mound of couscous on her plate.

Emily answered. "Absolutely. Couscous is a very traditional North African cuisine. There are lots of Algerians in France because Algeria was once a French colony," said Emily.

Gigi reached for a piece of bread and said, "The vegetables are delicious." She turned to Angie, who was still looking skeptical. "Go ahead and try it."

Angie scooped up a forkful and, after a short moment, reached for another. Melanie said, smiling, "Looks like we have a new convert! What *I* love, besides the taste of course, is that it's so cheap! Julie doesn't know what she's missing!"

The four ate for a few minutes in silence and after ordering dessert, Melanie turned to Emily and said, "You seem very familiar with everything here. Have you been often?"

"Gigi and I were just talking about that on the walk over. Yes, Ben and I have been several times." Emily continued, "What about you, Melanie? With your husband at the State Department, do you travel a lot?"

"Actually, no. Gary pretty much has a desk job."

"So why didn't he come this time? Doesn't he like to travel?"

Melanie said curtly, "Gary had a conference in San Francisco."

Emily was surprised at Melanie's tone. In a placating voice, she said, "That's too bad. I'm sure he would have liked to see people from school again. It must be an important conference?"

Melanie nodded. "Very." Her tone was still very short.

"Well, San Francisco is a great place to *have* to go for work. Why didn't you go with him? I mean—this trip looked great on the brochure, but I think if I had a choice between a college alumni trip or a trip with Ben, especially to somewhere like San Francisco, I'd choose to go with Ben." Emily pressed, feeling there was more to the story. Melanie was always putting everyone else on the spot. Why not give her a dose of her own medicine? And Emily really was curious.

Now Melanie looked annoyed. It was obvious Emily had hit a sore spot. Melanie gulped the last of her wine before replying. "*I* really wanted to come *here,* so that's when I thought about making it a 'girls only' trip."

"I'm happy for us, but won't Gary be frustrated to miss it?"

Melanie was silent at first, but then took a deep breath and said, "When I saw the brochure, I immediately knew I wanted to do this trip. I saw it as a way for Gary and me to go somewhere away from work and home. And I saw it as a chance for us to talk about what's going on with us right now." The sharing of this confidence changed the mood, and no one spoke, waiting for Melanie to continue.

"I looked at the dates in the brochure and knew pretty quickly I could make the scheduling work. I have my own business, working as a compensation consultant, helping companies figure out what sort of retirement plans to offer their employees. I was just finishing a couple of assignments, so the timing was good. And I knew Gary hasn't taken much time off, so I assumed it would work for him, too."

Here Melanie looked around at all of them and drew in a ragged breath. "Gary and I are not in a good place right now. I felt if he agreed to come on the trip, it would be a sign that he wants to work on figuring out—and hopefully fixing—whatever's going on."

Her expression became frustrated. "When I first brought it up, he told me about the conference, and why he *had* to attend. And I couldn't argue against it when he went through all the reasons it was so important." She paused. "So I was incredibly disappointed, but resigned. I thought that was the end of the discussion."

Melanie paused. When she spoke again, her voice was taut with anger. "But that *wasn't* the end. He went on this tirade about how he was *happy* that the conference conflicted with the trip so he wouldn't have to go on it with me! That he had no interest in spending a concentrated amount of time with me. That it would drive him *crazy*!"

Her voice dropped and they strained to hear her last words. "He doesn't care about me at all anymore."

There was a stunned silence.

Emily was the first to speak. "That sounds really rough, Melanie. I am *so* sorry. I had no idea."

Melanie looked miserable. "It was horrible. And for me, it felt like the culmination of a series of conversations we've been having—or to be honest, *not* having." She looked around. "You all know that Gary and I got married the summer after he finished grad school. Angie and Joe were there, but the rest of you had moved away by then." She stopped for a minute, looking stricken. "Um, I mean except you, Emily....Um...."

Emily interrupted. "I wasn't a part of the conversation at that point—it's okay, we all know that part already."

Melanie looked relieved. "Right. So anyway, we got married and moved down to the DC area. And life went along pretty well. I started working at a small consulting firm, learning the retirement business, and Gary got his job at the State Department. We had Craig a year later. We both had jobs we liked, and we found we agreed on most child-rearing questions. Things were going along pretty smoothly. We had our ups and downs, like any other couple, but Gary continued to move up the ladder at State, and I eventually started my own consulting practice. And through it all, Craig was a good kid—did well in school and in sports, and this fall, he started at UCLA.

"Sounds great, right?" She looked sad. "But last year, things started to unravel." She paused, searching for the right words. "Gary became more and more distant. He was always going to his office on the weekends to work on 'projects'.

Well, that's what he *said* anyway. He claimed he could only do his research at the office because he works with sensitive information."

Gigi said quietly. "That sounds legitimate. Why don't you believe him?"

"It just doesn't feel right. I mean—we used to talk about *everything*. Even his work, though he could never be too specific about what he was working on. He would at least share some of the stories and talk about the people in his office."

Melanie took another sip of wine. "Now we just kind of exist in the same house. No more fun conversations. Not even about Craig. And he *never* asks about my work. And if I ask him about his day, or show any interest in his work, he just gives short, brusque answers and stomps off."

Gigi spoke up again. "Is it possible that he has more work to do because there are fewer people? Has anyone quit recently or gotten fired? That could create more work for him and a need to go into the office more."

"Not that I know of. He always had a pretty small group in his office, but I don't think that's changed." Melanie paused before adding bitterly, "But since he's not talking to me, I wouldn't know."

Everyone was silent for a few moments. Finally Angie said sympathetically, "Melanie, I had no idea. You've never said a word about any of this. I'm so sorry. That does *not* sound fun."

Melanie's chuckle was forced. "'Fun' certainly does not describe my life right now."

Emily wanted to offer some comfort, but was afraid that anything she said would sound trite and forced. What did she know about Melanie? Certainly nothing of her life, or even really who she was anymore. She decided to try, instead, to change topics.

"What's Craig planning to study at UCLA?"

At the mention of Craig's name, Melanie's face brightened. "He has no idea, to be honest. We just dropped him off last week for Freshman Orientation. But he's already loving it, and so busy he hardly has time to even call."

Gigi smiled. "Melanie, that at least is good news. Congratulations! I'm sure UCLA is a very tough school to get into."

Melanie smiled. "It is—I'm very proud of him. He's always been a great kid." After a moment, she continued. "It can't have been very pleasant for him this past year with all the tension and the charged silences. He's certainly aware that Gary and I are having our issues, but he's never asked me about it."

Gigi spoke again, her quiet voice full of sympathy. "Dealing with kids can create stress in any marriage, but it sounds like this must be something different."

"Definitely." Melanie agreed. "Sometimes it seemed Craig was the only thing we had in common. During this last year, for example, we both kept going to his soccer games. It was one of the few things we still did together."

In the silence that followed, Melanie motioned to the waiter to bring the check and, in pulling out her wallet, saw the time on her phone. "Yikes—we've got to leave now or we'll be late getting back to the museum."

She looked around apologetically. "Sorry about all that. Thanks for listening and for letting me vent a little. I know we'll figure it out." She paused, then added, "But it's been very tough. I'm about at my wit's end."

Angie reached over to pat her hand. "You *will* find a solution. I have confidence in both of you and in your relationship."

Emily looked around the group with new eyes. Suddenly Melanie was the insecure one and Angie was the one in charge. It was too bad Julie hadn't been there to hear Melanie's story, because Emily was sure she would have had some good ideas to share. Emily resolved to fill her in later.

Funny how in just twenty-four hours, some of their old camaraderie was returning. And listening to Melanie's issues, she was glad to see no evidence of the judgmental attitude that had been so destructive back in Boston.

Melanie had always struck her as so strong and independent, but this lunch had shown a much more vulnerable side of her. It made her more approachable, and more human somehow. Her opinion of Angie had also shifted somewhat. She still struck Emily as lacking in self-confidence, but there had been a glimmer of something else there just for a moment. It was obvious that Angie had a good heart and cared deeply about Melanie.

"I wonder what Julie had for lunch?" Angie asked as they filed out of the restaurant. "It's funny—so far we've had Italian and North African, but no French cuisine!"

"I wonder if she even noticed," Emily said dryly. "My impression is that she was probably more interested in who she was with than what she ate. But I could be wrong."

Melanie welcomed the change of topic. "No harm 'window shopping' so to speak—it never hurts to look, right? Speaking of which, look at this!" She had stopped in front of a small shop to admire a bright green cardigan that was hanging in the window. The color reminded her of new spring leaves. "Too bad we're in a hurry…."

As the foursome made their way back to the museum, Melanie and Emily kept up a running commentary on the windows they passed. Angie noticed that all the clothes looked elegant, but *tiny*. She'd never find anything in her size to take back as a souvenir! She'd have to stick with something for her kitchen, or something to add to her various collections at home. The idea made her feel depressed. She certainly couldn't discuss with *this* group what it felt like to be too fat to buy a sweater!

Gigi was also silent. Hearing Melanie confess the problems in her personal life made Gigi want to open up and ask for help too. But she was not Melanie, and spilling her guts out loud was not her style. These women had been close friends in a past life, but it would take time for Gigi to feel comfortable with them again. She'd keep mulling over the situation in her mind, and when the right moment came, she'd hopefully have the courage to share with them all.

Julie rejoined them at the museum entrance, looking happy and dragging Sam and Todd behind her. For the next three hours, the seven of them talked their way through the various exhibits, all of them fascinating and well presented. Greg did not join them, and Gigi was thankful they did not have to deal with him. He was far too loud for her.

Todd, the quiet introvert, became quite talkative in the museum, bolstered by his thorough knowledge of medieval history and perhaps his two glasses of wine at lunch. His added commentary made each exhibit more interesting, and when he slipped ahead of them into the room with gargoyles and positioned himself like a statue, making a particularly ridiculous face, he had them all holding their sides and gasping for breath. He turned out to be entertaining and quite charming.

Too soon it was time to leave. It turned out that the museum was quite close to the hotel, so they decided to walk back. They all parted company at the lobby, with promises to sit together at dinner, which was scheduled for 8:00 at a restaurant called *Le Procope.*

Another late dinner, Angie thought, sighing. She panicked slightly when she realized she hadn't thought to buy any snacks during their afternoon walk. She hoped there was gum in her purse somewhere. This European lifestyle was killing her!

Chapter 8.

Coming out of her room, Gigi ran into Emily and Julie, who were also just locking their doors, and the three of them decided to ride the elevator rather than walk down. It proved to be a tight squeeze for three people, and as they entered the lobby they were laughing about how different it was from a hotel elevator in the States. Melanie and Angie were already standing with Todd and Sam. Gigi noticed with some trepidation that Greg had decided to join the group.

"Well, *there* they are," boomed Greg.

"Why did *he* have to join us?" Emily said under her breath.

"He's okay," whispered Julie. "He's loud, but harmless." Changing the subject, she said, "I don't see John anywhere. He must still be under the weather. He's going to miss an amazing dinner!"

It was a beautiful evening, so they all decided to walk to the restaurant. Angie had never done so much walking in her life, but she didn't want to give Emily any further ammunition by opting to take the bus. Gigi thought that Sam or Todd must have said something to Greg, because on their walk over, he spoke much more quietly.

Arriving at the restaurant, they were escorted up a beautiful curved stairway to a dining room that looked like it belonged in the private home of a wealthy French family. A beautiful chandelier shone gently in the center of the room, and the walls were a pale yellow. There were tables of varying sizes, all set with beautiful white plates, white linen napkins, and elegant silverware. Melanie found two tables next to each other that were set for four people each, so they divided into two groups. Gigi was relieved that Greg ended up at the other table. She was seated with Sam, Julie and Emily, and Greg was with Angie, Melanie and Todd.

As the waiters took the drink orders, Todd spoke up from the other table. "Did you guys notice the description of the restaurant's history on the back of the menu? It says it opened in 1686 and is considered the first café in Paris."

Julie said with amazement, "I had no idea. I've never been here, but I've heard great things about it."

The menu had lists of appetizers, main courses, and desserts, but there was also a pale yellow insert with *prix fixe* options for their group. The items on the insert were included with the price of the tour—but they could also order off the menu if they paid separately.

Sam ignored the yellow insert and perused the menu. "Look at the seafood platter appetizer. That looks amazing. Any of you want to share it with me?"

Gigi looked at the price and gulped. She, for one, was not going to volunteer for that.

Realizing his error, Sam said quickly, "My treat. I'll order two for the table."

"Thank you," said Julie. "I love all things seafood."

Emily turned to Gigi. "What are you thinking about for dinner?"

"I think I'll have the fish in puff pastry on the yellow *prix fixe* menu. How about you?"

Sam was still reading the entire dinner menu. Now he said, "Look! You could have snails, or steak tartare, or calf's head in a casserole—whatever that is."

Gigi laughed. "You can try those. I'll stick with what I know will be delicious and to my taste."

Julie smiled sweetly at Sam. "Thanks for those lovely suggestions, but I'm going to have *sole meunière.*"

Emily nodded. "I was thinking about that, but if you are having it, I'll have sea bass, so we all try something different."

Sam teased, "I feel that *someone* needs to try the calf's head casserole—it says it's a specialty and is prepared just the way they did in 1686."

"Well then, we'll leave that honor to you!" Julie answered. She knew she was flirting with Sam, but she couldn't help herself.

"Actually," he answered in the same tone, "I'm going to try the Revolutionaries' Beef off the main menu. It says it's beef cheek and duck *foie gras*. That *cannot* be anything but incredible."

Emily noticed his eyes were shining as he looked around the table, his gaze lingering for an extra moment on Julie.

After the waiter took their orders, Emily raised her glass. Above the hubbub of conversation she said, "I'd like to propose a toast."

Everyone at their two tables quieted and turned toward her. She continued, "To my husband, Ben, who I wish were here."

Then Todd raised his glass. "To a wonderful meal—and one that I hopefully can bring my wife back to share with me sometime soon."

Everyone smiled and clinked glasses. Emily thought she noticed a brief shadow pass over Sam's face, but he was soon smiling again.

The seafood platters and the appetizers arrived and there was no more time for toasts. Gigi noticed that Melanie looked sad—and that Julie had eyes only for Sam.

The rest of the meal was spent with everyone sharing college stories as well as stories from their lives. When it came time for dessert, Julie's flaming *crêpes* were served with a flourish, and there was applause and laughter.

Emily caught up to Gigi as they went down the stairs and out into the cool night. "Amazing! That was just amazing."

Gigi nodded. "I agree. I have to say, we eat well in Italy, but nothing like *that*."

Emily nodded. "And you didn't even have dessert! I don't know *how* you resisted. I think I'm going to explode."

They walked in silence for a few minutes before Gigi said thoughtfully, "I really miss Paolo and Mariella. I keep thinking about them as we see new things, and I keep wishing I could share the experiences with them."

Emily nodded. "Me too. Ben would love that restaurant. But I know whenever he starts doing research for a new book, he's buried for weeks. He barely surfaces to eat and sleep."

"That must be hard."

Emily nodded. "It can be, to be honest. But I'm usually busy, too. Until this fall, I was teaching community college—writing lesson plans, grading papers. If you walked into our house any evening from September through mid-December, you'd be shocked at the concentrated silence."

"Wow, that's the opposite of my house! With Mariella and her girlfriends, it's *never* silent."

Emily looked thoughtful and a little sad before saying quietly, "That wouldn't be all bad."

Emily's openness emboldened Gigi to ask, "Have you regretted not having kids?"

Emily's eyes were shiny with unshed tears. "I love Ben more than you can imagine and can't picture my life without him. But I would have loved to have had a couple of children." She fell silent. Then, with a forced cheerfulness in her voice, she added, "But I couldn't have both, and I've never regretted my decision or looked back."

Gigi tucked her arm into Emily's, and they walked along in silence for a moment before Gigi said, "I will tell you—having a child is simultaneously the most frustrating and the most fulfilling experience possible. I wouldn't trade having Mariella for anything, but there's no question children put stress on any marriage." Gigi realized she had said exactly the same thing to Melanie at lunch—but it was so true.

Emily said. "I'd like to meet Mariella someday soon. Since I don't have kids of my own, I like spending time with friends who do. I play the role of 'favorite aunt.'"

Gigi giggled. "She'd *love* you, that's for sure, with your amazing clothes and air of sophistication."

Emily looked surprised and pleased by the compliment. Gigi said, "I mean it. You have a way about you that exudes confidence and poise. Those are attributes I'd love Mariella to learn, and I'm just *not* that way."

Emily gazed critically at Gigi's outfit and said, "If I'm being honest—and I'll warn you that after three glasses of wine, I lose all sense of tact—I would agree that you don't have a sophisticated wardrobe, but what you *do* have is a quiet confidence. I'm sure she sees that."

Gigi's heart warmed. With a laugh, she said, "I won't take offense at the wardrobe comment at all, because I know that you're right. On showing confidence, I *try* very hard to be a good example for her. Thank you."

They continued the last part of their walk in companionable silence. As they approached the lobby doors, bright light and noise were spilling out onto the sidewalk, and in silent, tacit agreement, they swerved left to the smaller door that they knew would take them to the back stairs.

Ducking into the stairwell, they climbed the three flights and stood for a moment outside their rooms.

Emily grinned. "I'm glad we walked back together. And I'm *really* glad we came directly upstairs!"

"I've had enough socializing for one day," Gigi agreed. "It's not my strong suit."

"I wouldn't say that at all. I would say you don't seem to *need* it the way some other people do."

Gigi smiled. "That's a nicer way to put it." She reached over and hugged Emily. "Goodnight."

Emily's hug back was tight and filled with emotion. "Goodnight."

****

Angie, Melanie, Greg and Todd walked back to the hotel together. Greg and Melanie were so talkative that Angie and Todd said almost nothing. At the hotel, the two women caught the elevator to their room, at Angie's insistence. She had walked enough for one night and squeezing into a small elevator seemed a small price to pay.

Back at the room, Angie said breathlessly, "I'm going to call Joe and tell him about that dinner. At home it's only 2:00 in the afternoon. Why don't you take the first shower?" She was nervous and didn't want an audience if it didn't go well.

"Deal!" said Melanie happily.

Joe was not as enthusiastic as Angie had hoped he would be. In fact, he seemed very skeptical about everything she said. It suddenly dawned on Angie that at home she very rarely told Joe anything new. Her life was so predictable that they always talked about the things *he* wanted to discuss. Now, it seemed like he was waiting for her to tell him that she'd been wrong in coming. To tell him that he had been right all along. Earlier, she might have. But now his skepticism strengthened her resolve. Angie's enthusiasm for sharing her adventures vanished and she curtly told him good night.

By the time Angie finished her shower, the room was still. Looking over at Melanie's bed, she could see the slow movement of Melanie's chest and heard her slight snore. Angie slipped into bed and let herself think back over the last two days. Could it really have been such a short time? It felt like a lifetime ago that she had met Emily at the luggage carousel.

This evening's dinner had been a revelation. She had been struck by how fresh everything had tasted. She didn't know any other word to describe it. It made her realize how much processed and fast food she ate at home. She realized suddenly that she wasn't feeling bloated, which was her natural state at home. And she didn't feel sluggish. Could that all be a consequence of eating processed food? She had read that processed foods contained a lot of salt. And she loved the bread here! At home they never had fresh bread, just supermarket sandwich bread.

She turned the small light on next to the bed and pulled out her new journal. When she had been so upset that first day, Melanie had suggested that she start a journal. Melanie was always writing in *her* notebook about everything and everyone, and she had suggested it to Angie as a good way to lessen her homesickness for Joe and the girls. She had said that writing everything down was a great way to remember all the details to share when she got home. Angie had reluctantly agreed, and Melanie had immediately taken her down to a store near the hotel and bought her a small notebook and pen. It had been sitting in the bedside drawer ever since.

She opened it now and, glancing over to be sure Melanie was still asleep, she started to write.

I had an epiphany tonight and it's so simple that I feel silly writing it down, but I'm going to, because I want to remember it when I get back to Portland.

We had dinner at a wonderful restaurant called Le Procope. We could choose either two or three courses off of a 'fixed price' menu for no charge—well actually a small charge if you wanted the third course—but mostly included in the tour price. (That's what I chose.) Or you could order off the menu (which is what Sam and Julie did). I started with a simple green salad that had the most amazing dressing, followed by a yummy fish that was pan-fried with some butter and lemon and herbs and served on top of spinach. It was called "rouget" in French, so I'll have to look that up when I get home. I have always been afraid of trying to cook fish, thinking it would smell up the whole house, but this looked really simple and it didn't smell at all.

As I finished my salad and my fish, I realized that I actually felt full. I couldn't believe it! I'd had a couple of pieces of bread too, but still, I had not eaten that much.

So then it came time for dessert, and I didn't order any! I can't believe it, even as I'm writing it, and I know Joe will never believe it! But it's true. Part of the reason was the cost, for sure, but it was also because I was enjoying the last sips of my wine and I didn't feel like I needed anything else.

Then we walked home (I have *never* walked so much in my life!) and it was actually pretty easy. And *pleasant.* That's when I realized that I *never* walk at home. We're in a nice suburb, but there's nothing easy to walk to. The closest thing to us is the 7-Eleven, and that's probably a mile or two away. I'd never thought about it before.

None of the walks here have been too long, either, or I would never have kept up. Plus it never feels rushed. You've got time to look in the shop windows, and the people-watching is fantastic! People just seem to take life a little slower here ,and that's nice. And I can't believe all the different smells! At home, since I'm in the car, if I smell anything it's whatever is in the car with me—coffee, or food if I've picked something up. Here, there's the smell of the bus and car exhaust as we walk along, and whiffs of cigarette smoke as we pass the outdoor cafés. (I can't believe how many people still smoke here.) Then you walk by a bakery and get that incredible smell of baking bread! Makes my mouth water. Or a butcher and they have rotisserie chicken. Yum! Oh, and of course there are the *crêpe* stands. Sugar, or chocolate, or cheese! I'm definitely going to stop at one of those before we leave.

I'm also surprised that so many people have dogs. I'd think that would be tough in a big city, but they seem to take them everywhere, even into the restaurants sometimes. And no one seems to care. And they all seem pretty well behaved.

So here is my epiphany. <u>When I eat healthy food, and I walk, I feel better.</u> It's simple, but it makes sense. I think I can even lose some weight if I keep it up. But I need to remember this after the trip is done and I'm back home, driving everywhere. I'm going to say it to myself every morning and I'm going to try to figure out ways to walk instead of drive.

Maybe if I talk to Mary and Anne about it, they'll help me too.

Now I have to go to sleep, Wonderful Journal. I'm sure tomorrow will be another fun day.

She gently closed the journal and set it back on the shelf next to the bed. She fell asleep imagining describing her adventures, and Mary's and Anne's eyes widening in amazement....

****

Angie opened her eyes slowly, then glanced over toward Melanie's bed, noting the slow, steady movement of her breath. The bedside clock said 8:00, but the alarm had not gone off yet. *Wow, I'm actually getting used to Paris time,* she marveled.

Moving quietly, she went to the armoire to decide what she should wear. On the inside of the door was a small mirror. Glancing at herself, she stopped in shock. *She really did look fat.* Writing the journal entry last night had felt so good and now, looking at herself and seeing how she must look to others, she felt a moment of despair. Her first instinct was to call Joe and run home, but she forced herself to take a deep breath and push those feelings away. Why would she run home now, when she was just figuring things out about herself, and about how to have fun on her own? She knew she had been buying bigger clothes, but her family didn't seem to notice or care. Or did they?

Glancing over to be sure Melanie was still asleep, Angie lifted her nightgown and made herself really look at herself, at the bulge of her stomach over the old elastic of her underwear. *No wonder Emily had given her that shocked look at the airport!* It was funny how you get an image of yourself in your head, and how, over the years, that image doesn't change even if you do. She remembered her mother commenting on her own shock whenever she looked in the mirror and saw "that old lady," wondering if that could really be her, since she still felt the same inside as she had at twenty-five.

So what was she going to do? Dieting was nothing new—and it never worked. She always regained more than she lost. Maybe this trip would be her chance to approach the whole thing differently—to try to look at being more active as well as changing the kinds of food she ate. She was learning on this trip that she didn't have to give up everything she loved to eat—but she did need to learn to make better choices. And she was going to get Melanie to help her.

She heard Melanie waking up and stretching. "Good morning," Angie said.

Melanie, with a sleepy smile, answered back, "Good morning. You're up bright and early."

Angie came and sat on the edge of Melanie's bed. "Can I ask you to help me with something?"

Melanie, hearing the serious tone, propped herself up on one elbow. "What's up?"

Angie felt flustered, but made herself continue. "When I woke up this morning, I was thinking about how wonderful that meal was last night, and you know what I realized? I eat crap at home. I don't eat things like fish and vegetables. I eat at McDonald's or we get a pizza delivered."

Angie paused before continuing. "Melanie, I'm sick of feeling this way. Of eating badly and feeling tired all the time. I never really thought about it before. I was just doing what I'd always done. But coming on this trip took away that routine, and replaced it—without my permission, I might add—with a *new* routine that includes fresh food and much more walking. And after just two days, I already feel much better, physically *and* mentally."

Melanie smiled broadly. "That is *fantastic!*"

Angie continued. "Do you know that feeling of being bloated all the time? Well, I don't have that this morning. And my legs feel a little sore from the walking, but sore in a good way, you know?"

At Melanie's nod, she continued. "So here is what I want you to do, please. Will you help me continue to be aware of what I eat, and encourage me to walk? I really feel like this could be a start to a whole new 'me.'"

Her look was so earnest that Melanie reached over to hug her. "Good for you! Of course I'll help you. Hey, we could talk to the others about it and they could help, too."

"Oh no!" Angie's eyes looked wild. "I'm not ready for that yet. I saw the way Emily looked at me that first day. I couldn't take any more of her scorn."

"Emily wouldn't do that," Melanie protested.

"Oh yes she would! She's been looking down on me since we arrived." Before Melanie could answer, she said, "Look—let's not talk about that. But can we keep it between us for now? I really want to see if I can get into some good habits while I'm here, and then keep up with them when I get home. You'll have to be my long-distance coach then!" She paused and then added, "I'm not ready to let anyone else in on my plan quite yet. I've only just figured this part out for myself! Please.... You can't tell the others because they'll tell *her*—and then I'd get that look again."

Melanie answered, "Okay, if that's how you want it. It'll be our secret for the moment. But I really think everyone would be happy to help."

Angie's look was grateful. "Thanks."

"Okay." Suddenly glancing at the clock, her tone changed and she said, "Hey! I've got to get moving!"

Listening to Melanie humming in the bathroom, Angie finished dressing. It felt good to enlist Melanie's help. She knew she'd need backup, because no matter how sure she felt right now about following through with these new ideas, she knew she'd fall off the wagon as soon as a Big Mac reared its ugly head. She couldn't even imagine how many she must have eaten over the last several years, and she shuddered slightly.

When Melanie emerged from the bathroom, Angie noticed for the first time what a difference Melanie's makeup made. On impulse, she asked Melanie to help her apply mascara and some eye shadow—two items she had never even held in her hands before. She'd always assumed makeup was expensive and time-consuming, and she certainly had no idea how to apply it. Melanie chose a soft eye shadow that looked very natural, and Angie was surprised at how good it made her feel. A touch of mascara and she was done.

They locked the door to their room and Angie deliberately walked past the elevator to walk down the stairs to breakfast. She felt like a new woman, inside and out.

Chapter 9.

Julie opened her eyes slowly. Her dream slowly faded.... What had it been? Oh, yes, it had been about Sam, and they had been dancing at some sort of nightclub, slowly swaying to the soulful wail of a saxophone. She felt like she could still smell his cologne and feel his hands pressing on the small of her back.

Stretching sinuously, she let herself imagine, for a brief moment, that he was lying next to her and that she could roll over and see him there, watching her....

"Ridiculous," she said out loud. "Get over this craziness—he's a married man, for God's sake!"

She hopped into the shower, knowing it wouldn't be quite warm yet. Its chilly sting took away the last remnants of the dream and she closed her eyes, scrubbing her hair vigorously. *There are lots of eligible men out there in the wide world—I need to stop mooning over one that I can't have!* She thought to herself.

But as the water warmed up, she let herself stand under it for a couple of extra minutes to think back to the previous day. What fun it was getting to know everybody again! At dinner, Gigi had tried her first (and probably her last) oyster, and the look on her face had sent everybody into gales of laughter. Gigi had been very good-natured about it all and obviously enjoyed the novelty of it.

And the chip on Emily's shoulder was definitely dissolving. She and Gigi had been arm and arm walking back last night, sharing some sort of confidences and giggling together.

But the best thing had been the way Sam had smiled at her during dinner every time she turned to tell him something—that look in his eyes that made her feel like they shared a deep secret.

By chance they'd had a few moments alone on the walk home, and Sam had really opened up. He'd talked about the long hours at work, and the travel it required, and he had started to talk about his frustration with life at home—how he and his wife, Helen, had been in counseling for some time. The conversation was just getting more serious when they had arrived back at the hotel, and Todd had come over to ask them to join him for one last drink at the hotel bar.

The group at the bar included Greg, Todd, and about six others, and the conversation gradually moved into a political discussion. After forty-five minutes, Julie had found herself stifling her yawns. Catching Sam's eye, she motioned that she was going upstairs. His look held understanding… and did she also detect some longing?

Standing now, drying her hair, she thought more about her feelings for Sam. She definitely felt comfortable around him. Certainly some of that was simply the comfort of familiar people and old, shared stories. But she *really* liked him. The spark between them was not just in her imagination, and she was sure he felt the same way.

What, then, should she do about it? Intellectually, she knew the right thing to do was to steer clear of him—to make sure she stayed with Melanie and the others. Emotionally, she knew she absolutely did *not* want to do that. Feeling this spark made her realize how much she'd missed it. She was feeling emotions that had been dormant for a long time. True, he was married and technically "off limits," and she would keep herself aware of that, but she would not deny herself the pleasure of his company entirely. Just chatting with him and hanging out with him was easing the loneliness that had started to seep into her days at home. Besides, she reasoned, if she started to actively avoid him, that would create awkwardness, since he and his friends and she and her friends were all getting along so well.

Glancing at the clock, she saw she had twenty minutes to get downstairs. Pulling on a pair of jeans, a long cashmere sweater, and her soft leather boots, she pulled her hair back into a ponytail, and chose a pair of dangly earrings that Melanie would lust after. With one last glance in the mirror, she reached for her purse and headed to the stairs. Today's schedule included *Notre Dame* and a walking tour of the *Marais* area, followed by a visit to the Pompidou Center's modern art exhibit. She had been to the Pompidou Center before, but had never walked through the surrounding area, so that would be fun.

Once downstairs, Julie paused at the door to the dining room, looking for her friends. They were all seated together in one corner. Angie was looking happier than she'd seemed thus far on the trip. Good—hopefully she had decided that Paris was actually an okay place to spend some time.

Though she told herself not to, she let her gaze continue till she found Sam. He was seated with his "gang," and she noticed that John had joined them. Well, that gave her a good excuse to go over at some point to check on him, right? *You keep telling yourself that,* she chided herself as she made her way toward her friends.

Emily smiled as Julie sat down. "Hey, you!"

"Hey yourself. I notice that John is back among the living. Apparently he caught something on the flight over and went straight to bed when he got here. That's why we only saw him briefly at our breakfast yesterday."

Emily nodded. "I feel bad for him. What a bummer to lose the first two days of the trip."

"He still looks a little pale," Julie observed. "I hope that he's okay."

Emily gave her a sideways look. "Really?" she drawled. "I thought you only had eyes for one man."

Julie blushed and ducked her head. "Now don't go talking like that. I'm just getting reacquainted with everyone." She did her best to say this casually, but Emily poked her.

"Yeah, right. Well, we'll leave it at that for the moment, as long as you keep me informed of further progress." Emily's look was sly and Julie laughed.

"I never could keep anything from you, could I?" They shared a conspiratorial smile.

Michel stood up from his table in the corner and cleared his throat. The room grew quiet. "First, I want to say thank you all again for coming on this trip. We love alumni who remain engaged and interested in Foundry, and programs like this one are a great way to stay connected. Secondly, welcome to Paris! Paris offers a wonderful opportunity to see history through its incredible architecture and you will experience some of that over the next few days.

"I also want to thank the staff at Foundry who found this hotel, which is so centrally located. If you walked back from the Cluny Museum yesterday, you got a good sense of how close we are to everything. Proximity was one of our most important criteria when choosing this particular hotel. Walking allows you to more fully experience life here, with its variety of sights and smells that are so different from life in the United States.

"We will be leaving shortly to walk to *Notre Dame,* one of France's finest examples of Gothic architecture. Construction on the church began in 1160, and it took more than a hundred years to complete. It has survived through several traumatic periods in France's history, but has suffered damage at various points, including defacement of many of its statues during the French Revolution. Personally, I think there is a wonderful feeling of calm and strength in the sanctuary itself, and I look forward to hearing your impressions. You can either just walk through the cathedral itself or, if you have the energy, you can climb the 387 steps up to the towers where you will be rewarded with a magnificent view of the city.

"We'll also have the opportunity to visit the *Crypte Archeologique,* which is located under the square in front of *Notre Dame.* The Crypt was officially designated as a museum in 1980, when they unearthed the remains of a variety of buildings that had existed on the site over its two thousand year history.

"As some of you may know, Paris began on the *Ile de la Cité* and was named for the first known occupants, the Parisii tribe. Since then, it has played an important role for a variety of civilizations, and we will learn more about that when we tour the Crypt. Over time, like many cities, Paris grew haphazardly and became overcrowded with buildings of every description and size. Some of those were torn down because of the terrible sanitary conditions in the 18th century, and then more were destroyed in the 19th century by order of the city Prefect, Haussmann, to create much of the open space and many of the wide boulevards you see today.

"After we finish our tour of the Crypt, we will proceed on foot to *Sainte-Chapelle,* which was built during the second half of the 13th century by Louis IX. The building that it is housed within, interestingly, is now an administrative building for the city of Paris, but of course it was a part of the Royal Palace at that time.

"*Sainte-Chapelle* has the largest collection of thirteenth century stained glass in the world. It also has several great religious relics, including Christ's crown of thorns and a fragment of Jesus' cross.

"After *Sainte-Chapelle,* you will be free to find a café for lunch—believe me, there are plenty to choose from—and then we will head over to the *Marais* area. The *Marais* spreads across the 3rd and 4th *arrondissements,* or districts, of Paris. It was, for a long period in history, the aristocratic district. In the 13th century, Charles I of Anjou, who was King of Naples and Sicily, and the brother of Louis IX, built his home there, and in 1361 King Charles V built a mansion there to house the Royal Court during his reign from 1364 till his death in 1380.

"The *Marais* remained the French nobility's favorite place of residence from then through a portion of the 17th century. We'll visit the *Place des Vosges* on our tour, which was designed under King Henri IV in 1605. Many French nobles built their urban mansions around that square.

"At the end of the 19th century and during the first half of the 20th century, the area became a Jewish community, populated by many Eastern European Jews. During World War II, the Nazis targeted that community, and many of its residents were deported. As you can imagine, the area then fell into disrepair. It was not until 1964 that General de Gaulle's Culture Minister made the *Marais* the first '*secteur sauvegarde,*' or literally, 'safeguarded sector.' During the following decades many of the historic buildings were renovated and restored, and several became museums, like the building that houses the Picasso Museum, and the *Hotel*

Carnavelet, which houses the Paris Historical Museum. Unfortunately, we do not have time to visit those on our walk today, so you will have to come back to do that on your own.

"We are going to finish our afternoon at the *Centre Georges Pompidou,* also known as *Beaubourg,* It was built in 1977 and houses the largest museum for modern art in Europe. The building also includes a large public library and the French Research Center for Acoustic Music. For anyone who is not familiar with that building, you will be shocked at its design—very modern and 'turned inside out.' For example, all of its functional elements are on the exterior and color-coded: green for plumbing, blue for climate control, and yellow for electrical wiring. We will be handing out a pamphlet later describing it in more detail. You'll have an hour or so to browse in the museum before we head to the restaurant at the top of the building for a drink and another fantastic view of Paris. *Allons-y!"*

****

As the group made its way across the bridge, Emily fell into step next to Julie and said, "Melanie told us a little about her home life yesterday, and I wanted to fill you in."

"Okay." Julie's look was questioning. "Is something wrong?"

"Yup. Life's not too good for her right now. She and Gary aren't talking much, and she's not sure what's going on." Emily turned to be sure Melanie was not listening before continuing. "I have to tell you, I saw a softer side to Melanie than I ever have. She's in a very vulnerable place. She really let down her guard, and I think she will actually let us help her. She's different from the old 'take charge and take no prisoners' Melanie."

Julie noted Emily's use of the word "us" and felt glad. "Interesting. Melanie was definitely the most confident of any of us back then—the one who always knew where she and Gary were going and what they were doing."

"Exactly. I can tell you she's not so sure now." Todd came up next to Emily to ask her a question, and that was the end of the conversation.

Arriving at *Notre Dame,* the entire group did a tour of the interior. Then the group split in two, with some deciding to brave the long climb to the tower and some going to the Crypt. Julie, Emily and Gigi decided to climb, and Sam, Todd and John joined them. Greg, Melanie and Angie all chose to go to the crypt.

To Gigi, the walk up the narrow round stairs seemed endless, but every so often there was a tiny window offering a quick glimpse of the city. She was fascinated by the way each stone step had been worn down in the middle by centuries of feet. As they came out onto the narrow stone parapet, there was a moment of silence as they all caught their breath and looked around.

Everybody pulled out their phones and cameras and posed for group photos, though the limited width of the parapet made it difficult. The gargoyles provided the perfect backdrop, and Emily immediately sent a picture to Ben that included a close up of a particularly menacing gargoyle, with a note about how much she missed him. Gigi sent a similar photo to Mariella and told her to share it with Paolo, promising that she would bring them back soon to see for themselves.

Everyone then proceeded up the second, shorter, set of stairs and out onto the top of the southern tower. This walkway was even narrower than the first, so people didn't take many group pictures, but they took a quick walk around to photograph the views before beginning the long walk back down.

Emily found herself behind John. Their progress was slow, hampered by cautious members of the group ahead of them, so she took advantage of the time to get re-acquainted. "I'm glad to see you're feeling better," she said conversationally. "What are you doing these days in your 'real' life?"

John smiled. "I'm a banker. I do commercial lending."

"Where?"

"I'm in LA. I don't know if you remember, but my family's there, and my father wanted me to come back to join his bank after business school."

"Are you married?"

"I am. A beautiful wife and three gorgeous daughters. Seems like poetic justice, in a way, that *I* would get three daughters, you know?"

He turned to look at her, confirming that she caught the irony. They both laughed and the initial awkwardness fell away.

"I guess you know about your reputation freshman year?"

"Yeah. Sam pulled me aside midway through the year and warned me, suggesting that maybe, just maybe, I might want to 'take it down a notch.' At the time, I was pissed off, but by the end of the year, I had figured out what he was talking about. I hit the booze less after that." After a pause, he added, "I actually drink very little now, but it's because I don't want to waste my calorie count on anything but the best wine!"

Emily laughed. "That makes total sense to me."

John continued. "My weight really crept up while I was focusing on growing my business. I just went along eating whatever I wanted at all the business dinners—I've always loved good food that's prepared well—and at the same time I was working late and not getting any exercise. Any free time I had was spent with my family, going to the various events in the kids' lives—like soccer games and music recitals. It felt selfish, somehow, to take time for myself and go to the gym, especially when my wife needed a break, too.

"But recently, I've started paying more attention to my lifestyle choices. You can't tell, since we haven't seen each other in years, but I've lost twenty pounds and have a goal to lose thirty more." He was obviously pleased with his accomplishment.

"Congratulations!" said Emily warmly.

As they reached the bottom and came out into the cool air, John continued, "My weight-loss plan actually started when I was here in Paris on business. I noticed that even though the food is incredible, people seem generally thin and fit. Obviously walking is part of it, and I also think it's tied to portion size. There are more courses, but not very much food in any one course, you know? Anyway, I'm trying to pay attention, and I'm definitely exercising more. I want what they have—great food without the big belly!"

Emily smiled. "They do seem to have it worked out," she agreed. "Ben and I both take our health very seriously, so I love your plan. And I think it's very *un*-selfish, because living a healthier life means living a longer life with your family!"

As John walked over to join Todd and Sam, Emily thought back over the conversation. She was thankful Ben had always been so health conscious—it had made it easy for her to get into good habits early in their relationship. She wondered about Angie again, and hoped that Angie's good mood that morning was a sign of a changing outlook on the trip. Could it lead to an even broader change of outlook?

****

Melanie found herself standing next to Greg during the tour of the Crypt. She noticed he was listening intently to everything Michel was saying about the various exhibits. *What had Michel said? That the Parisii tribe had settled there in 27 BC? That was amazing*. Melanie couldn't believe that human beings had actually lived and worked in this very spot for so long!

Melanie didn't want to interrupt Greg's absorption during the tour, but toward the end she turned to him and said, "It's fascinating, isn't it?"

Greg nodded. "Ancient civilizations have always been the most interesting to me. To actually *see* evidence of all those settlements through time—I mean, it's incredible, you know?"

"I'm glad there are actual ruins of some of the buildings. I'm a very visual person, so physical evidence helps me to get a clear picture in my mind. Give me ball gowns and diamond necklaces and I'm happy!" Melanie suddenly felt flustered, thinking how shallow she must sound.

Greg laughed loudly. "You know, I would have guessed that about you."

Melanie looked at him sharply. "Are you making fun of me?"

Greg suddenly looked distraught. "No, no, Melanie, I didn't mean that at all. I was just thinking that even when I knew you at Foundry, you always seemed like a very visual person. It's what I remember about you from class: you were always asking extra questions about the physical evidence of whatever period we were studying."

Melanie looked surprised. "Really?"

"Man, you used to drive me crazy with it sometimes. You would want to talk on and on about some detail on some dress of Marie Antoinette, or whatever, and I'd be thinking, 'Who *cares* about the stupid buttons or lace on a dress for God's sake?' But I could see that it was very important to you."

He blushed, and Melanie suddenly felt sorry for him. Behind his bluster, he was obviously quite shy. She gave him a friendly jab.

Melanie said, "I remember *you* made a huge deal about a traveling exhibit that came to LA—that one about Tutankhamen, I think?"

Greg looked startled. "You're right! How did you remember *that?"*

Melanie smiled. "Let's just say you were very vocal for weeks about all of the traditions around the burial of the Egyptian kings. And all *I* could think about was what a shame it was that the things that I liked to look at, like their clothing, had long since disintegrated."

Greg blushed again. "It's funny what we each remember!" He hesitated, then lowered his voice. "Hey, I want to apologize for being so loud at the restaurant that first night. And then again on the bus. Sam pulled me aside and told me I was being the classic 'loud and obnoxious American.' I've really been trying to pay attention since then." His look was pleading and Melanie took pity on him.

"You were definitely loud that first night, but let's be honest—we were all pretty noisy, aided by too much wine and too little sleep."

Greg nodded. "That's what I told Sam, and I've really been trying to be better since. Like last night at *Le Procope,* I was better, right?"

Melanie nodded, sensing her answer mattered very much to him. "Absolutely."

Greg added in an earnest voice, "I know I can make people uncomfortable, and I talk too much, and I don't want to be like that." He heaved a deep sigh and then confessed, "Back in Rochester, I don't have a lot of friends. I have some guys I hang out with from work, but I'm not sure I'd call them 'friends' really. More like drinking buddies, or football-watching buddies...." His voice trailed off and he looked sad.

Melanie reached over to touch his arm. "Hey, don't be so hard on yourself. I'm sure they consider themselves your friends. You're a great guy."

"Melanie, you're being nice, but I know I overdo it." He hesitated before adding, "Actually, I would appreciate your help."

"What do you want me to do?"

"I want you to tell me when I'm being annoying."

Melanie looked nonplussed. "Um, okay. But how am I going to do that?"

Greg thought for a moment, then said, "Look, here's what we'll do. If I start to get too loud, and you're close to me, give my arm a pinch. Or, if you're nearby but not right next to me, just wink at me. How does that sound?"

Melanie thought about it and then said, "That sounds okay." She paused. She wanted to say something further to reassure him. "Greg, we *do* know you're a nice guy."

"Thanks for saying that. I really do appreciate it. I *really* try, but when I feel awkward—which is most of the time—I can't help myself. I overcompensate and get loud." After an awkward pause he ducked his head, adding, "I can't believe I'm saying all of this to you, but I feel better having said it out loud."

"You know, Greg, if *I'm* being *completely* honest, I just might have to admit that I have some of those tendencies, too."

Greg looked astonished. "What are you talking about? No, you don't!"

"Now *you're* the one being nice, but I do know that I, too, can be overbearing."

Greg protested, "I've honestly never thought of you that way. I think of you as 'lively'."

Melanie smiled. "That's a nice description. I'm going to adopt that as my own image of myself. And you do the same!"

"Ha! I'm not sure I can pull that off, but I'll try!"

They looked at each other and laughed.

Greg reached out his hand and Melanie shook it solemnly. "Then it's a deal," he said. "You'll let me know when I'm overdoing it."

Melanie nodded and said, "And you'll let *me* know when *I'm* being too pushy."

"Deal." He smiled at her, blushing, and this time Melanie definitely felt he was flirting with her a little bit. It was fun to feel attractive to someone—even if it was Greg!

The group made its way to *Sainte-Chapelle*. Once there, Michel talked about the history and meaning behind the stained glass. Greg moved to stand next to Todd, but Melanie hung back, lost in thought. Now that she'd said it aloud to Greg, she had to admit it to herself. She *was* overbearing and loud sometimes. She liked to be in charge and know that others were following her lead. Could she, like Greg, be hiding insecurity behind a confident façade?

She thought about Gary, who seemed to be drifting further and further away. Was she too bossy and loud with *him*? Did she *really* listen when he tried to tell her about work—or when he had a different opinion than she did? She needed to think all of that through. She knew she could be a *little* bit opinionated. Okay, maybe she was *a lot* opinionated.

She followed the rest of the group as they made their way from the Lower Chapel—which Michel explained had been the parish church for everyone living in the Royal Palace—to the Royal Chapel above it. As Melanie stepped into the upper chapel, she looked up and stood completely still, her breath taken away. *This must be what it would feel like to be inside a Fabergé egg,* she thought. There was light and color everywhere. No description could match the reality. Michel was now telling them about the concerts held here, and how magical the combination of the classical music and beautiful stained glass could be. She vowed to herself that she would come back to experience that.

Coming out onto the sidewalk, Melanie realized that Angie was walking quietly beside her.

"You seemed a million miles away," Angie said quietly. "Everything okay?"

Melanie smiled. "Absolutely! Those gorgeous stained glass windows blew me away! Wouldn't you love to come back for a concert?"

"I guess so." Angie didn't seem to share her enthusiasm, and after a moment continued, "I thought maybe Greg had upset you in some way? I saw you talking to him earlier." Angie looked like a mother lion ready to defend her cub.

Melanie smiled and shook her head. "No, no. Actually it was a great conversation. It did make me think—but not in a bad way at all. He's a nice guy."

Angie's look was disbelieving.

"No, *really*, he is. He can be loud, as we've all seen, but he knows it and he's trying to tone it down." Melanie decided it was not appropriate to share any more of the discussion they'd had.

Angie looked relieved. "Okay, good. I was afraid he'd upset you." She thought for a minute before adding, "I guess he did seem better at the restaurant last night."

Not wanting to discuss Greg further, Melanie took Angie's arm. "Speaking of restaurants, I'm starving! Let's find the others and a place to eat. I could use some French onion soup—you know, with the bread in it and the cheese melted on top?"

Angie smiled. "That sounds delicious. We have until 2:00, when the *Marais* walk starts."

Soon all five women set off for a café that Emily assured them had the *best* French onion soup around. "In fact, you'll have to tell them if you want them to add sherry or not. Personally I can't understand why anyone would *ever* say no to *sherry*!" Emily said.

Gigi's eyes were gleaming. "I've never heard of that."

"Add this to your 'new experience' list, Gigi," said Julie. And all five laughed cheerfully.

Gigi chose a chair next to the window facing *Notre Dame*. The other four played musical chairs for a few moments, Melanie's laughter ringing out. Heads turned and Gigi grimaced slightly, embarrassed for a moment that Melanie was so loud and so *present*. She immediately felt bad about her negative attitude. She was very glad to be with the four of them—it was just that occasionally she felt on display when Melanie was being loud enough that others around them noticed. Gigi never called attention to herself if she could help it.

After some shuffling around and removing of scarves and jackets, Emily took control. "Does everyone want soup?" Nods all around. "With sherry?" Again, nods from everyone. "Anyone want anything else?"

Gigi shook her head and noticed that Angie shook hers as well. She would have bet money that just having soup would not have been enough food for Angie. To her surprise, Melanie was the one who said, "Does that mean that on the way back we can get a *crêpe* at that *crêpe* stand we passed?" Melanie tried hard to look innocent, but failed miserably.

Emily laughed. "*Bien sûr!* We should have just enough room for that!"

The waiter came over and after Emily gave the order, she turned back to Gigi. "Your 'new experience' list now includes an oyster last night, and sherry in your French onion soup—am I to conclude that your husband doesn't take you out to eat very much, or are you not a very adventurous eater?"

Gigi ducked her head in embarrassment. *Why did Emily always have to put people on the spot?* "I like trying new things. We just don't go out much." She knew she sounded defensive. "You know, when you have a child...."

Emily looked skeptical. "You only have one. And she's twelve, right? Perfectly old enough to go out."

Gigi nodded. "That's true, but Paolo goes out so often for work that when it's just us, he'd rather be at home. And he also likes my home cooking."

Emily was unconvinced. It seemed like Gigi used Mariella and Paolo as excuses for not doing much of *anything*. She opened her mouth to further press the issue when Melanie spoke up suddenly.

"What did everyone think of *Notre Dame* and of the Crypt?" Gigi threw her a grateful look.

Julie spoke. "I thought it was a fantastic morning—*Notre Dame* was incredible, and then *Sainte-Chapelle* was absolutely stunning!"

Talk turned to Michel and his wealth of knowledge, then on to tidbits each had learned about various people in the group. It was fun sharing their thoughts—it almost felt like Cambridge again.

Gigi fell silent and looked out the window. She hadn't really thought about it, but now that she had said it out loud, Paolo *did* prefer to stay home when it was just the three of them. He had to socialize a lot for work, talking to clients and prospective buyers, but she hadn't really thought about how, as a result of that, she herself went out very little. She had stopped her piano tuning business when Mariella was born, and though she had started it up again when Mariella had gone off to elementary school, she never had more than a handful of clients. And piano tuning was not a social activity anyway. In fact, one of the things she liked most about it was that it was a very solitary, peaceful job—time spent methodically working her way up the keyboard. The ninety-minute process required intense concentration and absolute quiet, as she listened to each note and then matched its tone to the neighboring keys. At the end, she was inevitably both fulfilled and exhausted. The level of effort also meant that she couldn't schedule more than one tuning per day.

Emily's question did make her realize that her social life had become very limited. And she *did* miss socializing and going out. She was not the "wild and crazy party" type, but she enjoyed small gatherings with close friends, and she loved going new places. She realized suddenly that Paolo seemed to be her only source of social life and conversation these days. When had her world gotten so narrow? She remembered large, fun group outings with friends—*his* friends, admittedly, since she had been the stranger coming from outside the area, but still, they were people who had become *their* friends over time.

Gigi remembered that after Mariella was born, her socializing had changed to being mostly with other women and their young children during the day. Then Paolo started to have more and more work commitments in the evenings, and Gigi stayed home with Mariella. Could she have chosen to go out on her own with their mutual friends in the evenings? She certainly knew them well enough, but it felt awkward. They were a fairly traditional group, and it was rare that anyone attended an event without a spouse. Add to that the number of invitations that Paolo had declined on *their* behalf, citing his work commitments, and suddenly there were no invitations coming in at all.

Gigi felt a spurt of anger, at him and at herself. Why had she let herself become so isolated? She had certainly not meant to let that happen.

She needed to re-think her situation. What about socializing with other women? She had gotten quite close to two women in their group, Christina and Sophia. But Christina had her own issues—she had three kids and seemed overwhelmed by them and by a very strong-willed mother-in-law. Sophia had called a couple of times to get together, but Gigi had had obligations at Mariella's school. She now realized that she had not made any effort since then to call Sophia back to schedule something. Sophia probably thought Gigi wasn't interested!

Remembering back to college, Gigi had always made a concerted effort to plan a few evenings out, which she could then alternate with quiet evenings in her room, and the combination had kept her happy and fulfilled. In Italy, she had let the solitary side of her personality take over. She hadn't even realized how much she had grown to depend on Paolo. That needed to change. She needed to be more independent, and to try harder to keep up with friends.

Looking up, she saw Emily looking at her expectantly and realized that she had asked her a question.

"Sorry. What?"

"Are you ready to leave? *Someone,*" she glanced toward Melanie, "wants us to have enough time to stop at the *crêpe* stand."

Gigi smiled. "Of course. Sorry. I'm ready."

As the five hurried up the street, Emily looked at her phone and realized they didn't have time for a *crêpe* stop after all. She changed direction and headed them back to the rendezvous spot. The walk back was silent, with Melanie sullen from the change of plan, Angie slightly out of breath because of the quick pace, and Gigi and Julie each deep in her own thoughts.

Chapter 10.

Spectacular. That was the only way to describe these views. In every direction, Angie saw panoramas of amazing architecture. She took it all in and couldn't believe where she was. The group had arrived at the top of the Pompidou Center right at cocktail hour and some of the group had spilled out onto the balcony area, laughing and filling the air with their conversation. Angie had made her way to the far edge and could not stop staring.

In the distance she could see the Eiffel Tower, its outline glowing with the setting sun. She had been told that it would light up once it was fully dark, and she was looking forward to that. To the north was *Sacré-Coeur,* the huge white church that she'd seen in her guidebook. She wondered if they were going to have the chance to visit. Melanie had suggested they might try to do that on Saturday, since it was an "open" day with no planned activities. The guidebook had said that *Sacré- Coeur* sat on the highest point of the city.

Through the windows of the restaurant to her left, she could see one of the two towers of *Notre Dame*. How could one location offer views of *all* these famous landmarks? No wonder Michel and Joelle had insisted that they finish the *Marais* walking tour here.

Angie had never walked so much in her life, but she had been so enthralled she hadn't even noticed. The *Marais* streets had been teeming. There were cafés and shops everywhere, and people in all of them.

Angie envied them. Everyone looked relaxed, some smoking cigarettes, some reading, and others laughing at each other's stories. The women were elegant and the men were handsome and slightly built, with suits that hugged their legs and buttocks. She couldn't help but notice that, could she? The men lounged with casual grace; their ties knotted perfectly, their shirts starched.

Angie realized that she was much more aware of appearances here, including her own. Now she realized where the "ugly American" stereotype came from. At home, people wore whatever they were comfortable in—sweat pants, baggy jeans, t-shirts, leggings, even pajamas! She had heard people call Portland a "granola" town, and she was starting to understand what they meant. People there did look a little "disheveled," and certainly more casual.

There were exceptions, of course. She'd been downtown at lunchtime, when there were more suits and general business attire, but no one had sharp edges to them like these Parisians did. She realized she hadn't seen a single person here she would describe as a "hippie."

Since arriving in Paris, Angie had also acquired a whole new understanding of the word 'disdain'. She'd seen it applied effectively by sales clerks, waiters, and other diners. Looking around now at her friends chatting casually, she noticed disdain in the glances of other patrons whenever there was a particularly loud laugh. Like Melanie's.

Melanie was with Greg and John, and waving her arms as she told a story. Good old Melanie. Angie smiled. Melanie had been a good friend to her for many years, and had seen Angie through several tough situations. She could be pushy and she definitely had an opinion about everything, but she also had the biggest heart of anyone Angie had ever met. Angie was very upset about Melanie's home situation. Melanie didn't deserve that kind of treatment. What was *wrong* with Gary?

Continuing her gaze around the room, she saw Julie and Sam standing over to one side, chatting with Todd. Julie was standing very close to Sam, and Angie could see their arms were touching. What was Julie up to? Julie knew Sam was married—how could she cozy up to him that way, knowing he had a wife and two kids at home? Julie laughed at something Todd said, then gazed back at Sam, and Angie could see that the look Sam gave her was more than just friendly. *Should she say anything?* Angie wondered. *Should she try to do anything? Was it any of her business?*

For the moment, she was finding it very pleasant to stand apart and just observe everyone. She had even forgotten to be uncomfortable about her weight. She wanted to remember all the impressions and thoughts she was having so she could write them in her journal when she got back to the room.

Angie looked out over the city again and felt a pang of regret. She loved her life, she loved Joe and the girls, but a small voice inside her wondered how life might have been different if she hadn't gotten married right after college. What if she had taken advantage of the semester abroad program at Foundry and had tried something totally different? She had been afraid—afraid of losing Joe if she went away for a few months, afraid of losing her friends and, now that she really thought about it, afraid of being alone.

She had never really been alone. She had wonderful parents who doted on her, and because she was their only child she had always been included in their activities. In high school, she'd had a couple of close girlfriends she'd done everything with, including the few social events they'd dared to go to. She'd had no boyfriends in high school, so when she met Joe at the Freshman Dance the first week of college and he had actually asked her to dance, she had fallen head over heels and had never strayed far from his side since.

They had gotten married right after graduation and had moved to Boston so he could get his graduate degree. There had been two trips to Europe with Melanie and Gary during those years, and though the trips were done on shoestring budgets, the experiences each time had made Angie look forward to going again when they had more money to spend.

They moved back to Portland after Joe got his degree, so Joe could teach at the University and live close to his parents. Angie had been pregnant with Mary when they left Boston, so she did not even look for a job. And then Anne had come along so soon after Mary that Angie'd had her hands full just caring for two babies under two years old. When the girls went off to elementary school she thought again about finding a job, but Joe's mother's health began to deteriorate, and Angie found that helping her and running her own household took all of her time. Someone always needed something, and Angie somehow was in charge of making sure that everyone else's life ran smoothly. It had never occurred to her, but she now realized that she had gotten very good at it.

The years had flown by, and the trip to Europe that Joe had promised "when they had more money" just never materialized. When it came time to actually buy the airplane tickets, somehow he was always too busy, or he had forgotten, or.... There were a million excuses. As the years ticked by, she became more and more stressed with waiting, and when she had finally confronted him a year ago, he confessed that he actually didn't *want* to go. He said that he had never really understood her interest in going back to Europe. He had promised to take her back because it was obvious how important it was to her, but in his view there was always something in Portland that presented a more pressing and appropriate need for their funds. Portland was great. They had everything they needed. Why would she want to go to a place where she didn't speak the language, the food was so different, and they didn't even use the same currency?

Angie had been stunned. She had thought it was a dream they shared. Joe's indifference made her question all the other things she thought she knew about him. She spent an evening and all the next day going through it in her mind, but concluded that inside she had always known that was how he felt. Joe was a homebody—he didn't even like going to Seattle to see his cousins, so why in the world would he *ever* want to go back to Europe? As he pointed out, he didn't speak the language, and he certainly didn't like the weird food. When she told him that she understood why he didn't want to go, it seemed to release a flood of words describing all the things he didn't like—look how late they ate dinner, and you had to take buses and subways to go anywhere, and…. The list went on and on. So Angie had to satisfy her desire to see the world by watching movies or hearing about trips friends had taken.

And then Melanie's email had arrived. Joe had been shocked when she told him she wanted to go without him. It had taken courage she didn't know she had to decide to go. After a day of questions and several repetitions of "Are you sure?" he had agreed to buy her ticket, as long as she *really* thought it was a good idea and *was sure* she could handle it on her own.

Angie had insisted, "Of *course* I've thought about it, and I know I can handle it." She had smiled and given him what she hoped was a totally confident look, but inside, her stomach had churned with doubts and concerns. And those doubts had not diminished in the weeks that followed. She had never gone *anywhere* on her own. She obviously couldn't speak French. She didn't even own a decent suitcase, for heaven's sake! But by the time the day came to leave, she was excited and very glad she was going.

The flights had been long—five hours to the East Coast, and then another seven to Paris. Next was the confusing walk through the airport, followed by a twenty-minute line at the passport control station. Then there had been more corridors until she had finally reached the baggage area. The final straw had been that horrible shuttle ride with Emily.

But thank God Melanie had made her stick it out. Here she was, looking out over Paris, feeling healthier than she had in a long time. Who would ever have thought it possible? Maybe she could even persuade Joe to come back with her one day!

Glancing back into the restaurant, she saw Emily and Gigi standing to one side. Gigi looked up at the same moment, and her smile was welcoming, but Angie had to decide if she was willing to face Emily. She convinced herself to join them by telling herself she could leave if Emily got to be too much.

****

When the group arrived at the top of the Pompidou Center, Emily ordered a *kir* and found a table with a good view of the entire restaurant area. The tart white wine and *crème de cassis* combination was refreshing, and she was taking a moment to savor it while letting the flow of conversation swirl around her. Everyone was getting more comfortable with each other and it was fun to watch the dynamics.

"What are you thinking?" Gigi quietly interrupted her reverie. Emily smiled. "I was just taking a moment to look at the group. It's only been a couple of days, but it feels much longer somehow, you know?"

Gigi pulled out a chair and sat down. She, too, had a *kir*—Emily's suggestion, and yet another "first" to add to her growing collection.

Emily continued. "It's funny how, in a school as small as Foundry, there were students I didn't know at all."

Gigi nodded. "That was true for me, too. As a Music major, I was always in the practice studios with a piano, or at choir practice at Slatherton Hall. So those were the people I knew."

Emily said, "Exactly. In fact, *we* would never have gotten to know each other except for the fact that we were both living in that front hall of Blandell. That was fun, wasn't it?" She looked wistful.

Gigi smiled. "Yeah, it was." She was silent a moment, thinking back. Emily in those days had been a wild party girl, someone who would come and go at all hours. Gigi had never understood how Emily managed to keep up her grades.

Emily was watching her face and she laughed. "I can see your mind churning, remembering my wilder days, right?" Gigi blushed and Emily reached over to pat her arm reassuringly. "Don't worry—you're right. I *was* a party girl. Up late having fun, then up early in the morning for yoga or to go for a run. I could never pull that off these days!"

Gigi smiled. "None of us could." With a shy grin, she added, "Most of us couldn't pull it off even then."

Emily's look turned serious. "I don't think you know that before college, my life was *very* quiet and *very* sheltered. I grew up in New England. Coming to southern California, with its free and easy lifestyle, was a shock to my system. And not having my mom looking over my shoulder every minute.... Well, I don't have to paint the picture. You lived it with me that year!" They both gazed out over the room and Emily added, "You know, I think my affair with Ben started out as part of that rebellious feeling. I was trying to shock my conservative parents." She took a sip of her *kir* and then said, "Luckily for me, Ben was actually the perfect guy for me and it all ended in the best way it could have—me marrying a great guy."

Gigi said in a tentative voice, "You always seemed a little on edge. Like you were searching for something and getting frustrated because you couldn't find it." She paused before adding quietly, "Ben seems to have been that 'something' that was missing."

Emily looked thoughtful. "You're right—I *was* looking for something. Though I don't know where that feeling came from. I can't blame my parents at all. They gave me a loving and stable childhood. I was just always restless and discontented." She fell silent.

Gigi let the silence continue for a couple of minutes, the noise of the bar filling the air between them. "You know what's ironic?"

Emily looked over at her. "What?"

"Look where you ended up. Back in Boston."

Emily laughed. "We New Englanders always come home, I guess." She added, "And in the end, my parents and I made up, after they had time to get over the 'shame' of the whole affair. They were sad that we never had kids, but Mom told me once that she really loved Ben, and that meant a lot to me."

Gigi looked over at someone and smiled, and Emily followed her gaze. She saw Angie moving towards them. Emily was pleasantly surprised to see that Angie looked—well—almost happy. She was wearing a dark sweater over her dark jeans, and she had added a jaunty little scarf at her neck. It gave the whole outfit a certain sense of style. Had Angie put it together herself or had Melanie helped her choose that combination?

Emily turned to Gigi. "What's our plan for dinner?"

Gigi shook her head. "No idea. I think dinner's open tonight."

"I know a great little place that isn't too far from here. I could call first to see if they have space."

Quietly, Gigi asked, "It's not too expensive, is it?"

"No, just a little family-run place. Not too many choices of food, but all tasty."

Gigi nodded. "That sounds good." As Angie got close, Gigi turned to her, saying, "Emily and I were just talking about dinner plans. Emily knows a good place near here. Do you want to join us?"

Angie answered, "Absolutely. Are you asking Melanie and Julie, too?" She wasn't about to disagree with any suggestion from Emily, but she wanted plenty of friendly faces around.

"That was our next step," said Gigi. "Why don't you come with me to ask them? Emily, we'll give you a thumbs up if they say yes."

Emily watched with interest as Angie spoke to Melanie, and then Melanie pulled Julie away from Sam's side. Julie did *not* look happy, but after a moment, Gigi signaled to make the reservation for five.

The four women made their way back to Emily's table, arriving just as Emily said, *"A tout de suite"* and hung up her phone.

"Looks like we're in luck. The restaurant can seat us if we get over there by 8:00." She glanced down at her phone. "Which is in seven minutes."

Melanie said, "Let's get going then!" Emily noticed that Julie was still looking irritated.

Emily led the way quickly down a couple of small streets to a green doorway. Old panes of glass in its center offered a slightly blurry view of the interior. The light spilling out of the window was welcoming, and when Emily opened the door, they could smell a tantalizing combination of garlic, fresh bread, and roasted lamb.

Once seated, Gigi glanced around. "Look at all the shelves over there. That's odd."

Emily spoke up. "Ben and I were told it was originally a pharmacy. It was closed back in the 1920s and then converted into a restaurant. The young couple who own it now have only had it for a couple of years."

"It certainly smells wonderful." Melanie took a deep breath.

Just then a petite woman came to the table and smiled brightly at Emily, launching into what was obviously a welcoming speech to a returning friend. Emily answered back with an equally long reply. The others were amazed to find out how fluent she really was.

Turning to the rest of the group, Emily said, "Martine says that she will bring the board over to show us what's available tonight, and she will bring menus in English as well."

"Sounds like you don't need that," Melanie said dryly, and was surprised that Emily ducked her head with a slight blush. "You've been holding out on us, girlfriend."

Emily looked abashed. "I never said I *didn't* speak French."

"Yeah, but you never said you spoke it like *that*."

"The French teachers at the University have been hosting French-only dinners for years, so Ben and I get lots of chances to practice."

Martine returned with the menus and Gigi was glad to see that the *prix fixe* menu was 24 euros—about $30, which seemed reasonable. It included either an appetizer and the main course, or a main course and dessert.

Emily looked up from her menu. "Anyone need help? Sometimes the translations are not very good."

Angie spoke up timidly. "Um…. What is this appetizer that has mushrooms?"

"That's a *veloute*. It's basically mushroom soup, but with the mushrooms blended so it's very smooth. Oh, and it has cream."

"Wow, sounds rich." Angie turned back toward her menu.

After a few more moments of silence, Emily motioned to Martine and started the ordering herself, getting the mushroom *veloute* and the rabbit stew.

Angie looked up from her menu and said, "Could you please ask for the tomato tart to start, and the scallops for my main course?"

Gigi chose the pork dish that came with cooked apples.

"Don't you want something to start?" Emily asked.

Gigi shook her head. "I would rather have the dessert," she said with a grin.

Emily laughed. "Got it. Melanie?"

"I'll start with the mushroom soup and then have the steak."

"Julie?"

Julie looked up from the menu and turned to Martine to give her order in French.

Melanie turned to her. "What did you get?"

"The same as Angie." Julie's tone was short and she turned immediately back to Gigi on her other side.

Emily ordered a carafe of wine for the table, and after Martine had left, Melanie, in a loud voice, asked, "Julie, what's up?"

Julie turned back toward Melanie. It was clear she was annoyed. "I don't like being told what to do, and frankly, I felt coerced into coming here." She turned to the rest of the table and with an apologetic tone, she added, "I don't mean I didn't want to have dinner with you all. I just didn't like feeling that I was *ordered* to attend."

Melanie's tone was defensive. "Excuse me—I didn't *order* anyone to do anything. I just thought it would be nice for the five of us to have a meal together."

Julie didn't back down. "It's not like we haven't done that a couple of times already. We've had lunch together every day and obviously dinners, too."

Melanie looked genuinely surprised. "Whoa, whoa, slow down. We all came on the trip together, so I just thought it would be nice to have a dinner without the crowd."

Julie was silent a moment. "I understand that. But I had other plans."

Everyone waited for her to continue, but Julie was silent, taking a sip of her wine.

Melanie spoke again. "Did you want to have dinner with Sam, by any chance?"

Julie sat still, but then nodded. "Yes." Her tone was defiant. "Yes, I did."

She locked eyes with Melanie and there was a moment of tense silence. Julie was the first to look away and her shoulders suddenly slumped. "I *do* want to have dinner with him, and lunch with him, and…." She didn't need to finish the sentence for everyone to know what else she wanted.

Gigi spoke up, her voice quiet, but insistent. "Julie, you know he's married."

Julie's look was miserable. "I know that, and believe me, I've really thought about staying away from him. But after the *Procope* dinner, when we were walking back to the hotel, he started to tell me how unhappy he is in his marriage, and how alone he feels because he has no one to talk to about it. All of his friends are married couples who know both of them and who run in the same social and work circles." This time she looked around at everyone as she said, "Don't you see? *I* know exactly how he feels, because I lived in that techie world, too, when I was married to Ryan. In that world, everyone knows everyone, and everyone is always poking into everyone else's business, personal and professional. And at Sam's level, you never know if people want to be your friend because they actually like you, or because they think you can be useful. It's all very artificial—lots of air kisses and 'let's do lunch.'"

Julie continued. "There's lots of money floating around, too, so you get all kinds of weird behavior around that—those who want to flaunt it, and those who go the other extreme and wear flip flops and torn jeans just to show they don't care."

Emily spoke next. "So why is he unhappy in his marriage?"

"He feels like he and Helen have drifted apart. As CEO, he has to spend a lot of time working—long hours when he's in California, and a lot of time traveling to their other offices around the world. He was just opening an office in Paris, and that's actually why he's here for this trip." She continued, "So when he does get home, he just wants to relax. He wants to have simple, interesting conversations. About…you know…whatever. Maybe something in the news, or maybe just a great restaurant he tried. All she wants to talk about, apparently, is her days at the gym, or shopping. Their worlds have completely separated. The only thing they still seem to have in common is the kids, and now they're both in college."

Melanie looked skeptical. "How many times have we heard the 'my wife doesn't understand me' story? I'm sorry, Julie—it could be totally true. But you have to admit that's a little weak."

Julie's eyes flashed. "He said they've been in counseling for a year and it isn't working."

Melanie looked unconvinced. "If he's busy all the time with work, what's his wife supposed to do?"

Angie spoke up for the first time. "Why doesn't she travel with him? I would have *loved* to have a husband who had to travel around the world!"

"Apparently she went with him a couple of times early on, when the kids were small and could be left at home with her parents. But when they got to high school, there was always too much going on in their schedules for them to take time off, and Helen was right there, pushing them to do more extracurricular activities and to get the best grades so they could get into the best colleges. Now that they're in college, they still email their papers to her for her review. Crazy!"

"Wow, talk about a helicopter parent," Emily's voice was sharp. When Gigi looked confused, she explained, "I don't know if this is true in Italy, but in the States now we've got these parents who are convinced that their kids can't do anything on their own and are always interfering. I had students at the community college whose parents would call me and complain if I gave their kid a grade on a test that they—the parents—didn't agree with!"

Gigi's look was incredulous. "Seriously? I certainly haven't seen anything like that in our school. I'm the one who feels like a helicopter parent because of how much I care about Mariella's education—and I don't do *anything* like that."

Julie went on. "So he and Helen have nothing to say to each other. It's obvious how much it means to him to have someone to talk to."

"Talking is one thing," said Melanie dryly. "It isn't the 'talking' part that I'm worried about."

Julie blushed, but couldn't deny her feelings. "I know—I keep telling myself that my relationship with him is an extension of how comfortable and relaxed I'm feeling. We all kind of 'grew up" together, you know? I love London, but I can't 'hang out' in the same way with my British girlfriends. They just don't understand."

"And your British boyfriends?"

"I don't have a British boyfriend at the moment, and the few dates I've had have made me wonder how the British Empire has survived this long—I've found no evidence of *any* romantic instincts at all!"

They all laughed, and Julie continued. "Sam needs a sympathetic ear, and I'm comfortable in that role. I can back off if it gets to be more than that. I don't think it will—he's married, and we both know that."

Melanie's eyes widened. "Sympathetic ear? I'm thinking it's already gone *way* past that!" Her face reddened. "Look at you tonight! Standing close to him, brushing arms, gazing up at him. That's what you call being just 'a sympathetic ear'? No, sorry, you can't get out of it that easily. You're already crossing that line, in your mind anyway, and moving things to a whole new level."

Julie's tone grew defiant again. "Okay, so yes, I may be letting myself feel more for him than I should. But I'm not sorry about that. When I'm with him, I feel like I'm on top of the world." She paused and took a deep breath, trying to slow her heartbeat. "It's giving me a *lot* to think about. And I take full responsibility for my actions." She paused, and when she spoke again, it was with quiet determination. "Melanie, this is not easy for me to figure out, no matter what you think. It's complicated, and I don't have the answers yet. But one thing I *do* know. I don't need *you* sitting here judging me."

Melanie's mouth tightened and she looked ready to shoot back a reply, but Emily suddenly spoke up. "Melanie, *calm down*. I've been on the receiving end of your judgmental attitude, and I wouldn't wish it on anyone. Leave her alone."

Melanie, Gigi and Angie all had the grace to look uncomfortable, remembering the heated debates they'd had about Emily's behavior.

Julie was right, Gigi thought. *Life was hard, it was complicated, and no one—not even Julie—knew what would happen next.*

Chapter 11.

Joelle had instructed everybody to be in the lobby the next morning at 9:00 sharp, ready to leave for Burgundy. They would be staying for one night, so they were told to pack lightly and leave the rest of their belongings in their rooms.

Gigi saw Angie sitting by herself in the dining room, writing in a notebook of some kind. Curious, Gigi walked over, pausing so as not to startle her. "Angie, how are you? You look rested this morning."

Angie looked up, closing the notebook as she smiled. "I really slept well, thanks. I was telling Melanie that I'm eating better than I ever do at home—and with all this walking too, I feel like a new woman."

"Good for you," Gigi said warmly.

"And I've started writing in this journal. It was Melanie's idea for getting rid of my loneliness, and she was right. I've never had a journal before and I had no idea it could be so freeing. I can keep track of all the things I want to share with Joe, but I can also write about situations that frustrate me or make me unhappy, and it helps put everything into perspective." She then added, "I've got *so much* to share with Joe and the girls when I get back!"

"That sounds like a great idea. I may need to try it," Gigi said as she sat down. As she waited for her *café crème* to arrive, she searched for a conversation opener. She realized she hadn't spent any time alone with Angie thus far on the trip, and she suddenly felt unsure of herself. What had Angie said about Joe not coming—that he had back surgery? That would do.

"So you and Joe have been in Portland since you left Boston?"

Angie nodded. "Having two children in two years didn't leave us any time or money for things like trips to Europe."

"Melanie mentioned Joe's back surgery in her group email. How's he doing?"

Gigi was surprised when Angie blushed and stammered, "Actually, he didn't have surgery."

"Oh, sorry. I thought that's what the email said."

"It did. I told Melanie that because it then gave me a good excuse to come on this 'girls only' trip. But that's not the real reason." Angie paused and took a bite of her croissant.

"I don't know how well you know Joe, but let me tell you—he's a real homebody. He *hates* leaving Portland!" Angie's expression changed to one of frustration. "About a year ago, Joe confessed to me that he had no interest in *ever* traveling to Europe. I couldn't believe it! I knew he generally liked to stay home, but he seemed to have a good time when we all traveled together from Boston." Angie looked at Gigi for confirmation, and Gigi nodded, shocked. She certainly had the impression that he had enjoyed himself on those trips.

Gigi didn't know what to say. She wanted to support Angie, but she could see Joe's point of view, too. Timidly, she said, "Well, there's nothing wrong with being a homebody, right?"

"No, you're right." Her expression changed again. "To be honest, it was one of the things that attracted me to him in the first place. It made him seem so solid—the kind of guy who would always be there for you—who would always be dependable.

"And I still feel that way—don't get me wrong. But after I read Melanie's invitation and I looked at the brochure, I really wanted to come. And Joe couldn't understand that *at all*. We had a big argument."

Gigi looked sympathetic, and Angie took another bite of croissant. "And then when I got here, the rest of you all seemed so cosmopolitan, so worldly. I couldn't bring myself to confess that Joe didn't even *want* to come. It seemed so lame. I mean—who wouldn't want to go on a trip to Paris and wine tasting, for God's sake?"

"Angie, I think it's great that you decided to come on this trip anyway. That took courage."

"Do you really think so?" Angie's look was uncertain. "I know some people do this sort of trip all the time. But it was a huge decision for me. I haven't been back to Europe at all since those early days, and I've *never* been this far away from Joe and the girls." She held up two fingers pinched together. "I came *this close* to backing out." She paused and added, "But you know what? It's turned out *so* much better than I ever imagined! All these new things I'm doing. Like starting to write in this journal. And eating good, healthy food. And walking." She smiled. "I had this moment yesterday, looking in the mirror, when I really *saw* myself, you know? And I thought, '*This trip will be a new start for me. I want to feel like this when I get back home.*'"

Gigi was amazed and touched. Angie was certainly taking charge of herself in a way Gigi wouldn't ever have imagined. "I'm so impressed that you're taking an honest look at your life and seeing this trip as a positive new start."

Angie's answering smile brightened the whole room, and Gigi felt good that her encouragement meant so much. It suddenly made her want to share her own situation, to see if Angie might be able to reciprocate with encouraging words of her own. After a short pause, she said, "I want to do the same thing."

It was now Angie's turn to look surprised. "*What are you talking about*? You have a gorgeous Italian husband, a lovely daughter, and a life in Europe that sounds like a dream!"

"The first two are certainly true, but what I've realized this week is that I'm not taking full advantage of the 'life in Europe' part. I've let myself get very isolated. Because Paolo does a lot of socializing for work, he doesn't want to go out when it's just us. And we live in a fairly conservative community, so it's not always easy to go out on my own—or rather, without him. I've let that become an excuse for not going out at all.

"Being with all of you on this trip has reminded me that I *do* very much like socializing with friends and I miss it." She looked thoughtful before adding, "And it's created tension at home that I hadn't really understood until now."

"So what are you two so deep in conversation about?" Emily's voice startled Gigi, who looked up to see Emily, Julie, and Melanie pulling up chairs to join them.

Gigi panicked, not sure she was ready to share this discussion with the full group, but looking at them all, she knew it was the right moment. Taking a deep breath, she said, "I was just telling Angie about my home situation." She proceeded to tell them about her sense of isolation and lack of socializing at home, then added, "And there is something else

I wanted to ask you all about. I'm worried about Mariella." She turned to Emily.

"I had never heard the term 'helicopter parenting' before, but when you talked about that, it made me realize that *I'm* a helicopter parent. I don't get involved with exam grades or things like that, but I *am* very concerned about Mariella's education in a more general sense. The elementary school in our little town was fine, but I'm not happy with the middle school, and I want to make some changes.

"I've been talking to my sister in Chicago about her daughter, Megan, who is Mariella's age. She's doing all kinds of complex computer projects at school. Mariella's school doesn't even have enough computers for everyone to work on!"

Julie spoke up. "But don't you work with her on your computer at home?"

"It's not enough. Paolo doesn't really care about using the computer except as it relates to his business. He has no patience with the sorts of games and projects that Mariella is interested in. And I'm just not that computer savvy, so she's already *way* better than I am at doing research and finding what she wants on the Internet. And on top of all that, our Internet service is undependable and very slow.

"I'm sure the schools in the more urban areas, like Rome, offer much more, but we need to live where we do because of the vineyards. If Mariella is ever going to succeed at an American college, she needs those computer skills."

Gigi was silent for a moment before continuing. "I want her to have an American education because I want her to be comfortable in both cultures. She has family in both places and I would like to help her avoid some of the awkwardness and insecurity I felt in my early years in Italy."

Julie spoke up. "Gigi and I talked at dinner that first night about how hard it is when you don't understand the cultural references in conversations and interactions. Even speaking the same language, British and American are two very different cultures. It's exhausting because you have to be on your guard all the time. I have to remember to say 'football' instead of 'soccer,' and if someone offers to 'knock me up' it just means they will 'wake me up'!"

Everyone laughed, and Gigi spoke up again. "Mariella speaks English pretty well, but she's learning it from me, and I haven't lived in the States for twenty years! I'm not up on the latest slang. Yesterday, for instance, I learned from John what 'first world problem' means! I don't know that kind of stuff."

"So do you have a solution, or should we just start throwing out ideas?" Melanie asked, her eyes gleaming. It was obvious she was enjoying the idea of helping to find an answer.

"I do have an idea, and I need you to tell me if I'm crazy. I think Mariella should go live with my sister, Suzanne, and attend middle school with Megan. It would give Mariella exposure to American culture, improve her English, and give her exposure to technology in a way we can't give her at home."

Melanie looked thoughtful. "That's not a crazy idea. It actually sounds practical and cost effective to me. So what's the problem? Is Suzanne not on board with it?"

Gigi's face fell. "No, Suzanne's fine with it. It's Paolo. He thinks her middle school is perfectly adequate, and he doesn't understand why she needs more exposure to computers when no one else there is getting it." Gigi's look was pleading. "And he *really* doesn't understand why the cultural aspect is so important to me."

Gigi looked so miserable that Emily reached over to take her hand. "I think it's a good idea. Lots of people in the U.S. send their teenagers abroad, through programs like Experiment in International Living. You'd just be kind of doing the opposite." Emily continued, "And I can tell you, having spent the last few years teaching community college, to be a successful student you do need a good working knowledge of all the basic computer programs just to do the research and homework."

Gigi nodded. "That's what I thought." She was silent, then added, "I would miss Mariella like crazy, but I could handle it if I thought it was what was best for her."

"I think there's another benefit," said Emily thoughtfully. "If Mariella were gone, you'd be able to go with Paolo on some of his buying trips, and do some of the things we've talked about that have been missing in your life. Travel. Trying new foods. Having new experiences."

Gigi smiled. "You're right! And I could learn more about Paolo's business. On the rare times I do get invited to his business dinners, I have no idea what they're talking about."

"Just one more question," said Emily thoughtfully. "You haven't said what Mariella wants."

Gigi was silent for several moments. "I haven't spoken to her about it. I don't feel I can until I get approval from Paolo to even consider the idea. But Suzanne and her family came to see us last summer and Mariella talked about Megan for months afterward. I think she would love to go. I'm convinced it would be a positive experience that would carry over into whatever decisions she then makes on college and where she wants to spend her life."

Everyone was nodding and Julie said, "I think you have a vote of approval from all of us."

As they all got up to go to the bus, Gigi said, "Thank you all. It's been really helpful to describe the whole situation out loud. I'll let you know how it goes when I get back." Her heart felt lighter as they made their way outside.

****

The first forty-five minutes of the ride were spent maneuvering through Paris itself and the southern industrial suburbs, but once they had gotten to the highway, the view became much more rural. Gigi was struck by the different colors of the fields they passed, from deep green to bright yellow. She loved how each field was separated from its neighbors by a stone wall so that, from the bus, the view resembled a patchwork quilt. When the bus left the highway and turned onto the smaller roads leading to Beaune, the fields gradually became interspersed with vineyards, their neat rows of vines stretching to the horizon, each heavy with ripe fruit. Back home, Paolo would be extremely busy right now, for it was time for the *vendemmia,* the grape harvest. She assumed that the harvest must be happening soon in France as well, and craned her neck, searching for any sign of workers in the fields. It still amazed her how much of the work was done by hand, but it made sense, considering how fragile the grapes were. She looked forward to taking pictures and trying to remember the details to share with Paolo.

Michel stood up, and everyone quieted. "I think it's time to give everyone a few quick facts on winemaking in general, and then some facts about how it is done here in Burgundy. As you may know, the fall is the time of the wine harvest, or *vendanges.* The actual dates vary depending on each year's weather, which determines how quickly the grapes ripen. The weather continues to play a role because the winegrowers are watching for the optimum moment, when the grapes are fully ripe, but before any damaging last minute rainfall or frost.

"Winegrowers have to look at every small detail. They have to decide the right number of grapes on each vine—too many can mean weaker flavor, but too few could mean a small overall production. They also look at how many leaves each vine has, to make sure that the grapes themselves are getting the sun they need. There are many, many elements that go into their various decisions. I won't go into all of that now, but please understand that this is a very scientific yet unpredictable process.

"AOC's, or *appellation d'origine controlee,* is a designation from the government that means 'controlled designation of origin.' It is used for wine and cheese and various other agricultural products and is a guarantee that the item in question was produced in the region specified using production methods that satisfy the regulating body. Burgundy has many small vineyards, and has more AOC's for wine than any other region of France. Much of the wine produced here never leaves France, because many of these smaller vineyards pre-sell their wine to a particular distributor, thereby guaranteeing a buyer and locking in a price early in the process.

"There is a very important word you need to know when looking at wine production in Burgundy: *terroir*. Do you all know that word?" There were some nods and some people shaking their heads, so he continued.

"*Terroir* literally means land. Each parcel of land is different, and the wine it produces is different too. Most white wine produced here is made from the Chardonnay grape, and red wine is produced from the Pinot Noir grape. There are a couple of other, smaller varieties, but the two varieties you need to remember today overall are Chardonnay and Pinot Noir. The type of grape is not always listed on the bottle of wine, as it often is in California. Here you choose your wine by the producer, not the grape variety. We will walk through the labeling protocol and you will see that it is possible to have wine from literally just one field, or a blend of several fields in a very small area, and the label will tell you that. Some of the smaller producers will also sell their grapes to the larger *négociants* who bottle the wine and sell it as a blend. We will be touring Louis Jadot today, who is one of the largest *négociants,* but they also have their own fields and produce their own wine.

"For those of you used to drinking Chardonnay from California, you will be surprised by how different this tastes. California producers age their wine in American oak barrels and it adds a very distinctive taste. I'm sure you have all heard 'oaky' or 'buttery' used to describe a California Chardonnay.

"Here in Burgundy, much of the white wine is aged in stainless steel casks, so there is no oak flavor. Also, in some areas the ground is very rocky and that adds a 'minerally' flavor. I'm looking forward to hearing your impressions.

"Back to the idea of *terroir.* Wines here are categorized as *villages, grand cru* and *premier cru.* A designation is given to the wine based on the land where the grapes are grown, *not* on the quality of the harvest from one year to another. In general, the *villages* designation applies to wines grown in the valleys. They tend to be a blend of several fields. Wine produced from the vines on the rocky slopes is *grand cru* or *premier cru*. Some people say that the wine from those areas is better because the grape vines have to 'work harder.'

"The designations assigned to each field have been in place for a very long time. A grower can petition to have the designation of its wine upgraded, if the quality has improved enough to justify it. The process is long and involved, however, and there is no guarantee of success.

"I also wanted to also tell you about where we are staying, the *Hôtel Le Montrachet* in Puligny-Montrachet. This is a tiny village, as you'll see, but the hotel itself is top quality and its restaurant and chef are renowned. We will stop there first so you can get your room assignments and drop your bags. Then we will proceed to the town of Beaune for a quick lunch, and then on to Louis Jadot for the tour.

"We will return to the hotel in the late afternoon, and dinner will be served at 8:30, complete with wine pairings by their sommelier, and you will see why the white wines of Puligny-Montrachet are considered some of the best produced in the world. The sommelier will be available to answer your questions, both about the specific wines that we taste, and more general questions you may have."

Michel sat back down and Emily turned to Julie sitting next to her. "I'm really sorry Ben isn't here. He would love all this information—as well as the tastings, of course."

Julie nodded. "I had no idea that the classification was based on the land that the grapes are grown on."

From across the aisle Melanie said, "This is really going to be interesting. I'm not a big white wine fan and I never buy anything that says Chardonnay."

Emily nodded. "Me neither—that 'oaky' taste that he was talking about is something I've never cared for."

Melanie turned to Gigi, who was seated next to her. "I assume that Paolo is an expert on French wines as well as Italian?"

"He has to be—they are his direct competition! He is always looking for ways to show how his wines are different, and of course better, than the French ones." Everyone laughed, and Gigi then went on. "I remember him saying that the wines in our area of Piedmont are sometimes compared to Burgundy in taste."

"You must have amazing wine at your house!" exclaimed Melanie.

Gigi smiled. "Of course! You'll have to come visit and taste it yourself."

"I would love that!" exclaimed Melanie.

Everybody returned to looking out at the passing scenery, and Emily turned to Julie. "You've been pretty quiet since we left Paris. You okay?"

Julie nodded.

"Thinking about Sam?"

Julie again nodded.

"I admit, I was surprised you sat next to me on this trip. I figured you'd be back there with him."

Julie said simply, "I felt like I needed to give myself a little space today to think things through."

Emily looked at her for a moment and then in a soft voice said, "Staying neutral when there is a strong physical attraction can be tough. I know from my own experience. I remember sitting in Ben's class watching him as he taught, waving his arms around for emphasis of some point, and I would tell myself that being attracted to him was foolish. That it could only lead to trouble. That he was way too old. That I was way too young." She paused. "And you know what? None of it mattered. I was attracted to him, physically and intellectually, and when the opportunity presented itself to act on that, *nothing* was going to stop things from happening the way they did."

Julie nodded. "I've admitted to myself that something could happen between us, and I'm not going to stress myself out thinking about that. I know I'm helping him by listening, and I love being with him." Glancing toward

Melanie, she added, "And I'm not going to apologize for *any* of that. Not to Melanie, not to Angie, not to *anyone.*"

"What you do is your business and no one else's."

"Thanks." Julie lapsed back into silence, turning her gaze toward the rolling hills and the rows of vines, and turning her thoughts toward Sam.

****

The bus pulled up to the front of the hotel and everybody gathered their bags, stretching and chatting as they headed toward the reception area. Julie found herself behind Greg and Todd and surreptitiously looked around to see where Sam was. He was standing to one side of the bus, his cell phone to his ear, letting people swirl around him. John was obviously waiting for him nearby.

After the women received their room assignments and keys, they gathered outside. Julie said, "I'm in the Annex."

Emily spoke up. "Me too. She told me it's over there across the street." She pointed to a narrow, four-story building. "Let's go."

They walked through the front door into a small hallway, which seemed dim after the bright sunshine. Their footsteps made no sound on the thickly carpeted stairs as they made their way to the second floor, and they found themselves opening their respective doors gently so as not to break the silence. After a few minutes to unpack, they met again on the landing, which was simply decorated in muted tones of green.

"Do you like your room?" Emily asked.

"Very much. It's bright, and the window looks over the square at all those beautiful trees that are just starting to turn color."

"It's wonderful to be in the countryside!" exclaimed Emily. "I think I might run tomorrow morning—depending how I feel after the wine-tasting and dinner."

"That's a good idea," Julie agreed. "In London, I usually run at the health club, but running through this countryside would be much more interesting!"

They went out to the bus, where Michel was gesturing for everyone to get on board. After a fifteen-minute ride, the bus entered Beaune, and shortly thereafter it pulled into a small square. The group was directed to the outdoor seating area of one of the cafés.

Melanie led the five of them to a table in the shade, and Julie was glad to see that Greg, Todd, John and Sam followed behind them and took the next table over. She could tell that Sam was bothered about something, and she felt an almost overwhelming urge to go over to ask him about it. But the waiters were arriving and taking orders, so she limited herself to a sympathetic smile and vowed to pull him aside after lunch.

After everyone ordered, Melanie looked around. "Michael is certainly knowledgeable! I'm trying to remember everything he told us."

Angie nodded. "Me too. I want to put it all in my journal so I can tell Joe."

Melanie grinned. "I'm glad you're enjoying writing."

Angie smiled too. "I really am. Now I understand why you like it so much."

Lunch passed quickly, with soft murmurs of conversation broken by occasional laughter. Gigi noticed that when Greg started guffawing, Melanie looked over at him and seemed to wink. *I wonder what that's about?* Gigi thought to herself.

An hour later, after everybody had finished drinking their espressos, they piled back onto the bus. This time, Julie followed closely behind Sam and sat down next to him near the back of the bus. She could feel the warmth of his thigh where it touched her leg.

"What's going on?" she asked quietly. "I don't want to pry, but you looked upset earlier."

"I was listening to a message from Helen. I had left a short message for her last night, and I think I ended it with some simple comment like 'things are going fine.' She left a long message in return, going on and on about how unhappy she was that I had not invited her to come, and how much fun she was sure I was having. It sounded like she'd had a couple of drinks and was really wound up. She called at 8:00pm her time, so I didn't get it until this morning." He sighed. "Apparently she's re-thinking my logic about her not wanting to hang out with my college friends for a week."

Sam looked out the window, and Julie admired his profile. He continued, "She can really get under my skin. She knows me well enough to know I was feeling guilty for not bringing her."

"Do you regret your decision now?"

His voice was firm. "No. Actually. I'm sorry to say I honestly don't." He turned toward Julie. "I've reached a point in my life where I know who I want to be with, and how I want to spend my time. And, unfortunately, she has no place in that world anymore.

"I know we're both to blame. When I married her, it was obvious that she didn't have the same intellectual interests I did, and even back then it was obvious we didn't have a lot to talk about. But she was gorgeous, and she was fun to be with, and I thought that we'd find common interests and pastimes through the years.

"Then I got busy building my career and I didn't have much time to spend with her. She chose to immerse herself in our children, which was a wonderful thing and I'm thankful for that. For a while, it seemed like we could make it work, even with our lives being so separate most of the time. But her focus kept narrowing and suddenly I was no longer a part of her world at all—*all* of her thoughts and actions were centered on the kids, and there was literally no time at all for the two of us as a couple. She wouldn't ever take a vacation without the children. And when I tried to include her in my work, through client dinners and events at the office, she always found some excuse not to attend. She forgot that I existed as her husband, and instead I became solely the funding source for whatever she wanted.

"She was no longer my wife. She was a devoted mother, and obviously that was great, but a marriage can't survive with only that.

So now, with the kids successfully launched, Helen and I have absolutely nothing in common and I don't see that changing. The kids will always be her priority."

He looked so sad and dejected that Julie felt a rush of sympathy. She laid her hand on his knee and he immediately placed his hand over hers. Its warmth spread up her arm, and she could feel that dangerous tingle starting in the pit of her stomach.

For a moment, they looked into each other's eyes, and suddenly Michel was saying loudly, "Everyone off the bus please."

Withdrawing her hand, Julie stood. Taking a deep breath, she started toward the front of the bus. She could feel Sam following her and his proximity had her nerves tingling.

C'mon, now, girlfriend, keep it together, she told herself. But her heart kept repeating those final words "Helen and I have absolutely nothing in common and I don't see that changing."

****

Exiting the bus, Julie and Sam became separated as Sam politely let others enter the aisle to exit. Sam knew it shouldn't matter, but it suddenly felt like Julie was miles away. By the time he got off and stepped onto the pavement, she was nowhere to be seen. He strode quickly to the main building to try to catch up with the others.

The entire group was crowded into a room with a large map of the area on one wall. He scanned the room and found her, wedged between Emily and the wall on the far side. Was she deliberately avoiding him? There was no way he was going to be able to get across the entire group to be near her, so he resigned himself to biding his time. She did not meet his gaze, and he felt frustration building inside him.

He was *such* an idiot! He had made the decision to get divorced two years before, but he had dragged his feet, telling himself that he would wait 'until the kids were in college.' That had finally happened last year, and he had actually met with an attorney and started the process. Then, in January, the Board of Directors had decided that they wanted to expand the company by opening offices in five new countries, and he had been on the road ever since trying to make that happen. The divorce got put on the back burner.

Now this wonderful woman had come back into his life as if by magic, and his loveless marriage was putting a giant roadblock in their path. Logically, he could understand her hesitation. But emotionally, he *knew* she cared for him. He could see it in her every gesture and her every gaze.

He had never felt so frustrated, or so helpless. He was used to being *in charge* for God's sake! He made himself take several deep breaths, and tried in vain to focus on the wine presentation. When that didn't work, he took out his phone and started instead to make a list…the timeline and next steps for a divorce settlement.

****

Julie made herself focus on Jean-Pierre, the young man giving them the forty-minute description of the history of wine in Burgundy. But it was hopeless—her thoughts kept turning back to the conversation with Sam. *It certainly sounded like his marriage was over.* The fact that it sounded like it had been over for a long time assuaged her guilt.

She came back to the present when Emily nudged her arm to indicate they were heading down to the *caves* area. In the dim light, she could see rows and rows of barrels. Jean-Pierre gave each of them a glass, which would be theirs for tasting all the wines. He then showed them the spittoons, which were large silver bowls on stands set at various strategic locations near the barrels, and explained the technique they should use.

"You take ze sip of wine into your mous and swirl it around so it touches all parts of your mous. Eef you can, pleez try to also take a breath wif your mous a leetle bit open, so that ze wine will be introduced to ze air." His slight French accent added a charming touch to the words. Emily and Julie tried not to giggle.

"Zen you will concentrate, and try to imagine ze flavors. I will also tell you my impressions. Zen you will speet into one of zese." He pointed at the spittoons. "And zere ees water for you to put in ze glass to rinse it before you add ze next wine." He broke them into groups of five and an assistant poured for each group.

Julie found it hard not to swallow automatically after each sip, and was soon feeling a little lightheaded. Her group consisted of Emily, Greg, Joelle and one other woman Julie didn't know. Sam was in the group next to theirs and was obviously disappointed by that fact.

As they worked their way down one row of barrels and then another, Julie started to take pictures of the labels on each barrel with her phone to help her remember the names later. How did *anyone* keep track of all these different varieties? She found herself a little dizzy, and attributed it not only to the wine, but also to information overload. She would have to go back and do more reading on the history of the area and the winemaking process to try to cement the information into her brain. She would *never* remember it all.

Sam's presence nearby was also proving to be a serious distraction. She felt so out of control. This was *not* her usual MO. Cool Julie, calm Julie, the one who everyone felt would be best in any crisis. She was seeing a side of herself that she hadn't known existed, and it was scaring her a little. She certainly didn't remember *ever* feeling this way with Ryan.

But it was exciting, too. All of her senses were heightened. For the first time, when Jean-Pierre would pronounce this or that flavor in a particular wine, she actually felt that she was getting some sense of it. Tobacco? Cherry? Plum? She had always scoffed at the descriptive words people used to describe wine, but as she tasted the different varieties the way Jean-Pierre had taught them, she was experiencing sudden bursts of flavor. It was exhilarating.

Next Jean-Pierre moved them from the barrels to a table that held a selection of unmarked bottles. There followed another round of sipping and savoring. Soon she stopped drinking and just watched as others continued. The comments from several people were getting louder and louder, and poor Jean-Pierre started to get a look of panic. Michel suddenly spoke up.

"Everyone, please give me your attention." The room gradually quieted. "I want to thank Jean-Pierre so much for his time, and for giving us such a wonderful tasting adventure." There was a round of applause and several whoops, which made Jean-Pierre cringe. "Now, if we could all go back upstairs and to the bus, we will proceed back to the hotel, where you will have a couple of hours to relax or walk around the small town of Puligny-Montrachet, before our dinner reservation at 8:30. We will come back to Beaune tomorrow, to a very nice wine shop that carries the Louis Jadot wine, so that you will have the opportunity to buy some bottles to take home with you."

There was a relatively orderly movement to the stairs and then out to the bus, where there was a festive air as they rode back to the hotel. Julie deliberately sat with Emily, and as soon as they got back to the hotel, she went to her room. She was running away from Sam and she knew it.

She lay back on her bed and let herself think back over the afternoon, dwelling on the moment Sam had taken her hand, and the look that she had seen in his eyes. What a roller coaster ride this had been. There was no mistaking their mutual attraction. The question was what to do about it.

This must be how addicts feel, she thought. The combination of push and pull, the inexorable feeling of sliding towards the edge, knowing that you shouldn't succumb. But oh, the anticipation of the pleasure waiting for you if you simply let yourself go....

The wine had made her sleepy, but it had also awakened her imagination. She let herself drift off to sleep imagining his lips on her neck, and his hands wandering down her body....

Chapter 12.

Julie woke with a start. The sun was shining directly into her face, and for a moment she felt disoriented. Sitting up, she saw that she had slept for two hours and that it was almost eight. Thank God for that well-placed window! Time to get herself organized and downstairs.

Going to the mirror in the bathroom, she touched up her makeup and reapplied her mascara. Several good, strong brush strokes took out the tangles in her thick, brown hair. She was lucky that she had never really had to do much to it besides blow it dry.

Coming back out into the bedroom, she took a moment to admire the room in the light of the setting sun. It was decorated in soft reds and oranges. The furnishings were a sharp contrast to the stark, modern rooms they'd left behind in Paris. The old-fashioned knobs on the four-poster bed matched those on the vintage dresser. The whole impression was soft and slightly fuzzy—like the close-up shots of the female heroine in the movies from the forties that she loved.

Moving to the dresser, she pulled out her black lace camisole and slipped it over her head, smoothing it carefully into place. She then went to the closet and chose a pair of black leggings and a brightly patterned sweater that fell down to just cover her thighs. Opening her jewelry case, she stood thinking for a moment. Most of what was inside reflected her conservative dressing style, but she had deliberately included two pairs of dangly earrings to remind herself that she was on this trip to push herself out of her comfort zone. Picking up the second pair, she smiled. They were a visual rejection of the accountant in her, and instead reflected another Julie, the adventurous Julie who had taken all the frustration she felt at Ryan's lack of interest and had used it to fuel her move to London. She then pulled out a silver necklace that was so long she had to loop it twice around her neck. It was simple, a pure strand of small, exquisite links that fell down to lie between her breasts.

Finally, she reached down to pull on her new, soft, black suede boots whose narrow heel was half an inch higher than her usual style. Looking at herself in the mirror, her legs looked longer, sexier. Not bad, not bad at all, if she did say so herself.

She texted Emily, "U ready to go?" and when the reply came immediately, tucked her phone and key in her pocket and headed out the door.

Emily looked her over and nodded her approval. "Nice."

Julie looked at Emily's outfit and smiled. "You too. Ben is a lucky guy!" Emily was wearing a small black skirt over tights and a pair of knee-length boots. Her dark green blouse peeked out from under a short jacket, which was covered in small squares of black, green, and blue. She had paired it with a small pair of green earrings and a necklace with a single, blue stone dangling just below her collarbone. Her dark hair shone, and Julie noted with envy that there was very little grey.

Emily's brown eyes sparkled as she tucked her arm into Julie's. "You ready?"

Julie knew the bigger question Emily was asking, and nodded. "I think so. Let's do this!"

They walked across to the main building, and at the entrance to the dining room were greeted by tantalizing cooking smells. Julie glanced quickly around for Sam, but didn't see him.

Members of their group were circling around tables at the far end of the room. As they approached they could see that there were place cards at each seat. Everybody seemed to be making a game of searching for their name. Julie felt a moment of panic that she wouldn't have Emily by her side for the evening, but then told herself she was being silly. *Was she a teenager or a grown woman, for God's sake?*

Melanie's voice greeted them excitedly. "Emily," she squealed. "You're over here with Gigi." She was practically dancing with excitement. Julie followed Emily, scanning the tables as she went. She had not seen her name yet. There was another squeak as Melanie found her own place card. "Oh, I'm sitting with Greg—what fun! Julie, how about you?"

"Looks like I'm at Todd's table." He was waving from a table in the far corner.

"Hey there," she said as she arrived at the table.

"Hey yourself!" Todd replied. He gazed at her appreciatively. "You look great, by the way!"

"Thanks!" Julie blushed with pleasure. She felt sure he did not dole out compliments easily. She noticed that he had abandoned his usual collared shirt and v-neck sweater combination for a soft brown turtleneck and a camel colored cashmere jacket. It worked well with his straight brown hair, which was cut short, and his brown eyes, which were warm with welcome.

"So who else do we have?" She tried to keep her voice light, but felt it was obvious what she was asking.

Todd seemed oblivious. "I've just made the circuit, and the good news is we have Joelle with us. Hopefully we can get her to give us personal lessons on this whole wine rating system. And the whole naming system on the bottles…."

Julie answered, while straining to read the other names near her. "Who knew how much we *didn't* know about wine? I have to tell you—I got completely overwhelmed this afternoon."

Todd nodded. "Me too. I'm not used to drinking that much wine, and certainly not in the afternoon."

They continued their stroll around the table, and Julie's heart sank as they came full circle and Sam's name was obviously not there. Trying to sound cheerful, she said, "We've got Judy and Wayne, too. Did you know Judy when we were in school?"

"No, I think she was in the sciences, and with all those labs, those guys had no time for socializing—even if they'd been so inclined, which is highly doubtful!" He grinned.

Julie scoffed, "Yeah, you're one to talk! Mr. Math Nerd!"

"Look who's talking!" he said with mock indignation.

She smiled back. "I guess you're right. Pot calling the kettle black, right?"

He started to respond, but was obviously distracted by something over her shoulder. "Hey, I'm sorry, but I'll be right back. John wants me for something."

Having a moment to herself, Julie's gaze again circled the room, surprised she hadn't seen Sam yet, but also interested in seeing what everyone was wearing, and who was talking to whom. Melanie and Greg were chatting, and Greg seemed more relaxed. She was thankful she couldn't hear his voice rising above the rest of the crowd.

And there was Angie, also looking at ease and, surprisingly, looking quite put together. She was wearing a long grey jacket over her black pants. *Where had that come from? Maybe Angie and Melanie had somehow found a clothing shop this afternoon after they got back from the wine tasting?* The jacket certainly didn't look like anything Angie would have brought, but it suited her very well. She'd have to ask her about that later.

When they had all lived in Boston, Julie had sometimes found Melanie overbearing—too pushy and always imposing her opinions and needs on others. Now, Julie was seeing her in an entirely new light. Melanie seemed very gentle with Angie, and her support had really changed Angie's outlook on this trip. Julie thought back to that first afternoon, when Angie had come to sit with her in the café. She had been such a mess—so miserable and so sure that she should turn right around and go home. Now Julie could see in her a newfound sense of confidence, as she stood chatting with Joelle. Angie held herself straighter, and her face was animated as she told Joelle some story. Well, *that* would be a wonderful gift to take back home with her—a heightened sense of her own self-worth.

Julie continued her gaze around the room and saw Emily and Gigi talking to a couple she didn't know. It made her realize that thus far on the trip, their group of five and Sam's group of four had spent most of their time together. Not a bad thing, but there were twenty-five people in all, including Michel and Joelle, so that meant there were another dozen or so people she had not really talked to yet. Julie wondered whose idea it had been to have place cards tonight. It was certainly a smart way to mix things up a bit and make sure everyone got a chance to meet each other. Obviously Joelle and Michel, in addition to serving as hosts because of their knowledge and language skills, had to make sure that people interacted and had fun.

Julie hadn't really thought about it before, but it made sense that the school would want to encourage trips like this and make sure that they were enjoyable. It was a way to keep alumni contributing to the school by connecting them to their past, and also a way to ensure they would want their own children to attend and benefit from the same sense of community. Julie had never thought about that aspect of alumni trips, and she looked around her now with a new perspective. Michel and Joelle were working the room, laughing with one group, then moving on to the next, encouraging conversation and interaction. She had to smile at the brilliance of it.

"What are you smiling about?" Her heart jumped, and she turned to face Sam, who had come up behind her. He was standing very close and she could smell his aftershave, a musky scent that went right to her head. She allowed herself one quick inhalation before taking a small step backward.

She made her tone neutral as she said, "I was just realizing how brilliant that darn Foundry alumni office is."

Sam looked puzzled. "Okay, now that is not *at all* what I thought you were going to say."

Julie smiled and took Sam's arm, turning him to look out over the group. His arm felt warm and solid. "Seriously, look around. Tell me what you see."

Sam did as she asked before his gaze came back to her. "People talking to each other. What's so brilliant about that?"

"No, silly. Look at *who* is talking to whom. Standing here, I realized that your friends and my friends have hung out together a lot, but there are more people on the trip that we haven't talked to yet, right?" At his nod, she continued. "Okay, so tonight, for the first time, we have place cards at the tables. I was asking myself why they would do that, and then I realized that it's in Foundry's best interest to have *all* of us talk to each other, to remember how much fun we had together, and also to be reminded what likable people we all are. Then we'll go home and make sure our kids, and our friends' kids, apply, so they can eventually be a part of it, too. See?" Her eyes sparkled and Sam laughed.

"A very smart move on their part. So you're saying Joelle and Michel are part of a conspiracy?"

"Absolutely. Look at how they're circulating and talking to everyone, encouraging people to talk to each other. Place cards are a natural way to make sure the same people aren't sitting with each other—again."

Sam smiled. "Makes sense." He didn't say anything else, but Julie saw the mischievous look in his eye. She poked him.

"What? What are you not saying?"

"Well," Sam drawled, "Your theory makes total sense and now that you've explained it to me, I think that's exactly what they wanted to do with the place cards. And they are succeeding, because we are all sitting with people we haven't sat with thus far." He paused and with a sly smile added, "Though Todd and I might have played with their system a teeny tiny bit."

"What do you mean?" She loved seeing the sparkle in his eyes, such a contrast to the sad, lost look she'd seen earlier.

"Well… Todd and I made one little *tiny* switch in the place cards. Maybe Todd is sitting at John's table now, and maybe I am sitting at *your* table now." She had to laugh out loud.

"You guys are *very* tricky! Well, well, well. Maybe I should tell the teacher?" She was flirting outrageously, she knew, and enjoying every minute of it.

"Oh, is that the kind of girl you are? The Goody Goody Two Shoes type?" His gaze swept down to her toes and back up again. "Somehow I just don't think so…."

How could she have forgotten how much fun this was and how giddy she could feel?

"Well," she answered back, "I am an accountant by training, after all. You must know that accountants march to the rules and see everything in black and white."

Sam paused and his look became very serious for a moment. "Somehow I don't think that's true for you." He paused. "You strike me as the type who can sometimes see the grey."

Julie's breath caught in her throat. The conversation had taken a very serious turn. She looked deep into his impossibly blue eyes. "Yeah, I guess I am an exception. I very much understand the grey in certain situations."

There was silence as they looked at one another. Then, suddenly, Michel was tapping a glass with his knife and calling for everybody to take their seats.

Over at Melanie's table, Greg pulled out her chair for her. Melanie was pleasantly surprised and very touched. *What a gentlemanly thing for him to do. When was the last time Gary had done something like that? No,* she admonished herself, she had to stop automatically thinking negative thoughts about Gary. That wasn't fair.

She turned to Greg with a smile. "Thank you, kind sir. That is very nice of you."

Greg smiled back. "I was always taught to treat ladies with respect."

Melanie gave Greg a mock look of horror. "Somehow, when you say it like that, I feel about a hundred."

Greg's look changed to one of concern. "Oh, I didn't mean…. I'm sorry."

Melanie interrupted with a touch to his arm. "I'm kidding, Greg," she said gently. "Don't freak out on me."

Greg shook his head ruefully. "Sorry. I really want to do the right thing, but I'm paranoid that I'm going to mess up."

"Greg, you need to relax."

"I'm trying, I really am."

"I know you are. Just remember, *you are a nice guy*. You need to make yourself believe that."

"Melanie, you're the first person in a very long time who has made me feel like I'm a nice guy. It's hard to adjust my own self-image overnight. Words I think of when describing myself are 'loud,' 'boorish,' and 'insecure.'"

"Well, think of this trip as your new beginning. You're going to go back to Rochester a new man."

Greg said wistfully, "I would love to believe that could happen."

"Start believing it. It definitely *won't* happen if you don't fully embrace the idea yourself."

Melanie smiled at Greg and touched his arm to reinforce her point. "Now turn to your right and try your newfound charm on the woman sitting on your other side." She gave him a last smile of encouragement before turning to the woman sitting on *her* left. "Hi, I'm Melanie Russell. History major. Nice to meet you."

Dinner passed smoothly, with course after course of delicious food, accompanied by sumptuous wines carefully selected by the sommeliers, who explained the reasons behind each choice. By 10:30, Melanie's head was swimming and she waved to a waiter to bring her more water. She was grateful when she saw that they were serving coffee as well. When the waiter arrived, she asked for a double espresso. She did *not* want a repeat of that first night.

People were moving outside to the terrace to finish their conversations and hear about after-dinner liqueurs. Melanie watched Angie as she stood to make her way outside, and gave herself a mental pat on the back. Melanie was very proud of her part in Angie's transformation in just three days. It showed how a change of attitude could change everything else.

The jacket Melanie had bought in Paris was perfect. She had found it when she and Emily were out wandering that first afternoon. Emily had scoffed at her for buying Angie something, but Melanie had been really worried that her dear friend was going to give up and go back home. Her hope was that a "Welcome to Paris" present might change Angie's mind. Luckily, they had passed a store that seemed to have a wide variety of designs and sizes, and when she saw the soft grey jacket, she knew it was perfect.

She had thought she would give the jacket to Angie right away, but that first night they had all been in a rush to get to dinner, and since then, somehow, the right moment had not presented itself. So Melanie had bided her time. On a whim, she had packed it in her overnight bag, and then tonight's dinner had provided the perfect opportunity.

Angie looked quite animated. People at her table were nodding and smiling as she finished telling a story. She was even wearing a little makeup. Joe was going to be surprised by the new Angie when she got home. Melanie hoped he would not also feel threatened.

Melanie stood and moved outside to a table in the shadows at the corner of the terrace. She leaned back and gazed at the stars, marveling at how bright they were.

At home, Gary would still be at work. She missed him suddenly, and she decided to skip the after-dinner liqueur lesson, and instead spend some time figuring out what was going on with their marriage. In the shadows, she could pass unnoticed for at least a brief time, and being full of good food and wine put her in a mellower frame of mind.

In the past, her attempts to work through the problem had always been triggered by something Gary had done to irritate her, which would, in turn, remind her of *all* the annoying things that Gary had ever done. This time she would try to be more logical and less emotional.

She took a deep breath and let it out slowly. The first question was: *When had things changed?* And she knew the answer—during the past year. The harder question was *Why?*

She decided she needed to try to take a dispassionate look at their life together and look for obvious big changes. Starting with her own consulting practice, she had to admit it had been a tough year. She had lost a couple of key clients, not because of any change in her abilities or in their confidence in her, but simply because the economy had slowed and she was considered a "non-essential" use of their resources. It had hurt when they told her, but she told herself not to take it personally. And she thought she'd succeeded in doing that. A consequence, of course, was that her income was down, and she knew that had created its own stress.

But Gary had been very supportive. He didn't make snide, negative comments, which she felt he did about other things. He had worked with her to update her marketing materials, and helped her create a new website. That should have lessened the stress between them, but it hadn't. Her stomach cramped in remembrance.

Why was she reacting so negatively? What was she reacting to? She understood why the clients had let her go. She knew her clients considered her to be capable, and she did not feel it would affect how she was perceived in the field in general. *Then what?*

That gut-squeezing feeling was fear. Okay, she was scared. But not about her reputation. This was something much deeper. And then it hit her. She was afraid of not having enough money. It was simple, really. It was a fear that had been a part of her since she was twelve, when her father had died of a heart attack. Melanie had watched her mother flounder helplessly, completely lost when her life partner was taken from her so suddenly. Her mother had been a traditional housewife and had left all financial matters up to her husband, confident that he would "take care of everything."

Suddenly left on her own, she'd had to learn about every aspect of their financial life. Did they have a car loan? What was the mortgage balance on the house, and who held the loan? How did you balance a checkbook? Most importantly, she had to then take this new knowledge and figure out how to make her small pension and his Social Security cover those costs. Melanie's mother had always been a positive person, and she had maintained that attitude even after her loss, but there was a new shadow in her eyes that betrayed her ongoing insecurity.

It taught Melanie the importance of being self-sufficient, and she knew that that childhood experience still shaped her decisions today. The change in her income meant she was more financially dependent on Gary, and it was obviously making her uncomfortable on some subconscious level. It shouldn't matter. But it did. She was confident she would build her business back up, but the fact that she had lost clients at all was fueling her insecurity.

So that was certainly a part of their problem, but it didn't seem like it could be everything. *So what else? Something related to Craig, maybe?* Craig had certainly been under a lot of stress applying to colleges, but he had been successful and was now at a university he liked. Craig was a good kid, and she felt optimistic about his future there.

So it wasn't related to Craig himself. Could it be somehow related to their interactions with him? Throughout the years, she and Gary had always agreed on parenting techniques and styles. Whenever there was a large decision to make, or a parenting policy to set, it had always felt like they were very much aligned in their views. But recently Gary had started commenting on how much she was still doing for Craig—how Craig would never be able to accomplish basic life tasks if he never had a chance to do them for himself. She cringed now as she thought about the conversation at the restaurant where Emily had talked about helicopter parents. Was *she* a helicopter parent? Melanie knew she liked to keep everything and everyone organized, but was she going too far? It didn't feel like it. After all, Craig couldn't be expected to know how to write a college application. He'd never had to do it before. Or know how to write a check. They'd opened a checking account for him just six months before he started college, and he was still figuring out how it worked. Or know how to pay for his college books, or set up his meal plan, or where to buy a lamp for his new desk. He'd never had to do any of those things, so she was happy to help.

Melanie stopped dead. *Oh my God!* Hadn't she *just* been remembering how helpless her mother had been when her father died? Wasn't she doing *exactly* the same disservice to Craig by not letting him do these things for himself? The parallels took Melanie's breath away.

He was eighteen! High time to figure out how to accomplish the daily tasks of college life.

Gary was right. She needed to let go. If things didn't always work out perfectly, well, that was part of the lesson, right?

She would sit down with Gary as soon as they were both home, and work out how much to give Craig per semester. His tuition and room and board were covered by loans, scholarships, and a college work/study job, but he needed to learn how to budget for books, pizza, and other "stuff." College was the first step toward life on your own, and living on a budget was a good lesson to learn early. And if he needed or wanted more money, well, they'd *all* have that discussion together.

She smiled, anticipating Gary's look of surprise when she told him her idea, and his look of shock when she admitted that he had been right all along.

She felt an enormous relief. It all made sense. So the final question in her mind was about all of his secret "projects" and his extra time at the office. She thought back to the lunch conversation with Emily, Gigi and Angie. Maybe Gigi was right. There could easily have been changes in personnel at his office, and more work for him as a result. Feeling guilty, she now vaguely recalled a conversation about his frustration at the office over something, but it had been when she was in the middle of the whole college application process for Craig, and she hadn't really been paying attention.

Melanie felt ashamed. She had been so busy being angry with Gary for not listening to *he*r that she had stopped listening to *him.* If they weren't having meaningful conversations any more, it was *her* fault, not his.

How had she been so blind? She had *never* meant to become such an unsympathetic wife. She still loved Gary. And he deserved better.

People were drifting back to the dining room, chatting, carrying their last glass of wine with them. Melanie moved to the terrace door and could see Emily and Gigi standing with another couple, laughing over a shared story. Angie was headed in that direction, and Melanie started towards them as well, feeling lighter in spirit than she had for a long time.

****

Julie hesitated at the doorway to the restaurant. She had excused herself to go to the restroom after the coffee and dessert were served. Now she took a moment to look around at the diners that were not part of their group. Many were older, and most were well dressed in a wealthy, "weekend in the country" sort of way. She heard snippets of English, German, Russian, and some Chinese or Japanese. There was the soft sound of conversation and the clinking of glasses. She could smell crêpes, chocolate, wine, and fresh-baked bread. She inhaled deeply, trying to imprint the moment firmly into her brain. She wanted to remember these smells, these tastes, and these feelings.

It had been a long time since she had felt such genuine warm pleasure from an evening with close friends. She was looking forward to inviting some of them to meet her inner circle in London. And of course, there was the giddy excitement from an entire dinner with Sam by her side. She had felt the unmistakable electricity between them, heightened by the wine they shared and the looks he'd given her.

"*Now* what are you thinking about?" a voice murmured behind her ear. His breath warmed the back of her neck and she allowed herself to lean ever so slightly backward, feeling his solid presence behind her.

"No. No, don't turn around. Keep looking into the dining room. I like looking at your profile."

Slightly breathless, she answered, "You scared me."

"Startled, I hope, but never scared," he replied, and he reached out one hand to gently pull her back more securely against him.

"What are you doing out here?" she asked lamely, searching her brain futilely for a pithy response.

"Same thing you are. I tried to be discreet, but I was hoping I'd catch you before you headed back in there."

"Really?" She could feel her heart thumping against her chest and tried to sound calm. "And why is that?" She felt his hands on either side of her waist.

"I think you know why. Do we really have to go back in there?" his voice was soft, but pleading.

"If we don't we'll miss our lesson on after-dinner liqueurs. You wouldn't want to miss that would you?"

"I have my own idea for an after-dinner activity."

Julie felt faint. "And what would that be?"

"Let's just say that what I have in mind doesn't involve drinking. But I *will* say it's about combining ingredients in just the right way." His right hand was now traveling up and down her back.

Julie felt her face flush. She was having a hard time breathing, and the tingling from his fingers was working its way into every element of her being.

Sam pulled her gently backwards into a darkened corner of the deserted hallway. He slowly turned her toward him, and she could feel his arms encircle her. Without thinking, she lifted her head, and his kiss was long and sweet, tasting of wine, and of him.

She drew back after a long moment, shaky. "Wow," she said softly.

He reached down and brushed her hair back from her forehead. "*Wow* is right."

They stood for a moment, arms locked around each other, sheltered in the darkness. She could feel his heart and it was beating as fast as hers.

"Where is your room?" he asked softly, rubbing the back of her neck with his fingertips.

"I'm on the second floor of the Annex. You?" She leaned into his hand. If she were a cat, she would have been purring.

"I'm on the third floor of the Annex. Up at the end of the hall. Want to come see? It's a great room, right under the eaves."

Here it was. The moment she had been dreading and hoping for since she had first seen him step out of that taxi. Her thoughts whirled, and her common sense waged a brief battle with her emotions. But she knew what her decision was. She'd known it for days.

"Yes. I'd love that."

She heard him let out his breath. "I was hoping *so much* you would say that." Gently, he took her hand, and led her out of the door of the hotel, across the street, under the stars, and into the Annex.

They climbed the stairs slowly, savoring the tension that was building in both of them. They reached the landing and passed her room to continue their climb. At the top of the stairs, he moved next to her, and took her hand to lead her to the end of the dimly-lit hallway. With his other hand, he reached into his pocket and drew out his key, inserting it into the lock with a gentle click.

Once inside, he let go of her hand briefly to turn on the lamp next to the door, then took her hand again to lead her further in, turning on another soft lamp as he went. Starlight came in through the dormer windows. Vaguely she noticed that it was a large room, with a bed to the left and a small seating area to the right.

The bed had been turned down in preparation for sleeping, and Julie suddenly felt awkward.

Sam turned her to him once more and, lifting her face to his, smiled down at her. "You are so beautiful," he said softly. "You won't believe it when I say this, but I swear you haven't changed at all since I danced with you in Cambridge."

She smiled. "What dance would that be?" she teased, though she knew it was the same one she remembered so well. She wouldn't confess how many times she had thought about that night and had imagined what might have happened.

"You know what I'm talking about," he answered gently. "That night at O'Malleys."

Julie nodded. "I do know," she confessed. "But tell me anyway."

He went back in time. "I remember that for once they actually had a good band in there, and we had all been dancing most of the night. Most of their songs were fast, and I was so glad when they finally had a slow one."

He began to recreate the evening. "I took you in my arms, just like this." He started to move slowly, dancing to the music of long ago. "We had a kiss...." At this, he lowered his head, and as she melted into his kiss, she was struck by how *right* it felt.

His tone changed. "And then.... your friend interrupted us and said she couldn't go to the restroom by herself. What *is* it with women needing company to go to the bathroom?"

He was laughing, but still slowly twirling her around the room. "I went and got more beer, and when I came back, you had vanished—like Cinderella!"

Julie laughed. "That was Emily, actually. When we got to the restroom, there was a huge line so we went next door to that Italian restaurant. We pretended to be patrons, which I'm sure didn't fool anyone, but they were nice and didn't argue the point. Anyway, that all took time, and when I got back, I couldn't find you." She stopped, wishing fervently she had tried harder. "After awhile, I gave up and just walked home." She was silent for a moment. "I never forgot that evening."

Sam's look was so tender that she looked down, terrified that the swirl of emotions she was feeling would show in her eyes.

Sam stopped dancing and simply held her in his arms. He spoke softly against her hair. "I thought about that night many times over the next several weeks, but in the end, I bowed to the pressure from my parents, and from my prospective employer, to finish at the top of the class. I threw myself into my work—as usual." His chuckle was bitter. "A pattern that continues in my life today."

He cupped her face in his hands. "I was so naïve about life, and about what would make me happy."

He stroked her cheek with his thumb. "I see now that I was happiest in Cambridge. I had *great* friends who really cared about me." He added, "It feels like the last time I had friends who liked me because of who I was, not because of what I could give them."

Gripping her arms more tightly, he added, "And you know what *really kills* me? You were right there, under my nose, and I blew it." He shook his head, amazed by his own stupidity. "If things had gone differently, maybe we would have found each other back then. You were amazing—you *are* amazing! You have reminded me what it's like to laugh, to share stories, to learn about new places and things, to love life. This world feels *real*—more real than anything I've experienced in all my years living in California."

"But..." Julie started to respond. Sam reached over and put his fingertips gently against her mouth.

"Sssshhhhh. What's important is that you're here—with me—and I'm not dreaming. Please.... come to bed with me."

Suddenly nothing else mattered. She moved into his embrace, pulling his head down to meet hers, and this time their lips met in urgent response. Her thoughts vanished, leaving only the taste of his lips on hers, the feel of his hands on her back, the sound of his ragged breathing. She was surrounded by his slightly musky scent. She held him tightly and let herself forget the outside world. She immersed herself in him and only him.

She felt him lift her gently to carry her to the bed, and with each kiss she could sense his loneliness, his pent-up frustration and his hunger. She let her mind go and felt herself surrender to his overwhelming need.

Chapter 13.

Julie woke slowly at dawn. She felt a weight on her chest and, with the realization that it was Sam's arm, came memories of their incredible lovemaking—the perfect end to a magical evening.

She looked over at Sam for a moment. His tousled hair fell over one eye, and he looked peaceful, and somehow innocent. She could see the gray streaks in his hair more clearly in the morning light, but without the worry lines his face looked boyish and just as she remembered it from all those years ago. Those creases were ever-present when he was awake—evidence of a life that included lots of responsibility and tough decisions.

Julie smiled. Sam was sleeping like a rock, his chest rising and falling evenly. Slipping out of bed, she quietly gathered her belongings and dressed in the bathroom to avoid disturbing him.

As she came out, he rolled over, and in a sleepy voice said, "Hey—where are you going?"

"I think I should go back to my room." She came back to the bed and kissed him gently. "The rumors will fly fast enough without me strolling out of your room later when everyone's headed to breakfast."

He rubbed his eyes and sat up. She couldn't help admiring his now-familiar broad shoulders and lean torso. Reaching over to grab her hand, he pulled her down to sit next to him. "I want you to know I have *no* regrets at all. I hope you don't?"

She shook her head firmly. "None at all."

"We need to talk about all of this."

She nodded. "Yes we do, but not now. We have a couple of days before going home. I'd like some time to think about everything. Okay?"

He looked concerned. "I want to be sure you know that this was *not* a crazy, one-night stand because of too much good wine."

Julie brushed hair from his forehead. "I'm glad to hear that, and I feel the same way. This was a big decision for me."

"Please don't take this night lightly. I'm not." The one thing Sam knew for sure was he did *not* want to lose her again.

"Don't worry. I'm not either." She squeezed his hand and rose to go. "I should leave."

"I don't want you to, but I understand. I'll try to act normal today, but I admit it's going to be hard."

"For me, too." She sighed. "We need to keep things very neutral in public. All anyone else needs to know at this point is that we're friends."

"Okay, just as long as that's not what *you* think." His look was questioning and she shook her head, kissing him again before walking to the door. He felt miserable, and kicked himself again for procrastinating on the divorce.

Julie quietly crept down to her room and once inside, pulled on her running clothes, feeling too restless to go back to sleep.

Tying her shoes, she popped her room key into her zippered pocket and stepped out onto the landing, focusing intently on not making any noise.

"Good morning," Emily said quietly. Julie looked up, startled. Emily was also dressed for a run. "Did you have a nice evening?" she asked as they walked down the stairs, giving Julie her best innocent look.

Julie grinned. "Yes. In fact, I had a *very* nice evening, thank you. You?"

"Me too. Amazing food and wine at dinner and we had a fun table. I thought the place cards were hokey at first, but I wouldn't have sat with that group otherwise, and they were all very nice."

They reached the bottom of the stairs and Julie said, "If you don't mind, I'd like to go on my own. I'm assuming you will be much faster than I will."

Emily could tell that Julie was not in the mood for confidences and nodded.

"See you at breakfast?"

Julie nodded, but it was obvious she was not really paying attention. Emily watched her set off down the street and silently sent good thoughts her way, hoping Julie would confide in her if she needed help.

****

Gigi took the stairs down to breakfast, thinking about how much fun she'd had the night before. She'd had Emily at her table, so she'd been able to overcome her initial shyness pretty quickly. And more importantly, she'd met Roger and Dawn, who were incredibly nice and also had a twelve-year old daughter! Roger had been a Political Science major at Foundry and he was now a professor at a small college in

Connecticut. Dawn was a potter, and by the end of the evening had shyly admitted that she sold her work at craft fairs as well as online. Gigi had looked at her website before breakfast and Dawn's work was beautiful—delicate bowls and platters, glazed in beautiful shades of green and yellow.

Like Gigi and Paolo, Dawn and Roger had just one daughter, and the two mothers had totally bonded over that, comparing notes and promising to use each other as a resource for future questions and concerns. Dawn had completely agreed with Gigi about sending Mariella to Chicago. At the end of the evening, she also suggested the idea of an informal exchange for their daughters, where each would spend two weeks at the other's house over two successive summers, with the parents coming for the second week each time. Gigi loved the idea, both because it would mean another fun experience for Mariella, but also because that arrangement would let all four parents spend time together.

Gigi also loved the fact that that *she* would be the one initiating some social activity, instead of always seeing Paolo's friends. She hoped she could convince Melanie, Angie, Julie and Emily to come visit her as well. What fun that would be!

She spotted Emily and Julie already sitting in the dining room and headed over to sit with them.

"Well, good morning!" Their warm smiles of welcome reminded Gigi again how thankful she was to have come on this trip.

A waiter brought a fresh platter of croissants and slices of buttered baguette to the table, and returned shortly with a *cafe crème*.

"How did you sleep?" Emily asked Gigi.

"Very well! It's so quiet here. It reminds me a little of home. It also makes me realize how noisy Paris was."

Julie nodded. "I live in central London, so I'm used to noise. The silence here is such a contrast!"

"Did you have fun last night? Melanie and Angie looked like they did."

Julie smiled. "I agree. And Melanie is a miracle worker! Angie has totally blossomed, and Greg seems to have really mellowed, and both were thanks to her. She's got the touch!"

Julie looked over at Emily, adding, "I know you had some issues with Angie early on, Emily, but she really has changed. Don't you agree?"

Emily nodded, though she didn't look totally convinced. "She did look great last night. I thought Melanie was crazy buying that jacket for her in Paris, but it was perfect." Her tone was still slightly grudging.

Julie gave her a small nudge. "C'mon, give her a break. *My* impression is that Angie takes care of everybody else when she's at home. This trip is giving her a chance to be selfish for once. She deserves some credit for deciding to take it to the next level and make some changes in her personal habits."

Emily nodded. "You're right. But you have to admit—she was *so* annoying and *so* whiny that first day!"

"I know. But some of that was jet lag, and I think some of it was insecurity. We can't all be as self-confident and skinny as you, you know."

Gigi, who had been silent through this exchange, spoke up. "Julie's right. We all deserve a second chance." Turning to Emily, she added, "No one knows that better than you."

Emily's face showed surprise, but then turned thoughtful. After a moment she said, "Touché."

Julie smiled. "You're a nice person, and *I* know that, but I'm not sure Angie does."

"Message received." Emily's smile was rueful.

"So this morning we're going back to Beaune to buy wine, right?" Julie asked.

Emily nodded and, looking at her phone, said, "We're supposed to leave here at 10:00. Let's meet out front at 9:45."

****

Angie rose quietly, showering quickly before Melanie was stirring. She took care drying her hair and carefully put on some mascara and some lip gloss. Checking to be sure Melanie was still asleep, she reached over to her bag and pulled out her journal.

Melanie has me thinking about myself in a whole new way. I just finished putting on the mascara and lip gloss that she gave me. I never even thought about makeup for myself before. When the kids were small, my mornings were taken up with getting them ready for school and getting Joe out the door to his office, so I didn't have time for anything else. And my appearance was not something that I even thought about. But now the girls are gone, and Joe and I are moving onto the next stage of our life. I need to think about what I'm going to do with my time, and how I dress could be an important aspect of that.

This is all still so new to me—the idea that I will have time for myself. I feel so lucky that Joe has always made enough money that I could stay home with the girls, but now what do I want to do with myself?? We still have Joe's dad to take care of, but that's not going to take up all my time.

So what should I do?? I used to think that Joe and I would travel when he retired, but I know now that he's not interested in that, unless it's to see the girls, wherever they end up.

As I think about it, this trip has shown me that I'm not interested in lots of travel either. I feel a lot better now than I did that first day, but it's been hard—adjusting to the time zone, to all the walking, and especially to the pressure of being social with so many new people. I do want to bring Joe and the girls back to show them some of the fun places we've been, but that's about it. I guess I'm more of a homebody than I thought!

When I think about what I've enjoyed most, I think it's been learning about French culture and history. What if I could find a job that would give me exposure to other cultures without actually traveling to other places? Maybe work in a library? That would give me access to books to read, but I think I want something that involves more interaction with people. I feel like I've learned a lot about myself, and I'd like to be better about meeting new people. Well, we do have a lot of people moving to Portland from other places. But how would I meet them?

Wait!! I remember seeing a notice at the library about a need for English as a Second Language tutors at the Community Center. That could be fun. I'd get to meet people from other places, but only a few at a time so it wouldn't be as hard as this has been. When I get home, I'll go back to look at that notice and see what's involved. I bet I could do that!

Okay, that's a plan. And I think Joe will like it, too. I'd love to talk to Melanie and see what she thinks.

Angie closed her journal and, putting it back in her bag, she walked down to the dining room. She saw Gigi, Emily and Julie just leaving on the far side of the room, and she wondered who else might be available to sit with. At the far corner of the room, sitting alone her nose buried in a book, was Nellie, who had been at her table last night. Nellie was an English major at Foundry, and she and her husband, Bob, now lived in Rhode Island. Nellie was an editor of some sort.

"Good morning," Angie said, and Nellie looked up with a smile, then patted the seat next to her. Remembering that just a few days ago she had been constantly in tears, Angie marveled at the change in herself.

Angie turned to the waiter to say *Merci* as he brought her a *café crème.* Nellie handed her the heaping plate of croissants and buttered baguettes, and she carefully chose one of each.

Nellie said, "Are you as full as I am? I tell you—last night's food and wine were delicious, but I felt like I ate enough for three people. I didn't think I'd be hungry for a week. Then I get down here and it smells so good that I couldn't help myself. I had *two* croissants!"

Angie laughed. "I'm always hungrier the next day when I've eaten a lot, so I know just what you mean." She changed the subject. "I had so much fun last night, getting to know you and Bob. Where's he this morning?"

Nellie nodded. "He headed out at the crack of dawn to do some bird watching. I opened one eyelid long enough to remind him to leave a key with me, then turned back over to get another hour of sleep."

"Melanie and I are sharing a room and she's still sleeping."

"She's the one who persuaded you to come on this trip, right?"

"That's right. She's *such* a great friend."

"I love hearing stories like that. I feel like the friends I met at Foundry are still the closest friends I have. I don't know if I told you last night, but my best friend, Jeanne, who was my roommate freshman and sophomore years, had to cancel at the last minute because of a family emergency. She and her husband live in Newport, too, so Bob knows them. He was really bummed when they couldn't come. He's pretty shy." Nellie paused, but then with a thoughtful look, continued. "But you know, he's done just fine. Everyone's been so welcoming, even though he wasn't at school with us, you know?"

"I do. Once you get over the first couple of awkward moments, it's not too tough." Angie stopped before confessing, "I'm kind of shy, too."

Nellie smiled. "You weren't shy at dinner. Bob and I really enjoyed your stories." She checked the time and looked surprised. "Uh oh. Time to find my husband." With a "Hope to see you on the bus!" she tucked her novel under her arm and headed out of the dining room.

Angie watched her go and felt very content. Another small victory and something to add to her journal. Last night, seeing all new faces at her table, she had been *very* nervous, but she'd done fine, even summoning the courage to tell a couple of stories. Now she'd come to breakfast on her own, had a very pleasant conversation with a relative stranger and, just as importantly, had managed to limit herself to just one croissant and one baguette slice. Who knew what else she could accomplish if she set her mind to it? Smiling to herself, she headed back to the room to roust Melanie and get them both packed and onto the bus by 10:00.

Wouldn't Melanie be shocked to find herself in the position of being bossed around for once.

Chapter 14.

Emily was exhausted. Melanie had been boasting to everyone about Emilly's fluency in French, and she had found herself being pulled to and fro to assist people with their purchases. Now everyone had piled back onto the bus, and Emily sat slumped in her seat next to Gigi.

"You okay? You look a little harried," said Gigi with concern.

Emily nodded. "I'll be fine. Just a little overwhelmed with my own recent popularity." Her tone was grumpy.

Gigi was sympathetic. "I know it was appreciated."

"Who knew I would become a wine buyer for the group?"

Gigi's tone was soothing. "You do speak the best French. Well, besides Michel and Joelle, of course. With twenty-five of us all trying to buy wine, we needed all three of you to help."

Emily's smile was grudging, but she looked pleased at the compliment. "What a madhouse that was—and honestly, with all those wines to choose from, and so many people not really speaking French, I thought the store salespeople were going to completely give up and just leave!" She laughed softly. "Did you see Greg trying to carry four bottles at once? The poor sales clerk was hurrying along behind him, trying to persuade him to let him help, and all you could hear was Greg, saying in his loud voice, in English of course, 'IT'S OKAY, IT'S OKAY.'"

Gigi laughed, too, sharing the memory. "Well, we seem to have gotten out of there with no broken bottles."

"That store will never be the same," Emily said dryly. She seemed to have recovered her good spirits. "So what's our next stop?"

"Joelle said that we are stopping in a small town on our way back to Paris for lunch. Apparently there is a restaurant that specializes in *coq au vin*."

"Have you had authentic *coq au vin?*"

Gigi shook her head.

Emily said, "Yet another experience to add to your 'firsts' list! It's really delicious. If it's really authentic, they include some of the grape skins and stems in the pot while it's slow cooking, to give it lots of that wine flavor. Of course, they strain those out when they pull out the chicken."

Gigi smiled. "That sounds wonderful."

Emily looked hard at her. "Gigi, I'm so glad you're getting a chance to try new things on this trip, and that you shared your home situation with us. Before the trip, I was so jealous of your living in Europe, with all the opportunities for culture and great food and wine, but then I really got worried when it looked like you weren't actually living the life that would expose you to all that. Now it seems like you're going to make some changes."

Gigi nodded. "No more drifting along with Paolo's plans. He's a wonderful man and a wonderful husband, but he is also a little oblivious." Emily was glad to see that Gigi had a good sense of humor about it.

Gigi continued. "And now I also have this whole exchange idea with Dawn and Roger and their daughter. I really think it will fit nicely with my bigger plan. Once Paolo spends some time in the States, I'm hoping he will understand what I'm saying about the social differences and why I want Mariella to be comfortable in both places. Who knows?"

"Let's hope so." Emily's look was approving.

The bus came to a wheezing stop, and everyone got out to enter the restaurant. It was quaint, with a small front patio that had clearly been set up for their group. The sun was shining and the vines that covered the wall of the restaurant were turning brilliant shades of red and orange.

Everyone was quickly seated at the various tables and Joelle stood up." Your attention, please. We wanted to finish our tour of Burgundy with a traditional Burgundy dish, *coq au vin.* There are *pichets* of red and white wine on each table, as well as wonderful bread from the local *boulangerie*. Enjoy!"

****

Julie was proud of herself. She had managed, throughout the wine-buying excursion and during lunch, to keep a calm exterior. She had tried very hard to act normally, but she found herself with a heightened awareness of where Sam was at all times. She had once seen him eyeing her with an intensity that both thrilled and terrified her, and she was enjoying the energy and excitement that his proximity ignited in her. At lunch, he had made sure he was sitting just behind her, and would occasionally reach out to surreptitiously touch her shoulder.

Now Julie was back in her hotel room in Paris. Emily had suggested that the five women all meet at 7:00 for a drink before meeting the rest of the group at *Le Relais de l'Entrecôte* at 8:30.

Plumping her pillow up behind her, Julie lay back on her bed, thinking back over the last twenty-four hours. She let herself re-live each moment of the evening at Puligny, and couldn't believe how wonderful it had all been. She knew she had slept with a married man, but she had no regrets.

She thought back to their first conversation at the café, and his frustration with the artificial way of life in California. She'd been sympathetic, because she had lived in that world, too. And then her sympathy had deepened on the walk back from that first dinner, when he had first talked about his marital problems.

But her feelings for Sam went way beyond sympathy. Even back in Boston there had been a sexual tension between them—a mutual attraction. But he had not been an active part of their group, and when he did show up, he was often preoccupied and distant. It was very apparent that he had a definite agenda, and that his focus was on his studies.

They were now in very different places in their lives. She was lonely in her life in London and ready for a relationship. This was a second chance with a man she had never forgotten, and she was not going to let the opportunity slip away again!

They had both known they were attracted to each other, and she could now say, after last night, that the physical attraction was not one that was only interesting from afar. She had been amazed at herself and the level of passion that he aroused in her. She briefly thought of Ryan, and how cursory and 'by the book' their lovemaking had been. She was a romantic at heart, and she remembered how much she had been looking forward to all the romance of their wedding night—the scented candles around the room, the soft music and lighting, the light in her new husband's eyes. But there had been none of those things. It had taken years of introspection and counseling to admit that, even though some of those things sounded superficial, their absence had been a critical missing element for her.

That lack of passion and romance had led to Julie finally asking for the divorce. Her steadfast belief in the possibility of finding romance in the future had been what gave her the strength to face the loneliness of leaving her old life and starting again. Now she finally felt that she had found someone who understood those needs and might be able to share them.

Her mother had said to her once when she was hurting after a particularly hard break-up in high school. "Julie, you will meet, and date, many men over your lifetime. When you find one that not only loves you, but truly *cherishes* you, hold onto him." Thinking back on that conversation, she realized that Ryan had never *cherished* her. He had loved her for a while, in his own way, but what he really loved was technology and discovering new ways to make things work. Even now, she could remember that particular glint he would get in his eyes when he arrived at the solution to a difficult problem he'd been working through. It was a look that held immense satisfaction and a sense of fulfillment. And she realized that she'd never seen any element of that fulfillment when he looked at *her*. She had grown to understand that it simply wasn't in him to care for her the way he cared for his work.

She deserved to be *cherished,* and so did Sam. And she wanted to be that person in Sam's life.

But it wouldn't be easy. The first thing to figure out would be the physical logistics. She lived in London, and he lived in California. She could certainly move back to

California, but she would not do that in haste. They both needed time to see if their feelings blossomed into a real relationship. She was happy in London. She had worked hard to establish a new and better life for herself there. She suddenly realized, as she thought about that life, that she very much wanted to share it with Sam. She wanted to show him her home and her neighborhood, and have him meet her friends. But he had a full life in California, and obligations there. That would all have to be discussed and worked out. She knew she had *no* interest in a long-distance romance.

Her thoughts swirled from one idea to another, but she didn't find any easy answers. After twenty minutes of torturing herself, she abruptly stood and, reaching for her purse and sweater, left her room and headed down the stairs to get some air, hoping not to run into anyone. Thankfully, she reached the front steps without being detected. Zipping up her sweater, she set off at a brisk pace. She didn't have a destination, but hoped that getting out and walking would inspire her and move her thoughts forward.

Julie made her way down one of the small streets that led away from *Place St. Michel*. Just two blocks down, she came to a small crêpe stand, where she ordered a butter-and-sugar crêpe to keep her company as she continued her walk. She focused her thoughts on the crêpe, on the sweet flavor of the sugar melding with the richness of the melted butter, the edges of the crêpe crunchy and slightly papery on her tongue.

Why couldn't love be as simple as this crêpe? Crêpes were not complicated—they were not full of surprises. You didn't have to question your reaction to them. You simply reveled in the smell and taste of them and that was their purpose—to simply provide pleasure. You couldn't even fool yourself into thinking there was any nutritional value there. But that was okay. You knew what you were getting into, and you accepted it for what it was. A few moments of sensual pleasure. Which led her to think of Sam for the thousandth, or maybe the millionth, time—the smell of his skin, and his warm, capable hands.

In the end, Julie decided not to decide anything. She wouldn't let herself make any assumptions yet about whether this was a relationship or simply a wonderful encounter. They would find time to map out a plan—together.

Making her way back to the hotel, her thoughts filled with all the mundane questions she wanted to ask him. *What did he like to read? Did he like movies? Did he like long walks? What were his politics? Did he have a favorite color, or country, or beer, or…?* She looked forward to finding out the answers.

Chapter 15.

Emily gave her dark hair one final brush and, after a last critical look in the mirror, ran down the stairs to the lobby. Melanie and Angie were already there, and Julie was just coming through the front door. Emily heard steps behind her as she reached the bottom, and turned to find Gigi, a little breathless from her descent. She had tied a bright orange scarf into a jaunty knot on one side of her neck, and her cheeks were flushed.

"Hey, is that new? It looks great!"

Gigi blushed. "Is it too much? I know it's kind of bright…."

Emily smiled. "Not at all! I was just thinking that orange is a great color for you."

"I saw it when I was getting Mariella's present and I couldn't resist it. It feels like something I would have worn in college—a little wilder than what I usually wear these days. I'd forgotten how much I like orange."

"I really like it," Emily said again. "Maybe we can find time to shop together. I'd love to find a fun souvenir too!"

In the lobby, Melanie saw them and waved them over. Seeing Julie come through the front door, she asked, " Where have you been?"

"Just taking a little walk. And I found something marvelous." She smiled but didn't elaborate, knowing the mystery would drive Melanie crazy—and hoping it would also distract her from other potential topics of conversation. "I'll tell you about it later."

They walked out and headed down the street, Emily leading the way to a small bar she knew called *"Le Cool."* It was tiny, with a single row of tables along one wall, opposite a bar that ran the length of the room on the other side. The walls were brightly painted with kaleidoscopes of color flowing around hand-drawn flowers.

"This place looks like a total throwback to the 70s," Melanie remarked, and Emily nodded. "That's why I love it. It's completely casual, and run by a couple of young guys who are both very friendly. You'll like them."

A young man with several tattoos and a lip ring came out to greet them.

"Bonsoir," he said graciously, and quickly had them all seated near the back with menus. Soon each had a glass of either wine or beer in front of them.

"There are quite a few places in Paris that now have 'Happy Hour,'" said Emily. "I don't know if you noticed it on the menu."

Gigi nodded. "I did. I thought it was funny to have it in English."

"The concept has become more common in Paris. Like in the US, 'Happy Hour' means that some drinks are cheaper—but we're not talking dollar beers or anything like that!"

Everyone laughed, and Melanie spoke up. "No, it's become obvious that nothing's cheap in Paris."

Emily shrugged. "True, but.... it's Paris, so who needs cheap, right?"

Everyone laughed again and Emily raised her glass. "To friends and reconnecting."

"Hear, hear!" They raised their glasses, and their host reappeared with a couple of small bowls of popcorn. When he had set them down, Emily said, "By the way, this is the only bar I've found in Paris that offers popcorn!"

Gigi was delighted. "Now that's something we could use in our little town." She sighed. "I do miss popcorn."

Melanie turned to Julie. "So what was your marvelous discovery?"

"Only the most delicious crêpe ever made!" Julie answered enthusiastically.

The group pressed her for details and Julie was happy to oblige, regaling them with a full recounting of the cooking process, the choices for what to put inside, and finally the messy, but delicious, eating ritual itself.

When she paused for breath, Melanie spoke up. "Was Sam with you?" She tried to keep her tone nonchalant, but didn't succeed.

"No, I was by myself."

There was a pause, and Emily reached over to touch Melanie's arm. "I don't think we need to—"

Julie interrupted. "It's okay. I feel like there's an elephant in the room." She paused a moment before looking at Melanie. "What do you want to know?"

Melanie looked flustered for a moment. "Well, I don't want to intrude, but at the end of the evening last night, I didn't see you anywhere, and I didn't see Sam anywhere, either." It was obvious she wanted to ask the question, but her sense of decorum was giving her an internal battle.

"You're right. I slipped out to go to the bathroom just after coffee and dessert were served. I didn't go back." She didn't need to say any more for everyone to understand.

Again, there was silence.

"How could you?" Melanie's face was red and she was obviously agitated. Realizing she had raised her voice, she spent a moment trying to get herself under control before continuing. *"He's married, for God's sake!* I can't believe you're letting yourself get involved with a married man."

Julie's tone was quiet and calm. "Unhappily married, yes."

Emily spoke up. "Melanie, is it really any of our business? We know Sam's told several people how unhappy he is in California and in his marriage. And his kids are now both grown and off at college."

Emily's voice trembled slightly as she added, "Might I also remind you that some of us have been the object of this sort of judgmental conversation before, and it's *not* a pleasant experience."

There was an uncomfortable silence as they all remembered their behavior back in Boston. There was no way to ignore the damage and longstanding hard feelings that had been the result.

Angie's quiet voice cut through the thick silence. "And who are we to decide what's right or wrong?"

Melanie turned to look at her, shocked. "Aren't you worried about Julie?"

"Of course I am. But there are lots of pieces to this puzzle that we don't know." She looked around at the rest of the group. "There are hidden elements to *every* situation, and they can have a huge effect on the final outcome. If you all don't mind, I'd like to share a story that I think illustrates the point."

She paused and the group had only a minute to recover from their surprise before she began speaking again. "You all know that Joe and I have been together forever, but what you don't know is that Joe came *very* close to having an affair about five years ago."

Their faces registered shock as the women tried to take in this new piece of information. Joe, of all people? Solid, steady, dependable Joe?

Angie continued. "I know it's hard to believe that Joe would even *consider* something like that. And it wasn't something I could ever have imagined, either. But as I said, *none* of us knows everything that's going on in other people's lives, even those closest to us. And that's why you can't judge them. You don't know what crazy combinations of events, or circumstances, may be happening behind the scenes."

They were all silent, waiting for her to go on. Now their faces registered sympathy and sorrow. " Joe and I had been having some rough times. Mary was entering her teen terror years. She was running around with a bad crowd, and no matter what we did to try to limit her wild behavior, she would rebel and go out anyway." She looked around at all of them. "If you have kids, you understand the fine line you tread in those years, between needing to be tough, but not wanting to create such anger that they threaten to leave—because if they are like Mary, they would do it, and then what would happen next?"

Gigi was looking terrified and Julie reached over to hold her hand. Angie continued her story. "Joe's mother was very sick and we were the main caregivers. His father was not handling it at all well. And I was doing what I always do when I'm really stressed, which is eat." She gazed around the group, and for a moment there was a warning flash of defiance in her eyes. She would no longer let herself be judged—not by Emily, not by anyone.

She paused and took a sip of wine. "So, just when all of this was at its peak, a new girl started working in Joe's department at the university. I think you all know that he's a professor at the University of Portland?

"The regular secretary had to have surgery, and she was going to be out for about six weeks. The temp was young—in her mid-twenties, so she didn't have much work experience, but they all figured she could cover the basics for the department for that period of time." She paused again and this time drained her glass of wine. Emily signaled the waiter for another round.

"Right about this same time, the university was going through a major overhaul of its hiring policies and tenure structure. There were lots of evening meetings and apparently lots of debate and controversy within Joe's department. And of course it was all kept very secret. Politics are a *huge* part of university life, and so are endless internal debates." There were nods and she continued.

"Anyway, I got a call saying that Anne had sprained her ankle in basketball practice. I went and picked her up, and did all the regular things you do, but she still seemed to be in agony. I wanted to talk to Joe to see whether he thought I should take her to an emergency room for x-rays, even though the school doctor had reassured me that it was not a serious injury. At around 5:30, I tried Joe's cell phone. I wasn't too surprised when he didn't answer—I assumed he was in yet another meeting, so I left a message. So then I tried the main number for the department, figuring that I would leave a message there with the new girl. The phone rang and rang and then finally one of his colleagues answered, sounding irritated. I quickly apologized for disturbing him, and then asked if I could I speak to Joe?

"He said, 'Joe? Joe's not here. He said he was giving Allison a ride home because her car broke down.'"

"I stammered another apology and hung up. I didn't know what to do! I didn't know whether to panic about Anne, or Joe, or both. Why hadn't he called and told me he was doing that? So I went back into Anne's room and I just kept putting new ice packs on her ankle and giving her Tylenol as often as the directions allowed, hoping that was enough. I also left two more messages on Joe's cell phone, because by that time, I was really starting to worry, thinking he must have been in an accident or something.

The good news was that by about eight o'clock, her ankle seemed much less swollen and she finally went to sleep. But Joe had not come home yet, and he had not called. I even called a couple of the local hospitals, but there was no sign of him.

"Joe finally got home about ten o'clock. I was sitting in the kitchen and, as soon as he walked through the door, I jumped up and grabbed him, blurting out the story of Anne's injury. I then started sobbing and yelling at him at the same time, asking him where the *hell* he'd been, and telling him how worried I was. He hugged me and apologized profusely for not being there. He said how sorry he was that he was so late, and that he never got my messages, etcetera, etcetera. I let him ramble on for a few minutes while I calmed down, and then we both sat down and I asked him again where he'd been, this time a little more calmly."

She looked up as the waiter brought everyone a second drink. "I didn't even have to press him. He took one look at me, and it all came tumbling out. How he had gotten in the habit of asking Allison to help him prepare his remarks before the departmental meetings. And that she'd started typing up his notes for his lectures too, after work, when she'd finished her regular department work. Then that afternoon, she had told him her car was in the shop, and he had offered to give her a ride home. She suggested they stop for a drink on the way, and then that turned into dinner. He kept meaning to call and let Angie know he'd be late, but one event just seemed to lead to the next and he never did. By that time, it was also obvious she had a crush on him—you know—the older man, and her boss. And he was flattered."

The others were looking at Angie with wide eyes. "When they got to her apartment, she invited him in, and apparently made her intentions abundantly clear. Joe confessed to me that he did kiss her, but he said it had felt horribly wrong, and he immediately mumbled an apology and rushed out. He felt hugely guilty about what he'd done, and didn't feel he could face me. He drove around the city for a couple of hours before finally coming home.

"Well, we talked for hours that night, and he kept apologizing, but the more we talked about it, the more we both realized it had happened because he was looking for relief from all the stresses in our lives. I was escaping through food, and he was escaping by spending time with someone who seemed uncomplicated and stress-free." She laughed bitterly. "*And* it turns out he was also going through his own separate crisis. He was worried *he* was going to be laid off. As a senior professor in the department, I wouldn't have thought that likely, but he said that part of the discussion had been the concept of 'dead wood professors'—those who had been around forever and who were getting a good paycheck, but not really contributing any more. He hadn't wanted to tell me and stress me out even more.

"The look on his face was so sad and so confused. One part of me was incredibly angry that he had not shared those concerns with me, but I had to admit another part of me was thankful. With everything else—his mother's illness, Mary's wild behavior—I had plenty on my plate already."

Emily spoke up first. "What ended up happening at the University? We've had some of those discussions at Ben's college, too."

"Fortunately, nothing too terrible. In the end, they did lay off a couple of the younger professors, and Joe had to teach two more classes. But an increase in his schedule was certainly much better than the alternative!"

Angie turned to Julie. "That was a long-winded way of saying that I don't *need* to know any details of your situation, because what I *already* know is that, in my experience, it's not the third person who breaks up a marriage. There's already something very wrong and they just provide the tipping point. In my case, Joe and I had a strong foundation, so we could work our way through what happened."

She then turned to Emily. "Emily, I hope you see now that when I apologized to you at the airport, I really meant it. I understand a lot of things that I didn't back in Boston."

Emily looked appalled and embarrassed, remembering how intolerant she had been at the time.

Julie waited a moment before saying, "Thank you, Angie, for sharing that story. I know that couldn't have been easy to talk about, and you're right. None of us ever knows what's going on behind the scenes in others' everyday lives.

"I want you all to understand that what happened was not a drunken one-night stand. It happened because of feelings I've had for Sam for a very long time—since Boston, in fact. And Sam feels the same way. I hope we get the chance to try to build something together. We'll see.

"But in any case, I'm going into this with my eyes wide open. I know it won't be easy to figure out. Our lives are both complicated, and he still has a lot of obligations in California."

"That's what worries me," said Melanie. Her eyes filled with tears. "What if it was just a fling for him? What if he has no intention of leaving his wife?"

"That is always a possibility," said Julie, but when she continued, her voice was confident. "But based on the conversations I've already had with him about their relationship, it was never very solid, and it started deteriorating years ago."

They sat, silently considering Julie's words, and the sounds of the bar suddenly crowded in on them—gay laughter and the clinking of bottles and glasses.

Melanie broke the silence. "I'm scared for you."

"Thank you," said Julie. "I know you mean well, and I do appreciate it."

Emily spoke up. "Julie, you are a generous, loving person, and you deserve happiness."

Julie said quietly, "Thank you. So does Sam."

In silence, Emily signaled for the check, and as they hurried back to the hotel to meet the rest of the group, each was lost in her own thoughts.

****

Sam was agitated. He looked at his phone for the fifteenth time. Only 7:15. Not quite time to go down for dinner. Why did each minute seem to take an eternity to pass?

After Julie had left his room that morning, he had lain back down, reliving every minute of the evening. Julie's sparkling eyes, her quick wit, her wonderful smell—a little flowery, but with a hint of some kind of spice? He'd forgotten how much fun it was to banter back and forth with a beautiful, intelligent woman. It was already obvious, from a couple of literary references, that she was an avid reader, and he looked forward to finding out more about her interests. He had hungered for someone to share an intellectual life with, and he now felt he'd found her. How great would it be to have someone who wanted to go to the theater and to concerts?

And her body! She was tall and slim, and fit perfectly in the crook of his arm. He had enjoyed letting his hands learn her body, and looked forward to another chance to find all the places where she was ticklish. She was warm and soft, but she was also firm, with strong legs and arms—evidence of her time at the gym.

Today had been much harder than he could have imagined. Julie had been so near, yet so far. He had loved being near her in the restaurant, and could not resist reaching out to touch her. He wished that they could go off somewhere to spend more time alone. He was used to being in control of situations, so it was frustrating to be hindered from doing what he wanted by the tour schedule.

All he wanted was to be with Julie—to see Paris with her, to take her to some secluded bistro and drink wine and talk the afternoon away, and then whisk her back to the hotel and lock the door. Instead, here he was in his room, trying to sort through all the logistics of this unexpected development in his life.

This trip had reminded him what it felt like to be really comfortable with people, and how relaxing it could be to just be himself. That first night, there had been shared laughter and genuine, spontaneous banter, and the knot that was always in his stomach had slowly loosened its grip. These were people who had known him before he was "someone." These were people who were not carefully watching what they said to him because of his job title. Hell, some of them didn't even know what he did!

Sam had always known he was physically attracted to Julie. That had been obvious back in Cambridge, and it was immediately obvious again from the first moment at the café. But last night had been incredible. Maybe it was the freedom of being in an unknown, and therefore safe, place, but he had felt completely free and uninhibited. For the first time in years, he was keenly aware of his own body. He had let himself drown in his need for Julie, laying his emotions out on the table, knowing that doing so could be a huge risk. For the first time in a long time, he had let himself be vulnerable.

But in return, Sam had felt her wonder, her passion. He could sense her loneliness, and her pain from her failed marriage. There had been a moment when he had looked into her eyes and her uncertainty and obvious fear of sharing had actually choked him up. He almost wished he had not seen it, because he never, ever, wanted to hurt her. But he also recognized and cherished the precious gift she was giving him.

This morning had been a moment to revel in the wonders of last night, but this afternoon, back in his hotel room, it was time to think dispassionately and to consider all aspects of the situation. The first thing to consider was his obligations in California, and of those, his first priority would be to work through the divorce with Helen. It would be uncomfortable, but not a surprise. They had both known for a long time that their marriage wasn't working. A critical part of that process would also be his conversations with Jack and Lucy, to make them understand that it would not affect his love for them or the time he wanted to spend with them.

He also needed to consider his responsibilities to Avanti and to his employees, for they were his family, too. He had worked hard to make the company successful, and he would not throw that away. His brief fantasy about throwing it all in and moving to London was quickly dismissed by the rational part of his brain. It was more complicated, and he knew that. But he also knew that he wanted Julie to be a part of his life from this day forward.

He abruptly stood, feeling the need to get out of his room and escape his own thoughts. Stepping into the lobby, Sam spotted John sitting in the small bar area and knew that John would be the perfect person to confide in. John was a very successful businessman in his own right. He would understand Sam's personal pride in what he'd accomplished at Avanti, and the emotional burden that went hand in hand with that pride. He also lived in California, so he would understand Sam's frustrations with the lifestyle and people there. And on top of all that, he was married with children, so he would also understand the conflict Sam was feeling about disrupting his home life. Sam moved toward him, but hesitated when he saw that John was looking very intently at his phone.

At that moment John looked up, motioning Sam over. "Hey," said Sam, as he eased his long legs under the small café table. "I know we said we'd all meet down here at 8:00, but I was getting cabin fever in my room. What are you having?"

"It's called a *citron pressé.* It's basically their version of lemonade—just a lot less sweet."

Sam smiled. "Seems a little light. It *is* after 5:00 after all!"

"You're right, but I'd rather wait for a better wine selection at the restaurant, plus I'm sure there will be amazing desserts. If I'm going to indulge, I want it to be worth it."

"Very sensible. But I don't have your willpower." He motioned to the waiter. *"Bière à la pression?"*

"Nous avons le 1664 ou Leff."

"1664, s'il vous plaît."

"Not bad," John said admiringly after the waiter had left.

Sam shrugged. "I've been over a few times, and ordering a beer is definitely on my list of priorities."

They were both silent as the waiter set down the beer. Sam spoke first. "Can I ask your advice on something, and ask you to keep it between us?"

John raised his eyebrows. "Absolutely." He glanced around the lobby. "We've got a good vantage point here, so we shouldn't get interrupted."

Sam looked down at his beer. "So…last night…."

John said, "Yeah—you and Julie, right?"

Sam looked relieved. "Yeah."

"And?"

"It was amazing."

"She's divorced, right?"

Sam nodded. "And I'm not, as you know."

Now it was John's turn to be silent for a moment. "So what happens next?"

"Last night, I would have said that it was perfectly clear. I was ready to leave my crazy, artificial, workaholic life in California and head to London."

"But now?"

"Now I have to admit to myself that it's not as simple as that."

John looked sympathetic. "Bummer."

"On the one hand, I have a wife who doesn't love me, so that part's easy. I didn't tell you before, but I've already been working with an attorney on a divorce. The process got put on hold this year when I had to be away so much opening the new offices for Avanti, but I can put that back in motion once I'm back. As part of that, of course, I need to talk to the kids. The good news is they are now both in college so, though it's not ideal, at least they are older. And I will make very clear to them nothing will *ever* stop me from keeping them in my life."

"I'm glad to hear you say that," said John. They still need you, and it's always hard on kids to have parents separate. What else?"

"My job. When I started at Avanti two years ago, it was in bad shape. I've made some big organizational changes and they are starting to show some results." Sam paused to take a sip of his beer. "And it may sound corny, but they are my family, too. I don't want to let them down."

"It doesn't sound corny at all. Your deep involvement and emotional investment are what make you so good at what you do. And I'm sure you get a lot of personal satisfaction and pride out of it as well."

"I really do. And to be honest, I'm not sure if the changes have been in place long enough to stand on their own. That's part of the problem. Do I abandon the people at Avanti to pursue my selfish desires?"

John was silent and stirred the lemon around in his glass. The soft clink of the ice cubes was the only sound for a few moments. He said, "Why do you have to go to London? Can't Julie move to California?"

"We haven't had a conversation about it yet, but I guess she could." He added quickly, "But it would be awkward for her. Remember her ex-husband is still a driving force there, and it's a small community that loves sticking their noses in other people's business.

"Plus, I think it's too early to ask her to do that. We need time first to get to know each other and figure out if this is going to work."

He continued, "And the final point for me is, even if Julie *could* move back to California, do I want her to? Are the benefits I get from my work at Avanti worth more than the frustration I feel from living in that self-centered, small-town, every-man-for-himself atmosphere? This trip has made me realize how much I hate that life and how far it's taken me from who I want to be." He added, "In my mind it's not just a question of wanting the two of us to be in the same place—it's about *where* that one place is."

"Do you want my opinion, or is this one of those conversations where you just want to say it all out loud and then make up your own mind?"

As Sam started to look indignant, John interrupted. "Whoa, don't get pissed. I'm asking because, being married, I now know, at least in my experience, that there are two kinds of conversations, one that requires input and one that doesn't. Sometimes I don't guess right about which one my wife and I are having, and then I get my head handed to me."

Sam laughed. "You're right. Are they asking you just to listen, or are you supposed to offer solutions?"

"Exactly." He paused. "Honestly, I won't be offended either way."

Sam responded, "I would be grateful for your opinion. I think you understand my problem from all three sides of the question—personal, business, and general lifestyle."

"Okay." John paused. "First, and I'm sure you've thought of this, obviously this is a *big* decision, and one that won't get fully figured out on this trip, right?"

Sam nodded, and John continued. "Second, although your primary job responsibility right now is in California, you just told me that you're also required to travel around the world to open other offices. Do you have an office in London?"

"That's on my To-Do list for next year."

"Okay, then figure out a way to spend some time in it once it's up and running.

"Finally, I think this is *exactly* the time in your life to be a little selfish. You're entering a new phase of your life with no kids at home." He smiled. "This is just a new and different take on the idea of being an 'empty nester.'"

He looked thoughtful for a moment. "Sorry, one more point on Avanti. I'm sure you *have* made a big difference there, and it's great that you feel loyalty to the company. But who knows what life brings? Avanti could suddenly get acquired, and your ability to make changes could be gone, just like that. If I'm weighing your personal happiness for the next forty years against getting a company on its feet, all I can say is—life's too short."

Sam was listening intently, his fingertips pressed together. After a short pause, John added quietly, "My wife had cancer three years ago, and though she's fine now, it changed my whole attitude towards life—and how important it is not to waste it."

Sam looked shocked. "I'm so sorry to hear that! But she's okay now?"

"Yes, thank God. For the moment. But it was a good reminder that there are things in life we can't control, so we need to make the most of the things we *can* control. Don't wait for something like that to happen to you. You've been lucky so far."

"You're absolutely right on all fronts," Sam said as he reached for the bill. Pulling out a 10 euro note, he pushed John's hand away when he tried to pay. "You kidding? You just gave great marital *and* professional advice. This one's on me."

As they stood, Sam turned back. "Thank you for listening. I *knew* you were the right guy to talk to about this.

You've really given me some good things to think about. And thanks, also, for being a real friend. Friendship and discretion are two things in short supply in California."

"Glad to oblige."

Just then, Greg's booming voice filled the lobby, and as Sam turned he felt a clap on his back. "Ready for dinner, my friend?"

Over the next few minutes, the lobby filled with the rest of the group, and Joelle motioned for silence. She raised her voice and said, "We are headed to one of my favorite restaurants, *Le Relais de L'Entrecôte*. It is renowned for its delicious *steak frites.* As you may have read in your brochure, you will start with a wonderful simple green salad with walnuts, and they will also ask you how you like your steak cooked. *Saignant* means rare, *a point* means medium and *bien cuit* means well done." She paused before adding, "I won't even suggest *bleue,* which is how many French eat it, but which is just seared on the outside and basically raw inside. I also don't recommend you choose *bien cuit* or you will get very strange looks." Everyone laughed and she continued. "The steak will arrive with a delicious butter sauce that *Le Relais de L'Entrecôte* is known for, and with *pommes allumettes,* which means French fries, cut very thin. You can have second helpings of the steak and French fries if you like—it's included in the price. When we have all finished, they have a wonderful assortment of delicious, traditional desserts, so keep that in mind when you are deciding whether you want more steak or potatoes." Again, there was laughter. *"Allons-y!"* There was much laughter as they all made their way out of the hotel and onto the bus.

Throughout the evening, Julie found herself sneaking looks at Sam at the next table. He always winked or gave her a secret smile. And she felt so relaxed overall. With this group, there was no need for pretense. No need for posturing.

Thinking back to her life in London, she realized that she was finally starting to relax and feel more comfortable there as well. Instead of just *telling* each other stories, she and her friends were now *sharing* experiences, and that seemed to be what made the difference. In her early days and weeks, she had worried about unwittingly offending someone. It was so much easier now that she had a better understanding of British language and social behavior. She really liked the British reserve, which many people found "stuffy." It was a refreshing change from California, where everyone was your 'best friend' as soon as you were introduced. And she loved the architecture in London, the buildings steeped in history.

This trip had also reminded Julie how important Angie, Emily, Melanie, and Gigi had been at a crucial point in her life. She wanted to hold onto the closeness they'd found again and make them part of new her life. She certainly had the money to travel, and few responsibilities to get in her way. And now she had a big reason to go back and spend some time in California as well.

She glanced over and caught Sam looking at her with such a caring, soft, gaze that she gulped and looked back down. It had been a long time since she'd even considered sharing her life with a man. Her failed marriage had hurt her deeply, and she hadn't met anyone since then who had even tempted her to give up her independence. Now she felt ready to throw herself into Sam's arms and forget everything else. It was ridiculous. It was unnerving. But it was also wonderful.

Chapter 16.

"Would you consider walking back to the hotel?" Julie heard his entreaty in her ear and felt his breath on her neck. A thrill ran through her.

"It's not too far?" she asked as she turned to face him.

"It's about a mile and a half. Is that too far?"

"Not at all." Julie could feel a silly grin spread across her face. She couldn't do anything to stop it—or the joy that swept through her.

Sam's smile was just as broad as he responded, "Great!"

"Let me just tell the others so they won't worry. They can then tell Joelle that we won't be on the bus."

"Perfect."

Julie hurried back toward Emily, who was talking to John. Emily excused herself, and walked over. "What's up?"

"I wanted to let you know that Sam and I are walking back to the hotel instead of riding the bus. Can you let Joelle know?"

"Sure. And you certainly don't have to get permission from anyone." Emily's tone was dry.

Julie laughed and looked a little flustered. "I know that, but I also know that if Melanie suddenly notices I'm not on the bus, she will make a scene – so I wondered if you would quietly let her know as well...."

"That's a good idea. Otherwise, *everyone* on the bus will wonder where you and Sam are!" After a pause, she added, "Um...I hope the conversation goes the way you want it to." She paused again before saying quietly, "No one can ever know what the future holds. I certainly would never have assumed my life would turn out the way it has." She looked directly into Julie's eyes. "I do know that things worked out just right for me."

Her tone was so obviously full of love for Ben that Julie felt a lump in her throat. They had all been so quick to judge Emily in those days, thinking so badly of her for breaking up a marriage. And yet it had been the right thing for everyone. Julie could only hope for as positive a resolution in her own situation. The irony of the similarity of the two situations was striking.

"Thanks." Julie's tone was filled with emotion. "I want to say again how glad I am we both decided to take this trip. You are exactly the person I need on my side right now." She hugged Emily quickly before turning away, heart pounding as she threaded her way through the crowd and out to the sidewalk. She was thankful the bus was actually parked slightly to the left of the entrance, so the crowd of talking and laughing people was headed in that direction. She took a quick, furtive look and saw Melanie fully involved in a conversation with Angie. Good! Julie turned quickly in the opposite direction.

"Oomph," Sam's breath came out in a rush as she collided with him.

"Oh! Sorry.... I didn't realize you were already out here." Julie fought a sudden urge to giggle. His solid warmth was reassuring. She added, "Why do I feel like I'm playing hooky from school or something?"

"I know—I think we're all a little afraid of Melanie. She's like that teacher you never wanted to cross." He turned her slowly, and she could see the glow from the streetlamp reflected in his eyes. She was struck again by how familiar he already seemed to her, and how comfortable they were with each other.

Sam guided her to the restaurant next door and they turned their backs to the group, pretending to review the menu posted out front.

Julie asked, "Should we wait here for a second to let the bus leave?"

"I think so. If we set off down the street now, anyone who hasn't already noticed that we're staying back will see us, and then we'll be the sole topic of conversation the whole way back!"

It took several more minutes for the last stragglers to make their way onto the bus. Julie leaned back, enjoying standing encircled by his arms. She could smell coffee on his breath and a hint of his cologne.

The bus slowly pulled away with a sigh of its brakes and a cloud of exhaust and they were alone. With a sigh, she made herself step out of his embrace and reached back to take his hand. "Shall we?"

They walked slowly down the street, her hand firmly in his. She felt intensely aware of the sights and sounds around her. The yellow light spilling from a door of a nearby café, the roar of a motorbike nearby, the distant sound of a siren, its singsong tone reminding her that she was in Paris and not London.

It felt good to walk. She didn't know who should start the conversation, so she contented herself with just walking and reveling in the sights and smells of Paris, burning them into her memory to relive over and over again later.

"A penny for your thoughts."

She turned to him, protesting. "Just a penny? Not even a euro?" She smiled at him, and their linked hands swung in time with their strides.

Julie was silent, gathering her thoughts. It was hard to believe it had been only twenty-four hours since their night together in Burgundy. Should she just blurt out her feelings and her hopes? *Well,* she thought, *Why not?*

Her voice was quiet as she said, "Last night was incredible. I can promise you that not only do I have no regrets, but that I will always remember it as one of the most special nights of my life."

Sam's voice was equally quiet as he answered, "For me, too."

They walked for several more moments and she noticed the traffic noise was quieting. They passed another café and she looked inside, enjoying the sight of a group laughing and toasting something. It reminded her suddenly of the brochure that had started this whole adventure and she smiled.

Julie continued, "I am going to be completely honest and say I would like to have more nights like that." She paused and took a shaky breath. "And days, and weekends." Her heart was racing. She had never said *anything* like that out loud before.

The next moment felt like the longest she had ever experienced as she waited for his answer. His voice was rough as he said, "That's very convenient…because so would I." He stopped to pull her to him for a long kiss.

When Julie could breathe again, she looked up at him and let herself drink him in. She felt she would explode with the joy coursing through her, but she worked to keep her voice light. "Thank goodness we got *that* out of the way!" They both laughed and Sam squeezed her hands. She teased, "Now, how are we going to accomplish that?"

They started walking again and Sam spoke first. "May I walk you through some of my thoughts?"

"Please do."

"The first obvious issue we have to deal with is that you have a life in London, and I have a life in California. At first I felt that my life in California was so complicated I could never leave." He paused, then added, "But I have since realized some of the things that have tied me to California in the past are changing."

"Such as?"

He continued. "My children. They are both now busy establishing their own lives. And in today's world, staying in touch with them, wherever they end up, is much easier than it used to be. With Facebook and Skype, I can keep in touch as often as I want, and if I want to visit them, I can get there from wherever I might be living."

They walked on in silence and she was struck by the fact that their strides matched, even though he was taller than she was.

"The next big thing to consider, which *is* still pulling me back there, is my job. I've made some great friends at Avanti, and I've worked very hard to create a better atmosphere of teamwork there. On my most optimistic days, I might even go so far as to say that the company could succeed in a big way because of some of those changes."

"I'm sure you're right," Julie said quietly. "It's obvious that you've built trust and teamwork, which are so critical for any company. Those things are especially difficult to achieve when you have two different personalities trying to work in tandem: the tech nerds on the one side, and the marketing people on the other. Each team speaks its own language and has its own view of the world."

Sam turned to her and smiled appreciatively. "So few people really understand that. It's a much larger difference than I can possibly explain to people who don't live with it every day." His tone was quizzical. "I'm sure Ryan had similar problems at his company. I wonder if he realized how well you understand the issues—and what he lost by not recognizing that?"

"He was not a great one for understanding people. He never would have thought to ask my opinion about something like that."

"Well he's an idiot, but it's my gain and his loss." Sam squeezed her hand.

They were now approaching the bridge that would take them back across the river to the hotel. Midway across, he pulled her over to the edge to gaze down at the reflection of the moon in the water. He was obviously thinking about the best way to express his thoughts, and it was a moment before he continued.

"So I'm afraid that if I leave Avanti, the bonds I've worked to create between the various groups won't be sustainable and it will all fall apart."

"Leave Avanti?" Julie sounded shocked. "I could never ask you to do that! Avanti is your baby. You turned it around when two previous CEOs couldn't." She was embarrassed to reveal how much she knew about him and the company's history, but it was too late now. She continued, "You don't have to leave Avanti to spend more time with me. Look, you're here now because you're opening a Paris office, right?"

"Yes."

"And you have to open several more over the course of the year? Is one of them London?"

"Yes."

"Then why couldn't you open the London office next and then use that one as a jumping-off point for the rest?" She could see his expression brightening, so she pressed her point. "I can also come to California and spend time with you there, though things between you and Helen would have to be resolved before I do that. We all know what a small town atmosphere there is there—it could be awkward all the way around."

Sam rolled his eyes in exasperation, but he knew she was correct. He would have to sort things out with Helen before Julie made an appearance.

Julie took Sam's hand. "Come to London. Please. I want to spend some every-day time together. I want to see if we can have fun shopping for groceries, or going to the movies or a concert. I want to see how well we get along when we're not surrounded by the magic of Paris."

Sam was now grinning. "I can make that happen." After another moment, his look turned serious and he took her face into his hands. Looking deeply into her eyes, he said, "Thank you. Thank you for understanding my life, and understanding me."

Julie could feel her heart's frantic beating and she couldn't seem to catch her breath.

"I love the idea of making London my European base." His look became exuberant and his voice got steadily louder as he said excitedly, "I want to take you to the theater. And to museums. And to the movies. I want to figure out what you love to do!" He paused to kiss her deeply, and she felt every nerve in her body responding.

His voice, when he spoke again, was rough with emotion. "Can we make a new start? Together?" His look was so naked, so open. She felt weak and leaned against the cool stones of the bridge. She needed to feel their solid presence to reassure herself that this was all real. She felt like crying and laughing at the same time.

She took a deep breath, and then another. She looked at him, taking his hands in hers. "Those are the most wonderful words I have ever heard. I hoped for this more than I dared to imagine." Suddenly she laughed and broke away, dancing up the street, twirling in circles. Sam raced after her. "I have never felt this happy in my life! *Please* hug me and tell me it's real!" She threw herself against him and flung both arms around his neck.

He laughed and pulled her close. "Does this feel real?" and he kissed her again. She let herself drown in the sensations he created in her.

When they finally broke apart, she took his hand again and they made the rest of the journey in silence, stopping occasionally to simply smile at each other, or to laugh, or to kiss. Julie reached out to touch his face and marveled at the feelings that this man evoked in her. She had never felt like this before.

And she would *never* let him go.

Too quickly, they arrived back at the hotel. Everything was quiet and they slipped past the front desk, with a quick nod to the night clerk and a *'Bonsoir, Monsieur'."*

As the elevator doors closed, Julie reached over to push the third floor button, and Sam stopped her hand. He instead pushed the "5" and turned to look at her, with a questioning look. Her stomach clenched with the understanding of his action. With just a slight hesitation, she smiled and stepped closer to lean her head on his shoulder.

They were silent on the ride up, and as they walked down the hall to his room. He quietly unlocked the door and motioned her inside. She reached to the right, where the light switch was in her room, but again his hand stopped her, and instead he turned her to him in the darkness for a lingering kiss.

"We don't need lights, do we? The moonlight is bright tonight."

"No, we don't," she said, a little breathless.

He led her to the bed. Turning her so that she stood in front of him, he sat on the edge of the bed and slowly began to unbutton her blouse. She stood absolutely still as he slowly undressed her, and she held her breath as he inched her underwear to the ground. Stepping out of it, she was self-conscious for a moment, then straightened her back, feeling beautiful in his gaze.

Oh my God," he whispered, "You are so amazing."

She reached down and gently began to unbutton his shirt. He stood to allow her to pull it from where it was tucked into his jeans, then he undid his belt and let his pants drop to the floor. They were both completely naked, in the moonlight, and they stood looking at each other for a long moment.

"We fit together so well," she whispered, as she moved into his arms, burying her face against his chest, breathing deeply.

He held her, kissing the top of her head. "Yes, we do."

He reached down to pull her chin up and her mouth met his, gently at first, and soon with more urgency. Lifting her slightly, he lay her on the bed, aligning himself along her side.

This time, their lovemaking was slower, more exploratory. Julie felt that she must be dreaming—these sensations were too pure, too joyful, to be happening between two real, live people.

But it was all real. He was real. She emptied her mind, letting herself sink into a world that was just sensation—and a world that narrowed until it held only the two of them.

Chapter 17.

It was late in the evening. The bus had dropped them off back at the hotel after dinner, and Melanie was already asleep, snoring gently. Angie knew she should sleep too, but felt too full of energy to close her eyes. Pulling out her journal, she opened to the next blank page and began to write.

I faced my biggest challenge of the trip tonight. We had dinner at a restaurant called Le Relais de L'Entrecôte. They specialize in steak and French fries, plus amazing desserts. We walked in there and the smells coming out of the kitchen immediately made my mouth water and my stomach growl. I haven't had a single French fry since I've been here and suddenly I felt all my self-control vanish and all I wanted was a huge plateful of them.

Melanie took one look at my face and grabbed my arm to steer me to sit with her and Greg and John. She knew what I was thinking. I have been SO good—I have eaten more greens than I can ever remember doing, I've only had dessert occasionally, and I'm not drinking soda at all here. And then I smelled those fries.

When our meals came, the sauce on the steak was even better than they had described. I mean, it was incredible! I could taste the butter, and the herbs, and mustard, I think. And I couldn't help myself—I scarfed up every bit of that steak and every French fry on my plate in about five seconds flat!

The waitress immediately took my plate away and I thought I was safe, but then she came back with it refilled! It turns out that at this restaurant, you can have as many fries and as much steak as you want! I knew I was in trouble.... Some people were just starting to eat and I was so embarrassed that I'd already finished my first helping. But then something amazing happened. Instead of eating, I made myself think about the profiteroles that I had chosen for dessert and by thinking about that and sipping my water, I ate only a couple of fries and a couple of bites of steak, leaving the rest of the food on my plate! It was one of the hardest things I've ever done, both because it was so delicious, and also because it went against all my training as a child to finish "<u>everything on my plate</u>*."*

It was a great moment for me. Visualizing the profiteroles had really helped me resist the fries. That was the first time I've ever done something like that.

When the waitress took my plate away the first time, I could see how disappointed Melanie was, though she tried not to show it. But when they took my plate away to make room for dessert, I got her to look at me again and I pointed out how much food was still there. She was so surprised! She laughed and gave me a thumbs up, so then Greg asked what was going on, and I had to come up with something about a "private joke" so I wouldn't have to explain anything. When the profiteroles came, I cut them each into several pieces and I ate them very slowly, and that helped too. And I really felt like I tasted everything more than I ever have.

I finished the meal with a tiny cup of espresso. It was a little bitter, so I added a little bit of sugar to it, but I felt very European drinking it.

I can't believe this week is almost over. I've learned so much about myself.

Angie reached back to adjust her pillow, then jumped when she heard Melanie's voice. "What are you doing? It's the middle of the night!" Melanie sounded grumpy.

Angie closed the journal quietly. "Sorry. I just wanted to write about the restaurant while it was still fresh in my mind." She waited till Melanie turned over, then carefully set her journal on the shelf next to the bed and closed her eyes. Just one day left. Angie felt a little sad that the trip was ending, and then felt amazed that she was sad. She really hoped she could persuade Joe to come back with her one day.

Chapter 18.

Gigi was glad she'd been able to reach Paolo first thing that morning. She had tried to stay calm while telling him about the wine-tasting trip, because she knew it was something he would have loved and he wasn't there. Plus she didn't want to sound like she was having *too* much fun while he was home with Mariella. But then she had told him about Roger and Dawn and her enthusiasm must have been infectious because he had laughed, sounding much less grumpy about her absence. He passed the phone to Mariella and she told her about Katie and the idea of an exchange, and Mariella got very excited. Paolo had even said he loved her before he hung up.

She smiled as she went out to get on the bus to the *D'Orsay* Museum, feeling totally happy. What a great idea this trip had been!

Joelle started speaking as the bus pulled away from the curb. "The *Musée D'Orsay* is housed in what was once a train station, built around 1900. It was used as a train station until 1939, but its track area couldn't accommodate the new, longer trains and it was abandoned. It was then used as a mailing center during World War II, and it has been the set for several films and was even used by a theater company. In the

1970s, it was going to be demolished, but instead it was put on the list of Historic Monuments by Georges Pompidou, the President at that time. Eventually it was renovated and redesigned as a museum in July of 1986. It now houses one of the largest collections of Impressionist and Post-Impressionist paintings in the world, many of which were in the *Orangerie* before, which you may remember if you visited Paris in the 1970s." There were several nods, and she continued.

"We have tickets for the current exhibit, which focuses on Van Gogh and the influence of Japanese art on his work. To control the number of people in the exhibit at any one time, tickets are sold for specific times, and our tickets are for 11:30. You are free to explore on your own until then. The bus will head back to the hotel at 1:00 for anyone who wants a ride back, but we have no further events planned for the rest of the day, so you may do as you please."

Gigi's first impression of the *D'Orsay* Museum was of light and air. Looking up she marveled at the glass ceiling, which arched over the entire space. She could certainly envision it as a train station. Various sculptures were scattered throughout the main hallway, and she could see glimpses of paintings through the arches at the entrances to the galleries on each side.

"Do you want to join us as we wander?" asked Dawn, and Gigi nodded happily. She saw Emily across the courtyard and indicated she would stay with Dawn and Roger. Emily nodded, and pointed toward Angie and Melanie. She noticed that Sam and Julie were heading off on their own toward the exhibits at the far end of the hall.

Gigi turned toward Dawn as they walked. "I spoke to Paolo about our exchange idea. We're still finalizing our plans for next summer, but he thinks it could work."

Dawn looked a little flustered. "Umm... *next* summer?" her voice trailed off.

Gigi saw her discomfort and felt a moment of panic. *Oh no! Had she misunderstood? Had Dawn just been making conversation? Was it something Gigi should not have taken so literally?*

Seeing the panic in Gigi's eyes, Dawn realized how her answer must have sounded. "Oh, I didn't mean that I'm not interested! I totally want to do it. I just hadn't gotten as far as thinking about the timing." She paused. "I guess the one thing that is a little daunting is that we already have some family obligations that will require travel in the spring and we have a limited travel budget...."

Gigi added quickly, "We were already planning to visit my sister in Chicago next July, so I was thinking we could just include a visit to you. Then the summer after that you three could come to see us in our little town."

Dawn looked relieved. "That sounds great! We don't have any plans yet for July. I was assuming that Katie would attend summer camp and we could enroll Mariella too. I think that could be fun for both of them."

Gigi smiled. "What a great idea! A camp would be a great way for Mariella to improve her English." She hoped her first impressions were accurate and that Dawn and Roger were thrifty with their money, like she and Paolo. The idea was a good one, but only if the camp was reasonably priced.

"It's run by the town and lots of the kids in Katie's school go there. There are various choices—a theatre option, several craft options, and a couple of different sports options. What kinds of activities does Mariella like?"

"She loves theater and drawing. And she plays soccer at home."

"Perfect! Any of those could work for Katie too." Dawn was quiet as she thought through the logistics. "We'd have to get Mariella approved as a guest, but that shouldn't be a problem. And we're members of a neighborhood pool nearby, so the girls could also spend time there." She turned back to Gigi. "I love the idea! And then you and Paolo can come the second week. Could we have dinner together tonight to work out some of the other details?"

Gigi nodded, feeling a little guilty for abandoning her friends, but sure they would understand.

Dawn smiled. "Now let's go enjoy this beautiful museum!"

****

As everyone existed the bus, Sam held Julie's hand, holding her back so they were the last two to exit. John and Todd set off together, and Julie noticed Emily was heading off toward Angie and Melanie.

"Here's our first chance to see if our tastes coincide! Where do you want to start?" asked Sam.

"Well, I know a little about the Impressionists, but I haven't seen many of the original paintings. Why don't we start there?"

"Good idea. Plus that gallery is on the top floor, so with most people starting down here, we can get ahead of the crowd."

Julie smiled. It was exactly what she'd been thinking. She took Sam's hand, and he gave her a huge smile. He loved the idea that they had the whole day to spend together.

As they entered the gallery, Julie was immediately drawn to a Renoir painting and pulled Sam over. "Look," she said excitedly, "This is one of my favorites. 'Luncheon of the Boating Party.'"

Sam looked at it a moment before asking, "Why?"

"For me, it's a great portrait of the time and of the different classes of people. Look at the men in the front. They're wearing some sort of very informal shirt, almost an undershirt, and a casual hat. And now compare it to the men in the back—look at that one! He has a top hat and is dressed very formally. Working men at the front, richer society men in the back."

Sam nodded. "I never thought about it that way before."

"Did you ever read the book 'Paris' by Rutherford?"

"No."

"It's long, so it's a slog sometimes to get through, but it has some great descriptions of people and life in the late 1800s and early 1900s. I think these people in the painting look just like the people he was talking about."

"I'll have to read it, since you liked it so much."

"I really did. There's a detailed description of the construction of the Eiffel Tower that discusses all the people who worked on it. I really felt like I had a much better understanding of that whole era after I read it." She smiled at him and he smiled back.

"Okay, that's on my To-Do list now. And I like Renoir's paintings, too. Next?"

They walked slowly through the gallery, each commenting on the paintings that particularly appealed to them. Before they knew it, it was time to go back downstairs for the Van Gogh exhibit.

They headed down the escalator. This time, as they stepped off and moved toward the group, Sam kept her hand firmly in his. Julie could see that several people noticed, and for a moment she thought she should withdraw her hand—but it was obvious that Sam had done it deliberately. Looking over at him, she could see that his expression was defiant—almost daring people to say something negative. Emily spotted them and smiled her approval. Melanie looked shocked at first, then more accepting.

At 1:00, the group wound their way through the gift shop and then out to the exit. Gigi was exhausted, but exhilarated.

"I'm so overwhelmed!" she exclaimed to Emily. There was just too much to see. I definitely need to come back with Mariella and Paolo."

Emily nodded. "It's one of our favorite places in Paris. Ben makes the art come alive when he describes the history around it." Her look was wistful. After a moment she added, "I hope there will be a chance to meet back here again, with our spouses, so Ben can give you the tour."

"Paolo wouldn't have the first idea about any of the art, but he would enjoy learning."

Emily smiled and turned as Melanie and Angie joined them. "I'd love to walk back to the hotel," Emily said. "We could find a good place for lunch on the way. How does that sound?" They all nodded, and as they started to walk out, Melanie said, "Should we try to find Julie?"

"I don't think so," the rest all said in chorus. They all laughed.

They found a traditional looking café just two blocks off of the main street, and after a quick look at the posted menu, entered and ordered lunch.

Melanie spoke first. "So it looks like Sam and Julie have made some decisions."

Emily nodded. "She talked to me a little at breakfast this morning. They had a good discussion during their walk home last night, and they're trying to spend as much time together as they can these last two days."

Melanie looked worried. "Are you sure she isn't going to get hurt? That he isn't going to just go back to California and dump her?"

"From her description, he'll be seeing her very soon again in London."

Melanie looked puzzled.

Emily continued. "He's opening an office there, so they'll have a chance to spend more time together."

"I just hope it all works." Melanie didn't look ready to stop fretting about it.

Angie spoke up. "I think it's going to work out just fine." She said it with such quiet confidence that they all turned to stare at her. "I watched them in the museum, and I think there's a wonderful spark there."

Gigi raised her glass. "To Julie and Sam."

Melanie realized she needed to let go of her concerns and just be happy for them like everyone else. After all, this was not something in her control, nor would it ever be. She smiled and raised her glass with the rest. "Okay, here's to love for the people we love."

Talk turned to a discussion of their plans for the rest of the trip. Melanie suggested that they all go to the *Marché aux Puces,* the large flea market that was at the far northern end of one of the subway lines. Gigi had been there once before, and described it to them.

When there was a pause in the conversation, Emily turned to Angie. "Tomorrow night is the big farewell dinner, but tonight is open. Want to get dinner together?"

Angie felt a moment of shock and disbelief, but recovered and said, "Sounds great! Do you have any ideas?"

"I was thinking of walking over to the *Île Saint-Louis*. That's the little island between the Left and Right Banks that's just behind Notre Dame. There's a small restaurant there that one of the new young chefs has opened. And across the street is *Berthillon*, where you can get *incredible* ice cream."

Angie smiled. "I'd love to go."

Melanie overheard her and answered. "That sounds great! Can I come, too?"

"Absolutely!"

They all turned toward Gigi, who blushed. "Actually, I planned to have dinner with Roger and Dawn. We're working out our summer exchange trip. Do you guys mind?"

"Not at all!" Melanie gushed. "I'm glad that's working so well. Should we ask the guys to join us?"

"No, I don't think so." Emily's tone was firm. "I thought it would be fun for just us." She turned toward Angie. "If that's okay with you?"

Angie nodded, feeling like an important part of the group for the first time. "We can ask Julie, too, but I don't think she'll come."

"I agree. It's the polite thing to do, but highly unlikely she'll say yes." Finishing their espressos, all four rose and started to walk back to the hotel. Angie couldn't stop smiling. She felt very aware of everything around her—the bright yellow lettering on the dark red awning of the café they passed, the small dog sitting daintily next to an older woman at one of the tables there. She no longer wanted to *be* that woman, but she was glad to have *seen* her, and those like her, and experienced Paris for herself. She wanted to remember the sites and smells for a long time—the smell of the crêpe stand they passed, the air and light of the *D'Orsay*, even the smell of cigarette smoke. As Melanie and Gigi walked on ahead, Emily dropped back and matched her stride to Angie's.

Turning to Angie, Emily said, "Listen, I just want to say how sorry I am for my behavior at the beginning of the trip. Um…I know I was incredibly rude to you that first day, and I have no excuse." Her voice was quiet, but very sincere.

"Thank you for saying that, but you don't need to apologize. We were all tired and jet lagged and *no one's* behavior was what it should have been." Angie's smile was an acknowledgment of her own whininess that day, and they both looked over at Melanie, remembering her loud stories that first night.

"What if I buy you an ice cream after dinner tonight to seal the deal?" Emily's smile was genuine.

Angie was more than happy to start over. "I'll take you up on that, as long as it's a small one." They both laughed, and as they arrived at the hotel, Angie thought she would have some time to write in her journal before they went out again to Emily's restaurant. Emily had suggested they go over early so they could walk up and down the main street on *Île Saint-Louis* and look at all the shops.

Chapter 19.

The next afternoon, Julie exited the elevator into the hotel lobby just as Melanie, Angie, Emily and Gigi came in from their shopping expedition.

"Hey, guys, did you have any luck?" Julie asked. She had decided not to join them on their trip up to the flea market so she and Sam could spend the last day of the trip together. "You were certainly gone a long time."

Melanie looked around with curiosity. "Where's Sam?"

"I left him in a map store not too far from here. He couldn't decide which maps to get of the various wine regions and I got tired of waiting for him." Julie smiled as she said it, and Emily gave her a knowing look.

"Sounds like what happens when Ben gets into the museum bookstores."

Julie nodded. "I was just going to get a glass of wine across the street. Want to join me and show me your treasures?"

Melanie nodded, holding up her stuffed bag. "It was fabulous! You won't believe the great stuff!" She continued to exclaim about their day as they all made their way over to the café where they'd sat the first day.

"Feels like forever since we last sat here, doesn't it?" Emily said as they seated themselves.

Angie said, "It *does* feel like it was ages ago. I can't believe we're going home tomorrow." Her voice held such a tone of regret that Melanie patted her hand in sympathy.

They took turns pulling out their purchases and regaling Julie with the stories behind each item. She sat back, watching their interactions, the stories tumbling out, some overlapping but all sounding fun. She felt a momentary pang of regret for missing the shopping trip, but she would not have traded her day with Sam for anything.

The bags were finally emptied and Melanie turned to Julie. "Enough about us. What did you and Sam do?"

"We actually headed the same direction you did, but we stopped at *Sacré-Coeur.* That's the beautiful white church on the top of the hill in Montmartre. Do you all know it?" There were nods all around and she continued. "It's a very beautiful and holy place. I can't even begin to describe it. The history, and the quiet peace...." She paused before continuing. "Anyway, when we left there, we wandered down the hill and stumbled across the Dali museum. It's tiny, down in the basement of an old building. And then we found the most adorable little restaurant next to it called *Chez Plumeau,* and had a wonderful late lunch on their outdoor patio." Her eyes got dreamy and her voiced faded away.

Emily shook her head. "You've got it bad, don't you?" Her tone was teasing, but she said it softly.

Julie nodded. "Yep, I have to admit it." She paused and then added, "It was a wonderful day."

Gigi spoke up softly. "I'm glad things are going well."

Julie nodded, looking around the group. "It's been wonderful. Better than I could ever have hoped for."

Melanie looked relieved. "I'm just glad to hear the feelings are mutual."

Gigi turned to Melanie. "What have you decided you're going to do about your situation with Gary?"

Melanie looked thoughtful. "Getting away has definitely given me some perspective. I've realized that *I* was the one with the chip on my shoulder, not Gary. I think I actually drove him away, making him spend more time in his office—and then his being away would just get me madder, and then I'd do or say something else that would make *him* madder, and it would start all over again. It was a never-ending spiral and I couldn't see that until I got physically away from it." She smiled. "I'm looking forward to getting back and talking it through. I want to prove to him that I *do* know how to listen and not just talk all the time." Emily started to interrupt and Melanie stopped her, saying, "I know—I do a *lot* of talking, and not so much listening, but I'm going to really work on being better about that."

Emily smiled and said, "Actually, I was going to say I think you have proven on this trip what a great friend *and* listener you can be. Angie, wouldn't you agree?"

Angie nodded enthusiastically. "Melanie, it was you who wouldn't let me drown in my self-pity, and then you introduced me to my new addiction—my journal!" She smiled broadly. "Now I feel like I'm going back to Joe and to my life with a whole new attitude and certainly some great new habits! And Emily's right—I have *you* to thank for all of it." She raised her glass and they all toasted Melanie.

Melanie blushed and her eyes filled with tears. "I can't tell you how much that means to me," she whispered, and there was a moment of silence before Melanie turned to Gigi. "And how about you, Gigi? It seems like you've made some new friends and have some plans for when you go back, too?"

Gigi nodded. "With Roger and Dawn's help and friendship, I think Mariella will have some great American experiences—and I think they'll also help me persuade Paolo to let Mariella go to Chicago. So look out—we're coming to the USA!"

Gigi turned to Emily. "And Emily, thank *you.* You reminded me how important it is to try new things." She turned back to the group. "And you *all* have reminded me that I have a social side, so you have to promise to come visit and drink our wine!" Turning to Julie, she added, "I hope you'll come soon—it's really not very far from London." She added shyly, "Maybe you could bring Sam."

Julie nodded and smiled. "That would be wonderful! And you have to bring Mariella to London so I can show her around and spoil her. She's a perfect age for understanding some of the history—and I think she would really enjoy the shopping, too!"

Everyone laughed, and then Emily cleared her throat to get everyone's attention. "I have to thank all of you, and Julie in particular, for reminding me how special your friendship was to me. When I arrived, I was worried, and still angry, and at the beginning I was sure that I had made a terrible mistake." She looked apologetically at Angie.

Julie asked curiously, "If you were so convinced it would be unpleasant, why did you come?"

Emily looked humbled. "First, because Ben convinced me it was a good thing to try. But also because I have wanted to reach out for years but was too much of a coward to take the first step. I'd think about those fun times in Boston, and almost do something to contact one of you, but then I'd get angry all over again." She paused. "How crazy is that? *I* ended up being the one with the huge chip on my shoulder and the judgmental attitude, not you." She looked around. "But that's all changed. I hope you will all take me back into your lives again." She raised her glass, toasting each of them individually, and everybody raised their glasses.

"What's all the toasting about?" came a booming voice, and Greg, John, Todd and Sam came around the corner. "And why weren't we invited?"

Melanie shook her head, laughing. "None of your business, Greg. Girl Business. But come on over. You guys can certainly join us now. We were resting after our hard day of shopping."

Greg came to sit next to Melanie and Angie, Sam next to Julie, and John and Todd between Emily and Gigi. After a new round of drinks had arrived, Greg raised his glass. In a quieter voice, he said, "To reunions and reconnecting with old friends."

Everyone toasted, looking around at the now-familiar faces.

"Let's not wait twenty years to do this again," John said.

They all chimed in, "No way!" "No!" and "Absolutely not!" Though their voices were in unison, each was thinking about his or her particular journey. Greg's gaze stopped at Melanie and turned wistful for a moment. Angie smiled at everyone, knowing this was the start of a new chapter in her life. Julie turned to smile at Sam, imagining the moments they would share in the future. Gigi was already mentally planning a trip to London. Emily was calculating when Ben would be at a reasonable stopping point in his research so they could come back to Paris—with perhaps a side trip to London. And Melanie let herself feel particularly proud of the part she had played in bringing together old friends and new.

The End

ABOUT THE AUTHOR

Marty Almquist's first book was *Four Sisters in Paris*. She lives with her husband in Arlington, Virginia. She has two grown sons and an everlasting love for Paris, where her novels take place. Her blog, *I'd Rather Be in Paris,* is at www.martyalmquist.com.

22441393R00159

Made in the USA
San Bernardino, CA
06 July 2015